THE GINGERBREAD GIRL

Seven-year-old Cora, recovering from a serious illness in hospital, has a secret visit from her mother. Biddy manages to pass her daughter a gift, a gingerbread man, which Cora is to treasure always. When Biddy dies, Cora and her little sister are lovingly cared for by Eliza, their mother's great friend. Cora's feckless father, whom she hardly knows, is unaware of the tragedy, but just before the Second World War he unexpectedly reappears wishing to make amends. As Cora grows up she is irresistibly drawn to a man very much like her father. Will fate repeat itself?

THE GINGERBREAD GIRL

The Gingerbread Girl

by

Sheila Newberry

Magna Large Print Books
Long Preston, North Yorkshire,
BD23 4ND, England.

British Library Cataloguing in Publication Data.

Newberry, Sheila
    The gingerbread girl.

    A catalogue record of this book is
    available from the British Library

    ISBN   978-0-7505-2945-7

First published in Great Britain in 2007 by Robert Hale Limited

Copyright © Sheila Newberry 2007

Cover illustration © Len Thurston by arrangement with
P.W.A. International Ltd.

Published in Large Print 2008 by arrangement with
Robert Hale Limited

Magna Large Print is an imprint of Library Magna Books Ltd.

Printed and bound in Great Britain by
T.J. (International) Ltd., Cornwall, PL28 8RW

I dedicate this book to Sally Bowden,
friend and former editor.
Also to the fond memories
evoked of a favourite uncle,
and his version of an
enduring song.

ACKNOWLEDGMENTS

My thanks to: John, Pat, Glenys, Allen and Gill, whose generous help with my research is much appreciated.

PART ONE

1936-1945

PROLOGUE

1936

To Cora there appeared to be a mile of echoing hospital corridor ahead. She had not walked so far for many weeks. Her wobbly progress was exacerbated by her footwear which was new to her, but a size too large, like the starched cotton frock and the cardigan which swamped her spare frame. She'd heard the whispers of two of her fellow Charity patients as she left the ward where she had spent the final days of her recovery.

'Bet that lot ain't been paid for yet!'

This was true, Cora had no doubt. Beg or borrow from the neighbours, that was her mother's way; her daughter couldn't blame her for that. Piecework from the rag trade was poorly paid.

Now, young Cora Kelly was leaving the orderly life she had come to accept; the long rows of narrow hospital beds with their red-rubber protected mattresses, clean starched sheets and pillowcases; impeccably tucked-in cotton coverlets. She would miss the nourishing food here, now that her appetite had improved. Milk, and plenty of it, not stewed tea with a teaspoon of condensed milk from a sticky tin, which attracted the flies.

The young nurse accompanying her placed a steadying hand on her back. 'Take your time,' she said kindly.

'But me mum will be waiting.' Cora's lip trembled. She felt the sudden onrush of hot tears to her eyes. She recalled her mother's face, white and anxious, the evening the ambulance men rolled up her little daughter in a rough red blanket and carried her out of the building. The rest was a blur. She had been very ill indeed with diphtheria. There had been an epidemic in their crowded East London tenement. Most of the children there had not been vaccinated against the disease. Many were immigrants. Cora's own great-grandparents on both sides had come from Ireland around the middle of the last century in search of work. This had also been her feckless father's excuse when he left home, such as it was, when Cora was a few months old. You didn't miss what you'd never had, she thought, regarding herself, but it was much harder for Mum. Bertie Kelly's visit last Christmas had been totally unexpected. For four days they'd seemed like a family, but it didn't last. He'd left them in the lurch again, after pocketing the rent money, with no forwarding address. Biddy had been inconsolable for days.

'I'll see you tomorrow,' Biddy Kelly had

promised Cora, hoarsely. It was a pledge she couldn't keep. Visitors were barred from the fever hospital. But last week she had at least heard her mother's voice and was aware she was near. The heavy-breathing stout woman who swept under the beds every morning had smuggled a note to her.

Be in the end lavvy at two o'clock. The window will be on the catch. I will be outside, with something for you.

The patients were supposed to be having their afternoon rest at that time. The curtains were drawn across the windows in the wards. Cora had tiptoed out; she was fortunate that her bed was not far from the swing doors.

There was no lock on the door, but the lavatory block was deserted. Cora wrinkled her nose as usual at the powerful smell of carbolic. She crossed to the window.

'Mum?' she called uncertainly.

A hand wriggled through the tiny gap in the window, a shadow was revealed against the frosted glass.

'Cora? Yes, it's me. Among the dustbins! Wish I could see you, darlin'. Put the lid down on the lavvy and kneel on the seat. Are you all right?'

'Yes, Mum. I'm coming home soon, I hope. They say me nose swabs are clear at last. What about you?'

There was silence for a moment, then Biddy said: 'I miss you. I can't stop, you might get into trouble, so might I, and that nice cleaner what helped me. Just hold my hand for a minute, that's it.'

'I love you, Mum,' Cora blurted out. Biddy's hand was chilly; Cora tried to warm it with her own. It reminded her of her mother's numbed fingers turning the handle of the sewing machine, as she hunched over her sewing in the winter.

Then her hand was released, her mother's withdrawn. Almost immediately a small packet was pushed through the opening in the window.

'Goodbye, darlin', never forget, I love you, too. Get back to your bed now.'

Cora retrieved the package; when she looked up the shadow had disappeared.

She didn't examine her present until she was safely back under the covers. A hard-baked gingerbread man, slightly battered in his fall. Cora couldn't eat him, for he was a precious reminder of her mother. The biscuit was tucked in her cardigan pocket now, having escaped the daily inspection by Matron.

When they arrived at the reception desk a small woman rose from the chair where she had been sitting for almost an hour and greeted Cora with relief. This was her mother's good friend, Eliza Quinn, who shared their rented rooms. She'd supported the family through many a scrape. Eliza was single, no dependants, and served in the local baker's shop. When left-overs came her way she passed them on. A breakfast treat for Cora was a slice of stale bread dipped into hot water then fried in sizzling dripping.

'Here you are at last, Cora dear!' She'd never lost her husky Liverpool-Irish accent.

'Eliza, where's me mum?' Cora asked anxiously.

Eliza had been silently rehearsing her explanation. Now she replied quickly: 'Your mum's not too well just now. The hospital board don't feel she's up to caring for you for a while. They consider you need to go convalescent.'

'What's that?' the child demanded. Her pallor contrasted with her cropped black hair and dark, long-lashed eyes. Eliza observed that Cora had shot up in height. She was no longer doll-like and pretty, but a skinny and gawky seven-year-old.

'You need good fresh country air, a long summer holiday. No school for a bit. Your mum asked if I could help. Well, I thought of me aunty. She and her sons run a farm. You'll like it – all the animals and that. She's got a big heart, Ginny Brookes. Brought *me* up, you know, when me mum couldn't cope with all us kids in Liverpool. Twins, two sets in one year! Ginny was newly married, no family then of her own. She said you should come, and welcome, Cora. We're going there today, by train.'

'Can't I see Mum first?'

Eliza hesitated. 'She says she'll visit you as soon as she's feeling stronger. Now, Nurse, I'll sign the release paper, and then we must catch a cab to Liverpool Street!'

As they waited on the station platform Cora clung to Eliza's arm. After the quiet of the hospital the noise seemed horrendous. It made Cora flinch. People hurried backwards and forwards, a goods train shunted in the sidings, a disembodied voice boomed out, from nowhere it seemed, announcing the arrival of their train.

Steam billowed, doors opened, folk disembarked. Porters appeared with trolleys to transport luggage. Cora and Eliza stood back until the chaos cleared, then Eliza helped her young friend aboard. They walked a short way along the corridor then entered a carriage. Eliza placed their bags on the luggage-rack. Doors slammed shut.

For the moment, they were alone.

'Sit down, dearie,' Eliza advised as the train lurched forward. She plumped down on the seat beside her, took off her round felt hat, shook her head in relief, the bright red curls bouncing on her shoulders. Her hair and laughing freckled face made her appear younger than her twenty-eight years. She was actually the same age as careworn Biddy.

18

'Where are we going?' Cora ventured.

'*Californy, here we come!*' Eliza sang out sweetly, with a smile.

'California, d'you mean? That's in *America!*' Biddy had a sister there. They received a card from her each Christmas enclosing a photograph of her growing family.

'This one's in Norfolk. Not far from Great Yarmouth, where I sent them bloaters from, last year. Settle down, it'll be hours, and a change of train, before we get there.'

The final stage of their journey was in the early evening. They bowled along the winding lanes by pony and trap, driven by Ginny Brookes, small and round like her niece, with a man's flat cap on a bundle of hair which was faded but still streaked with red.

'Look!' Eliza pointed out to Cora. 'Californian poppies!' It was June, a bright, golden evening, and they caught glimpses of the sea below the cliffs before they veered inland.

'They're yellow,' Cora observed, 'not like the ones on 'membrance Day.'

They drove down a long track to the old house at Westley Farm. The roof was uneven where the original small structure had been extended over the past century or so. There were crumbling bricks on one side, and newer red bricks on the other, not yet taken over by the encroaching ivy. There was a chorus of barking from the dogs in the yard

19

and chickens squawking and flapping out of the way. Seagulls wheeled overhead. The door stood open, welcoming them in.

'Boys'll be in to supper, they're busy right now,' Ginny told Eliza. 'It'll give us time for a chat, eh?' She helped Cora down from the trap. 'Come upstairs and tidy-up. I'll show you your room. Eliza, you're in your usual bed. How long can you stay?'

'Only 'til tomorrow,' Eliza said regretfully. 'Got to get back to work. The boss lost his wife recently; I'm doing a bit of housekeeping for him and his son, too, extra hours for extra cash.' She added softly, with a quick glance at Cora, 'I'll help with her keep...'

Cora was to sleep in the little box room, immediately above the kitchen. She shared the space with some interesting items, long stored away but not necessarily forgotten. When Ginny opened the door and ushered Cora inside, she exclaimed:

'So this is where Aunt Poll's box disappeared to! I never noticed it yesterday when I made up your bed. It's well-aired, lovey, don't you fret about that. Granny Jules's old washstand, see, you're honoured! Hope you don't mind the artefacts.' She rubbed her finger over the lid of the square enamelled box on the windowsill. 'I must have dusted it. Would you like it to keep something from home, inside?' She opened the box to reveal the empty interior. 'Aunt

20

Poll put her baubles and beads in here.'

'Ta, it's loverly,' Cora said politely, as her mum had taught her. Then she yawned widely, forgetting to cover her gaping mouth with her hand.

'You're worn out,' Ginny told her. 'Why not get undressed and jump into bed? Eliza'll bring you up some supper. You can meet the rest of the family tomorrow, eh?'

Dear Eliza helped her to spoon up the hot bread and milk with honey. Cora's eyes were closing as Eliza sang again softly:

Californy, here we come,
Right back from where we started from. ('Well, I did, anyway,' she added)
Where bowers, of flowers bloom in the spring...

She gently removed the half-empty dish, placed it on the bedside table while she tucked the bedclothes round her charge.

Cora awoke some time later, and it was only then she allowed herself to cry. She turned the feather pillow over when it became too damp. The mattress was plump, 'well shook-up', as Ginny said. The box sat on the bedside table. Inside was the crumbly gingerbread man, which she'd guessed came from Eliza's shop.

When Cora stirred again it was morning. Eliza came in to the room carrying a tray.

21

'Breakfast in bed!' She beamed. 'Sit up and rest this on your knees. A boiled egg, see, with your name on it – now how did *that* get there? Ginny cut the top off for you, and made you some dippy bread-and-butter strips, soldiers, don't you call 'em? Not that these are standing to attention. Eat up. I'll put the glass on the little table. Fresh from the first milking, that was. Did you hear the clanking of the milk pails?'

'No. Ta,' Cora said. She looked at Eliza. 'Why are you wearing your hat?'

'Time for me to make ready. A train to catch,' Eliza said regretfully.

'Can I come and see you off?'

'You'd like to do that, would you?'

Cora nodded her head. She was intent now on eating her egg, she wasn't going to be left behind here on her own.

'The clothes you wore yesterday are already in the wash, they smelled of the hospital, but you've another set in your case.'

'I saw that, when you took my nightie out last night and the new toothbrush and that. Where did they come from?' Cora drained the glass of milk. It was a bit too creamy for her taste and still warm, but she wouldn't have dreamed of being impolite and saying so.

'A friend at the bakery gave them to me for you, her daughter had outgrown them. Good as new, see? Must be a careful child!

22

Let me take the tray. I'll bring you up a jug of warm water to wash with. Privy's off the scullery, in the yard. Oh, I forgot to say,' Eliza gestured at the washstand cupboard. 'The jerry's hid in there.'

'It's all right,' Cora assured her, 'I guessed!' She grinned. 'I turned up the nightlight when I had to get out. I ain't daft, you know.'

'Getting your old spirit back, dearie, that's good, your mum'll be pleased to hear that.' Eliza paused. 'Make the most of your holiday, won't you?'

'I'll try,' Cora promised.

Eliza patted Cora's shorn head. 'That awful pudding-basin cut,' she said ruefully, 'I suppose they had to chop your hair off because of the fever. Still, by the time Biddy sees you you should look more yourself, eh?'

The following two months passed happily. There was so much to do on the farm although it was really more of a smallholding these days. Ginny rented out some of the fields when her husband died, and reduced the stock.

Cora quickly became involved. Ginny bought her some wellington boots; it was always muddy in the yard because Mal gave it a hose-down after the milking, when the small herd of cows went through to the field to join the pony. There were half a dozen lambs being fattened up in a smaller paddock which they shared with an aged, bearded goat, and two young male pigs wallowing in mud in a pen. Cora was nervous of these last, she skirted them hastily as they stuck their inquisitive snouts over the fence and blinked at her with their beady, bright eyes. She was soon given a morning task to herself: gathering the eggs from the hen house. She'd apologize to a hen on the nest:

'Sorry to disturb you! Let's just feel under you and see...' Then she would hold up a warm brown egg with a clinging feather or two and add: 'Ta very much!'

The hens, a hybrid assortment, with wings unclipped, often escaped from their pen, like they had the day Cora arrived, but they mostly went back to lay, and to roost in their quarters at night.

Many feral cats lived in the barn. Cora approached that place with caution, for Ginny had warned her about the rodents who shared the cattery. The sacks of corn were the main reason, and other animal feed was also stored in here. Cora would push open the door, cry, *'Scat!'* fearfully, then pour skimmed milk from a jug into a big dish for the cats. The only one to come near her was a young ginger tom, who didn't object to a brief tickle behind his ears while he lapped his milk. Once he leapt from a beam on to her shoulders, startling her; he had a somewhat rusty purr and as he kneaded

24

with his paws she winced as his sharp claws dug into her flesh. Her exclamation of pain made him drop to the ground and shy away.

'You can't make pets of them, dearie,' a concerned Ginny said later as she applied soothing ointment to the scratches. 'Got to watch out these don't turn septic...'

Mal was the older of Ginny's boys. His hair was bleached like straw by the sun, he had a ruddy face and red hands, because they were often in cold water. He was responsible for the cattle as he had been since losing his father six years ago, when he was fourteen. He was a chap of few words; Cora was in awe of him. She wanted to ask him about the beehives he tended, and how the honey was produced, but all he said in his gruff way was to be respectful of the bees, then they wouldn't sting her.

Jimmy was different. He was almost sixteen, still growing, with a mop of sandy curly hair which made him look angelic, but he was a bit of a dare-devil. He rode the old dun pony bareback round the paddock, and sometimes he was to be seen vaulting on to the back of one of the cows, hanging on to her horns as she attempted to throw him off. Jimmy was always the last up in the mornings – he'd left school this summer, but when he wasn't up to mischief he always had his head in a book.

'We'll never make a farmer out of him,' his

mother would sigh indulgently.

Mal and Jimmy didn't argue over the younger brother's attitude to the family business. It was understood that Mal would inherit the farm, and that at some point Jimmy would leave home and make his own way in life.

Cora secretly adored Jimmy. He was willing to amuse her after supper with a game of tiddlywinks or snakes and ladders. She learned to be a good loser because Jimmy made no concessions to her age. He always had an answer for her questions and she believed him implicitly, even when he had an impish gleam in his hazel eyes.

Once, she couldn't help herself, she whispered in his ear as she wished them all goodnight: 'When I grow up, I'm going to marry you, Jimmy Brookes!'

He grinned, whispered back; 'Some hope, Cora Kelly!' She wasn't quite sure what he meant by that. She knew he had a girlfriend, for he went to the village social every Friday evening with Helen, from the big farm further up the lane. Cora watched from her bedroom window as they cycled off, avoiding the ruts, chatting animatedly.

When Cora was grown up, she'd sigh that these were the happiest days of her life, at Westley Farm, except her mother wasn't there, too...

It was coming up to September. Time for Cora to return home to go to school.

Ginny said very little as they drove to the station to meet Eliza, except to remark, as they glimpsed the sea, 'I meant to take you on the beach for a day. You would have enjoyed that. We're always too busy on the farm.'

'I don't mind, honest,' Cora replied. 'Did Eliza say if me mum was coming, too?'

There was a pause, Ginny flicked the reins, then she cleared her throat.

'She can't come, dearie.'

'Oh, well, I'll see her soon. Are me and Eliza going back to London tomorrow?'

Ginny nodded. 'By the way, would you like to keep Aunt Poll's box? A little farewell gift from me, eh?'

'Oh I *would*. Ta.' I'll share it with Mum, Cora thought, *she* deserves a present, too. I wonder if the gingerbread man is too stale to eat now?

Eliza said to herself, as she gathered her things together in the train, we'll arrive at the station in five minutes. I must powder my nose. When will I break the news? *Lord give me strength to do so...* She firmly believed in the power of impromptu prayer.

She waited until after supper, when the boys went out, and they'd cleared the table.

'I'll wash up. You two have a talk, eh?'

27

Ginny bustled into the scullery.

'Come and sit by me on the settle,' Eliza said. She hugged Cora close.

'Why are you crying?' the child asked.

'Because ... I have some very sad news, Cora. Your mum–'

'What about me mum?'

'You remember she wasn't well, that's why you came here...'

'She never wrote, not once,' Cora said in an injured tone.

'She couldn't. She wanted to, but she couldn't. She had a little baby, Cora, she should have told you she was expecting it, but, you were so ill too and...'

'I ... don't understand.'

'She ... passed away soon after the baby was born. Last week, it was. You've got a tiny sister, Cora. Your mother asked me to look after her, and you. Mr Norton, my boss, has been so kind, I'm to be housekeeper for him now full time: you and the baby, the three of us, we'll have a proper home there in a nice part of Stepney.'

'What's its name?' Cora asked. She didn't appear to comprehend what had happened to her mother.

'The house has a number, not a name. It's not too far from the shop.'

'I meant, the ... baby.'

'Deirdre. Biddy decided that, after her own mother. The baby's still in the free hospital, the nurses call her Dede. We can take her home when we're ready.'

Thank goodness, Eliza thought, she hasn't asked who the baby's father is. Poor Biddy: who else could it have been but Bertie? If I can help it, that wretched fellow'll never know about the baby. Biddy's children are *my* responsibility now.

If only Biddy had gone to the hospital earlier and asked for their help, she might have been saved. If only I had arrived home from work earlier that day ... the shock of finding she had given birth, all by herself ... that will haunt me for ever.

Eliza gave herself a mental shake. *I'll try not to let you down, Biddy. I promise.*

ONE

June 1939

Cora hurried home from school each afternoon, satchel bumping on her back, the now obligatory gas-mask box slung around her neck at the front. Dede, her little sister, was getting on for three now, a lively child with a saucy grin, big blue eyes and a mass of ringlets. Cora's hair had grown again, straight as pump water, just like Biddy's, as

Eliza told her. She was old enough to see to her own hair, but Dede yelled blue murder when Cora attempted to brush her tangled mop in the morning.

Then kindly Mr Norton would pass his hand over his own bald pate, and sigh as he read his paper at the breakfast table. He'd recently retired from the bakery, but he still attended to its finances, busy in his study each morning.

'I'm sorry, Mr Norton,' Eliza apologized, bringing in his morning kipper, glistening with melted butter. 'There's no need for her to make so much fuss. Cora's very patient with her sister. Like a little mother, I say.'

Mr Norton looked up. 'Thank you, Eliza. Is haddock a possibility tomorrow, d'you think? Don't worry about a tantrum or two. She'll grow out of it, no doubt. We,' he said tactfully, instead of 'you', 'shouldn't expect too much of Cora, she's still a child herself.'

'You're very understanding, Mr Norton,' Eliza said gratefully. She was glad that his son Neville, a master baker like his father, was not around at this time. He left at dawn for the bakery. He was a moody individual in his middle thirties, unpopular with the staff. He resented the children's presence in the house. If anything should happen to his father... Eliza offered up a silent prayer that Mr Norton's chronic chest complaint, caused by his occupation, would not see him off before the

30

children were independent of her care.

Now, as Cora turned the corner into the quiet street of substantial terraced houses, with the fan-shaped stained glass adorning each front door, she spotted Nev alighting from his parked motor car, then opening the ornate iron gate set in the communal front brick wall, with the broken glass on top, to deter any child thinking of walking its length. Not that there were many youngsters on their side of the street, which was mostly occupied by retired prosperous tradesmen, who, like Mr Norton, had moved on from rooms above business premises, and white collar workers.

She slowed down. She didn't want to encounter Nev. He always found something to complain about. He'd go upstairs soon after his arrival, have a bath, then rest on his bed until called for dinner. It was Cora's task to take Dede out for a while, before it was time for their tea, eaten in the kitchen, so that Nev could have peace and quiet at this time and Eliza could concentrate on cooking the evening meal for the two men.

Dede was already strapped in her push-chair in the hall.

'I waiting for you!' she called out reproach-fully, as Cora pushed open the door. Nev must have seen her coming, she thought, as he'd left it ajar.

Eliza stood at the kitchen door with her

finger to her lips. 'Shush!'

'We'll go round the block,' Cora said. She hung her bag on the hallstand.

'Here.' Liza beckoned. She brought out from her apron pocket a small poke bag.

'Dolly mixtures!' Dede guessed, holding out her hand eagerly.

'Share them with your sister ... see you in about half an hour, Cora.'

'Got lots to look at today,' Cora informed Dede as they trundled along the pavement. 'They're delivering air-raid shelters in the next street. They're for people to sleep in when the war starts, and the siren goes. We'll get one soon, too. It'll take up most of the garden, I reckon. Mr Norton says the top will be covered in mud and grass and then it will look like a giant molehill from the sky... Mr Norton laughed when I said I would help dig the hole, he said he's going to pay the men to put it up, he's too feeble himself these days and Nev hasn't offered to do it ... are you listening, Dede?'

Dede had a mouthful of tiny sweets; there was a multicoloured trickle of dribble on her chin. She nodded her head, held out the empty bag to her sister.

'Too late,' Cora said ruefully.

Dede had the last word. 'Mr Norting is – *Moley!*' she giggled. *The Wind in the Willows* was her current bedtime story. She preferred the pictures to the text. Cora took books out from the library for both of them every week. Eliza said that was the way you gained a good vocabulary. Then you'd be considered clever and get a proper job.

Cora thought, Nev is ... *obnoxious,* that's the word! Like Mr Toad!

Eliza was buttering some split fruit scones for the children when Nev came into the kitchen, surprising her. He looked more approachable with his thinning hair ruffled, not slicked back, in his casual evening attire, an open-necked shirt with spotted cravat and baggy, belted grey flannels, but this was an illusion. He was a mean man. No cakes came their way from the bakery, only bread still on the shelves when the shop closed.

'Seen my lighter?' he asked curtly.

Eliza knew that he usually had a smoke before he settled down for his afternoon nap. Like his mother before her, she had the task of emptying the ashtray each morning without his father seeing. Not that Mr Norton wasn't tolerant, she thought, putting up with surly Nev.

She reached once more into her capacious pocket and handed him the silver lighter. 'I found it on the floor in the hall just now. I couldn't come up with it, you were in the bathroom by then,' she said.

Nev didn't say thank you. He stared at her, as if he'd never really seen her before. Eliza felt distinctly uncomfortable, aware that having put on weight since she'd lived here, her figure was rounder than ever, her full breasts straining the buttons on her house dress. She'd undone the top two, because it was a warm afternoon, and the gas oven radiated heat in the kitchen. She thought: me face must be as red as me hair.

'Where's Father?' he asked suddenly.

'Gone for an evening paper, we need to keep up with the news,' she gabbled.

'Come here,' he commanded.

'What ... d'you mean?'

'What do you think?'

She moved uncertainly forward. She closed her eyes, flinched, as he fumbled at her cleavage, followed by a cruel pinch on the soft fold of flesh around her waist.

'Think I fancy *that*? You're mistaken.'

Eliza brought her hand up and slapped him hard on the left side of his face.

Nev caught hold of her wrist, twisted her am behind her back.

'Don't think I'll forget that ... wheedling your way in here with your encumbrances–'

'They're not that!' she flashed back. 'And you're not my employer, your father is!'

'Got hopes in that direction, have you? Feel obliged to repay him? You're half his age. He's past it,' he jeered.

'He's a decent man. I respect him, and he ... he respects me. Let me go!'

Voices in the hall; Mr Norton had obviously met Cora and Dede.

Nev turned on his heel, left without another word.

Quaking inside, Eliza cut two slices of still warm Victoria sponge and added these to the children's tea plates. There would be enough cake to serve up later with a dollop of jam and hot yellow custard for the men's pudding, she thought. They wouldn't realize.

Eliza and the children slept in the big back bedroom. Mr Norton had moved into a single room after his wife died. Eliza and Cora shared what had been the marital bed, with its fluffy blankets in winter and puffed-out maroon eiderdown, and now, in the summer months, Egyptian cotton sheets and a counterpane, also in white, with an embossed pattern. Dede still used the metal meshed cot which had been Neville's as a child.

'I bet *he* was a bed-wetter, too,' Cora said, with feeling.

'Don't be rude about your elders,' Eliza reproved her, but her tone was mild. 'No doubt Dede'll grow out of it. Give her a chance, eh?'

The late Mrs Norton stared down disapprovingly at them from her portrait over the bedroom mantelpiece. Her hour-glass figure was tight-laced, and she was buttoned-up to her jutting chin. Eliza wasn't

surprised the picture had been left *in situ.*
Though she wondered how, with such defensive 'armour', the Nortons had managed to produce Nev!

Cora sometimes pulled the sheet up over her eyes and muttered: 'She doesn't like us being in her bed!'

The young housekeeper was responsible for everything in the household, cooking, cleaning, washing, ironing, so really she was more a maid-of-all-work, she sometimes mused wryly, but she appreciated the perks of the job, like the good bed linen, and the bathroom, although she disliked clearing up in there after Nev's daily bath. She picked up his discarded clothes 'twixt finger and thumb, with a disdainful expression.

I wouldn't do this, if I didn't have to, she thought. If I ever get married, Lord help the man who thinks *I'm* his slave!

'Come in,' Mr Norton called out when Eliza tapped politely on the study door.

'You said you wanted to have a few words, after lunch?' she asked diffidently.

'Ah, yes. Do sit down, my dear.' He paused, as if thinking what to say next.

Eliza couldn't help it: had Nev made some spiteful comment about her, intent on revenge for the slap in the face she'd given him?

'Have ... have I done something to upset you?' the words came out in a rush.

'No, of course not.' Mr Norton smiled reassuringly. 'Look, I'll come to the point. War seems to be inevitable – all this pussy-footing around by politicians! – it's not official yet, but there will be mass evacuation of children from London and other cities to safer, rural areas shortly. Cora's school is likely to be involved.' Mr Norton was on the board of governors, and also attended the council meetings open to the public.

'I had heard rumours, I saw the posters, one said it was a mother's duty to send her children away, but another said, don't do it...' Eliza bit her lip. 'I suppose I didn't want to think about it...'

'Women of your age will be eligible, like the young men, for military call-up, or war work. Mothers with children under school age would be exempt from that, but might well be evacuated, too. Some families will make private arrangements. How about your aunt, the one who looked after Cora before you took the children on? Might that be a possibility for you?'

'Well ... the farm is on the coast, of course...'

'Ah, it could become a restricted area, I suppose.'

'What about you, Mr Norton? I couldn't leave you in the lurch.'

'My dear,' he leaned forward in his chair, patted her hand, 'your safety, the children, that's what concerns me. You would have a job to come back to, I promise.

'Why don't you take a short break in Norfolk, when the school holidays begin, and then you can discuss the situation with your family?'

'That would be nice...'

'Good. I am very willing to help with the cost. Write to your aunt today, I should.'

Even as Eliza made to leave, her employer was struck by a fit of coughing. She rushed round to rub his back, until he got his breath back.

'Are you all right now?' she enquired anxiously, noting a blue tinge round his lips. 'Shall I fetch you a glass of water?'

It was his turn to reassure her. 'Thank you, Eliza, don't worry about me.' He paused, then added diffidently. 'I shall miss you, if you do decide to go, you know.'

Eliza had Wednesday afternoons off. The bakery was shut then, and Nev came home at lunchtime. She usually took the opportunity to go for a jaunt along the Mile End Road. There were always shops open there. It was more window-shopping than actual buying, she thought, but it was a lively area to be, with lots of friendly faces. She'd sometimes meet up with someone she knew and have a yarn. Later, she and Dede would catch the bus back to meet Cora at the school gates. Sometimes they would go on to the cemetery and put fresh flowers on Biddy's grave. There wasn't a headstone, but Eliza had asked permission to mark the place with a simple wooden cross.

It was nearing the end of term. After the summer the future was uncertain. Eliza and the children were off to the farm on Saturday. She and Ginny intended to make sure that Cora and Dede enjoyed the golden sands at California, before it was too late.

She was looking wistfully at some children's beach clothes in a window display, when a hand touched her arm. She whirled round, alarmed.

'Bertie Kelly!' she blurted out. She recognized him instantly, despite his gaunt face. Where had he been these past years, with that waxen complexion?

'It is indeed. I'm glad to see you. I called at the buildings but no one seemed to know where Biddy had gone. They don't open up to strangers, it seems. Then I asked after you, and I got the headshake again. I went to the baker's shop, but the woman there said you didn't work there any more...'

Eliza blessed the loyalty of her former workmate, but fate had played into his hands, anyway, she thought.

'Mummy,' Dede complained, jigging in her pushchair, eager to move on.

Eliza had asked Cora if she minded Dede

calling her that. She'd thought about it, then said simply: 'Well, you *are* our mum now – especially Dede's – but I prefer to call you Eliza, like I always have, is that all right?'

Eliza had hugged her and said, choked: 'Of course it is, me darling...'

Now Bertie was looking at Dede, and back at Eliza and smiling, 'Well, well, I never thought of *you* as the marrying kind–'

'I'm not!'

'Ah ... but the baby, she's yours, I can see, same curly hair, if not the colour. What's her name?'

'Dede.' Relief was the main emotion she experienced now. Be careful, Eliza, she told herself, he doesn't know.

'Now, how about we go for a cup of tea and a bun for the little one, and you can tell me what you know about my wife, eh?'

'I ... mustn't be too long...'

'All right. But I expect the truth. I reckon Biddy told you I stole from her? Well, it wasn't quite like that. I promised to pay her back as soon as I got a job, but I was unfortunately detained for a while.'

'Detained: are you trying to say you were locked up?' Eliza demanded, but she allowed him to escort them down the road to a busy little café.

'At His Majesty's pleasure, yes. I missed the coronation in '37!'

'I imagine you deserved it,' she said tartly.

'I was easily led, but it was fraud, not burglary,' he admitted, pushing open the café door. 'I'm determined it won't happen again. I want to get back with my wife and child, make it up to them.'

The weary waitress swished a damp cloth over a table, removed dirty crocks.

'Now,' he said, as he stirred his tea, and winked at Dede as she took a bite of her bun. 'Where will I find my family?'

Eliza made a snap decision. 'Poor Biddy is dead, Bertie. No easy way to put it.'

His cup rattled in the saucer. 'When? How?'

'Three years ago. You left no address. I couldn't let you know. She ... she died of a haemorrhage...' That was true, even if it gave a false impression.

'Consumption?' he hazarded a guess.

'I ... I'm not sure.'

'Cora? Was she taken away?' He sounded genuinely anguished.

'No. The authorities allowed me to look after her. She thinks of Dede as her little sister.' May I be forgiven for lying, but it's for the children's sake, she thought.

'Can I see her?'

'She hardly remembers you–'

'How d'you know that?'

'I have to go now.' She made to rise.

'I want to see her, you know, surely I have that right?'

41

'Tomorrow, will that do? We're going on holiday on Saturday. I can't put that off.'

'Where shall we meet?'

'Here? After school, four o'clock, it's the last day of term,' she said, thinking, I'll have time to warn Cora then, and Mr Norton can advise me what to say.

'You'll turn up? Promise?' His large hand covered, held her small one on the table.

She nodded, strangely flustered by the contact. He was still a good-looking fellow, with that wavy hair, the pencil moustache like Ronald Colman's, despite his pallor. Hadn't Biddy always loved him, despite all his shortcomings?

'You can be sure of that,' she said stiffly.

TWO

'He's not going to take me away from you!' Cora said fiercely, when Eliza explained as best she could in the privacy of their bedroom. 'And what about Dede?'

'He, your dad, thinks Dede is mine. It seems best to leave it like that.'

'He wouldn't want *her* anyway; he never came to see me when I was that little, did he? But now I'm nearly old enough to leave school–'

'That you're not! Your teacher told me you could get into grammar school if you work hard, and then, who knows?'

'Do I *have* to see him?' Cora asked.

'I promised,' Eliza said solemnly. 'Anyway, I felt sorry for him when I saw how upset he was about Biddy. I told him, too, that we're off on holiday on Saturday.'

'You didn't tell him *where*, did you? You didn't say, to *California?*'

'No. He might plead different, but I reckon this was supposed to be one of his flying visits, don't you? Now, don't worry, get a good night's sleep, eh? I have to go down to do my evening chores.' Eliza leaned over the bed, kissed Cora. She peeped in the cot, felt the sheet under Dede. 'Not damp, yet. Don't read for too long, will you?'

Mr Norton was ensconced in the sitting-room, fiddling with the knobs on the wire-less. 'Mustn't miss the nine o'clock news ... take a seat. Did you speak to Cora?'

Eliza nodded. 'She's not at all keen to see her father. Anyway, there's the chance he may not turn up. Mr Norton, d'you know, have I a *right* to keep her?' she appealed.

'You are officially their foster mother. Biddy's husband would have to go through the courts to obtain custody.'

'I feel guilty, you know, because I have Biddy's personal papers, you know, birth and marriage, and sadly, her death certificate.

Also a few family photographs and other things which I am keeping safe for Cora when she is older, and of course, Dede. He didn't ask me about the certificates, and I didn't say...'

'You must decide what's best, in this instance. However, may I offer other advice?'

'Please, I wish you would!'

'If Biddy's husband wants to keep in touch with Cora, a letter now and then, a visit, it would be generous of you to allow that. I would say she has a right to know her father, especially if he is determined to lead a more stable life.'

'But what about Dede?'

'You must be the best judge of that, my dear. Now, is there any chance of another cup of coffee? Why don't you join me? Nev's out, playing billiards, and I won't have the pleasure of your company for a while, eh?'

She rose, and on an impulse crossed over to his chair and kissed him on his whiskery cheek. His look of comical surprise made her giggle.

Then he said quietly: 'I wish I was thirty years younger, Eliza, but I'm not.'

'You wouldn't be so wise then,' she said, embarrassed. 'Time for the news. I'll be back with the coffee pot.'

Bertie Kelly, standing outside the café, as he had been for most of the afternoon, expelled

44

a sigh of relief when he saw Eliza and the children approaching.

Eliza gave Cora a little push. 'Say hello to your father, Cora.'

Cora regarded him for a long moment, then held out her hand defensively. No hugs, she hardly knew him after all.

'Hello Dad,' she said, as they solemnly shook hands.

'Hello Cora, it's good to see you.' He hesitated, then called out to Eliza, 'We'll go inside now, shall we?'

Bertie did not appear to be hard up. He ordered a pot of tea, slices of slab cake. They settled themselves at a table by the window, screened by grubby net half-curtains. Cora, staring up and out at the street beyond, avoiding eye contact with her father, watched a succession of heads and shoulders passing by. She wasn't at ease in this dingy place with its overflowing ashtrays and mingled cooking odours.

'The milk's not too fresh,' Eliza observed, stirring her tea, 'but the cake's not bad. I wonder how it turns out so yellow?'

'They don't use real egg,' Cora suggested.

'Well, Cora, you haven't said you're glad to see me yet,' Bertie said.

She looked at him then. '*You* haven't said how much I've grown; I must have, because you haven't been around for nearly four years. I was in hospital for *months* after the

45

last time you came, I had my seventh birthday there that May, and then Mum died and, well, thanks to Eliza, I'm all right. I don't need you, Dad,' she stated baldly.

He flinched, but managed a wry grin. 'I reckon I deserve that. But I came to make amends this time, only to find it was too late, that Biddy wasn't here to forgive me, as she always did before. I did think of signing on for the army, doing my bit, but I took some advice from ... where I was, for a while.' He gave Eliza a quick look, had she told Cora he'd done a stretch in prison? She gave a little shake of the head. 'I went down the mines as a lad, and experienced men will be needed when the young ones go to fight for their country. I've got a job in a coalmine in Kent, and a place to live. I had something to offer Biddy, and you, at last, but now... I can see you wouldn't want to come. I have to leave here tomorrow. So, I suppose this is goodbye, Cora.'

Eliza ended her silence. 'It doesn't have to be that, Bertie. You came with the best of intentions, after all. We'll exchange addresses, and let each other know of any changes. You're Cora's father: keep in touch, for dear Biddy's sake.'

Cora's lips were compressed in a mutinous line, but she didn't comment.

The waitress took the payment for the bill. Bertie felt in his pocket and brought out a

46

further coin, a half-crown. He placed it on the table by Cora's folded hands.

'Here, Cora, buy yourself something from me.' He wrote his address on a piece of paper which Eliza produced from her bag, together with a pencil. Eliza in turn, neatly printed out their own address in return.

'You live in a nice area,' he noted.

'I'm housekeeper for my old boss at the bakery. We have a lovely home, and want for nothing. See, we're on the telephone, you can ring in an emergency.'

'Best go,' Bertie said. He stretched out his hand again to his daughter. 'Goodbye for now, Cora. I'm sorry I left it too late.'

They waited until he had disappeared down the road before they ventured out.

'Can we buy some flowers with the money he gave me?' Cora asked Eliza. 'Then we can put them on Mum's grave, but they'll be from *him*...'

She'd observed the unshed tears in Bertie's eyes as he made his apology to her, even though she couldn't bring herself to respond as he wanted her to.

At around midnight Eliza awoke with a start. There was an insistent rapping on the bedroom door, then she heard Nev's voice: 'Eliza, I *need* you!'

She scrambled out of bed, reached for her flannel wrapper, hanging on the bedknob, and felt for her slippers in the dark. She opened the door a mere crack; surely, she thought, he's not thinking of ... not with the children here and all.

'Yes?' she hissed.

'It's Dad. I just found him, collapsed, in the sitting-room. He obviously hadn't been to bed. Eliza, you'll have to help me move him!'

She tied the belt of the wrapper tightly round her to conceal her night-attire, then opened the door and followed him downstairs.

Nev bent over his father, who was lying in an untidy heap on the rug by the fireplace.

'It looks as if he'd been going to wind the clock on the mantelpiece, the key's in the hearth. Thank God there's no fire alight this time of year, or–'

'Is he breathing?' Eliza managed, aware that she had been holding her own breath fearfully for a minute or two.

'I can feel a pulse in his neck. It must be a seizure of some sort. Can you help me lift him on to the sofa – let the end down, will you? So we can make him comfortable.'

When they had Mr Norton safely on to the cushioned seat, had removed his tie and loosened the tight collar of his shirt, Eliza fetched a blanket from the airing cupboard to cover him. His eyes were still closed, but he was stirring.

'Telephone the doctor, we need him to

come out,' she urged Nev.

His hands shook violently as he picked up the receiver and spoke to the operator.

'He'll be here in about ten minutes. Said to spoon a drop of whisky, not brandy, into Dad's mouth. Eliza, can you...?'

'Sit down, you've had a shock. I'll pour some for you, too,' she said, taking charge.

Later, the elderly doctor told Eliza: 'You've done well. Best to let the patient stay where he is for tonight, I think. I'll call again in the morning and decide whether he needs to be taken to hospital or not. At the moment he appears to be stable, after a heart attack. He'll need watching, though: are you able to provide such vigilant care, Miss Quinn? What about the children?'

'School's out for the summer. Cora's a helpful girl, she'll look after her little sister while I'm busy. I'll stay down here with Mr Norton.'

'Choose a comfortable chair, then; you should get some sleep while Mr Norton is doing the same. The injection I gave him will keep him sedated for a few hours.'

When the doctor had left Nev appeared uncertain as to the role he should play.

'Go back to bed, Nev. You'll have to be at the bakery in three hours' time. I can manage, like I said to the doctor.'

'Eliza, I'll have to close the shop for a while, with you going away on Saturday–'

'My aunt's on the telephone; I can ring her and postpone our visit. She won't mind. I can't leave your dear father like this! The last thing he'd want is for you to shut the shop, even for a few days. 'Specially now. He says folk are going to rely on their local tradesmen more than ever, if, when, the war comes.'

Eliza moved Mr Norton's big chair close to the sofa, sat down with a cushion behind her head and another spare blanket unfolded over her legs.

'Thank you,' Nev said awkwardly. 'If you're sure...?'

'Yes I am. Goodnight, Nev,' she insisted firmly.

He turned at the door, hesitated, as if he had something to impart. Then he went.

By the look on his face, Eliza guessed, he'd been about to apologize for the other day, but, he couldn't bring himself to do so.

She yawned, closed her eyes. Morning would come soon enough.

Cora hid her disappointment as best she could. She'd told Dede so much about the farm and the animals. Eliza had given them the news first thing, in their room, when she came up to wash and dress.

'No brown eggs, no honey,' Dede said reproachfully. 'No choo-choo train.'

'No, not yet, but next week perhaps. When Mr Norton's feeling better. I'll take you

50

down the park later on.' Having coaxed Dede into her clothes, she picked up the dreaded hairbrush. 'Be good, don't make a fuss. Be as quiet as you can, Eliza says.'

Downstairs in the kitchen, she shook cornflakes into breakfast bowls, poured on milk, added sugar. There was no sign of Eliza, but the kettle was still steaming. She used the pot-holder as she had been taught and made a small pot of tea. Dede drank milk-with-a-dash, but Cora was allowed a proper cup of tea, since she'd turned ten.

Eliza looked in on them, briefly. 'Doctor's here. I'll be busy for a while. When Nev comes home after lunch we'll have to move Mr Norton's bed down to the study – he won't be fit to climb the stairs for a while. That means I'll have to sleep on the sofa for a night or two, just in case. I rang Ginny, she understands, sends her love. Be good!'

Cora carried her gas-mask case, but she'd removed the rubber monstrosity inside and hidden it under the bed. The box made an ideal container for the marmite sandwiches and biscuits wrapped in greaseproof paper, for their lunch.

'Don't stay out too long,' Eliza warned them. She hesitated. 'There are a lot of folk milling about, trying to find out what's going on in the world. Don't talk to strangers!'

'We won't,' Cora promised. She wondered privately why people weren't *doing* anything much, just walking about and gossiping on street corners.

As they went through the park gates towards the swings and slide in the children's playground, they saw a few familiar faces, children from Cora's school.

'We're going to be evacuated with the school, dunno when yet!' a little boy confided, helping his younger brother into one of the baby-swings.

Cora, doing the same for the impatient Dede, replied, '*We're* going to have a holiday first...' Saying it made it seem less doubtful.

'Push me high, up in the sky!' Dede sang out, rattling the swing chains.

Some time later, after a few goes on the slide and giddy turns on the roundabout, they sauntered off, looking for a seat by the tennis courts, deserted today.

Delving into their lunch box, they were startled as someone spoke to them.

'Cora? Didn't expect to see you today!' It was her father, looking rather crumpled and unshaven, carrying a small attaché-case.

'Didn't expect to see you!' she returned smartly.

Bertie sat down at the other end of the bench.

'You said you were going to Kent.'

'I was. I am. Need to tidy up a bit first.'

'I can see that.' Cora wiped a smear of marmite off Dede's face with her hanky.

'Well, I'll tell you the reason. Couldn't afford another night in a hostel. I had ten bob in my pocket and my train ticket when I came, but I hoped to stay in your old place and then move us on to my new abode. I spent the night on one these seats; blimey, it might be summer but it was freezing in the early hours! Got a sandwich to spare?'

She nodded. 'Bread's a bit lopsided, I had to cut it myself. Eliza was too busy.'

'Getting ready to go away, I suppose? Thanks. No chance of a cup of tea?'

''Fraid not. We usually have a drink at the water fountain, but there's always a crowd round that. The water tastes like sucked pennies if your mouth touches the spout.' Cora didn't want to tell him that it was now unlikely they'd be going away for a bit as it struck her that Bertie might try to persuade her to accompany him instead.

'Here,' she offered. 'I've a shilling left from what you gave me.'

'Had a spend-up, did you?' He managed a wry smile.

'Bought some flowers, from *you*, actually – for Mum's grave. She'd have been pleased. I don't need it, you can get some breakfast at the station.'

'Thank you, Cora.' He stood up, as if uncertain which direction to take. 'You look like your mother, the sweetest woman I ever knew! But some of Eliza's spirit has rubbed off on you, thank goodness. I like Eliza.'

'She doesn't like you!' Cora said bluntly.

He had that rueful look again. 'I can't say I blame her. Well goodbye, Cora.' Then he moved off, without looking back.

'*Dad?*' Dede murmured, choosing a biscuit.

'Yes.' I reckon he *is* her dad, as well as mine, Cora surmised, even if he doesn't know it. But he's walked away from us again.

THREE

Friday, 1 September

'We're not leaving you and that's that,' Eliza said firmly to Mr Norton.

He tapped the newspaper, open on his lap. 'Look at the shocking headlines; Poland's been invaded – there are reports, not yet confirmed, that Warsaw and other big cities have been bombed. By tonight our country will have its lights well and truly blacked out. That's official. Most of the children, the handicapped and sick have already been evacuated from this area. *You* should have been on the train to your aunt's last weekend as I insisted. Oh, Eliza…'

'I've had time to consider it, since you were took ill,' Eliza told him. 'This is our home, you can't move, because of the business, and Nev, you say ... well, we'll take our chance. There's the Anderson shelter in the garden, and air-raid precautions everywhere – it's not just a rumour any more, there will be a war, there's no disputing that. If things turn out badly, well, I'm prepared to think again, as far as the children are concerned. You don't really want us to go, do you?'

'You're like family to me, the family I never had.'

'There's Nev...'

'I can see I should have told you. I adopted Nev as a little lad when I married his mother, who was widowed before he was born. I'd been a lonely bachelor, he took my name, and I brought him up as my own, as you are doing now, with your two girls.'

'Does ... he know?'

'I'm afraid we neglected to tell him until he was too old to appreciate the fact.'

That accounts for him having such a chip on his shoulder, Eliza thought.

'I believe I've done the best I could for him, encouraging him to follow me into the bakery; the business will come to him in due course.' Mr Norton paused, then: 'I'd like to ensure that you, the children, can stay here, after...'

'Don't say it!' Eliza pleaded. 'You're much better, the doctor says so.'

'Ah, he also told me privately that with my

heart in the state it is, it's all too likely I will succumb to further attacks. Eliza, it wouldn't be fair of *me* to offer to marry you in view of this, but, how would you feel if *Nev* decided to pop the question?'

'He ... *wouldn't!*' Eliza said immediately. *Lord, please let it be so.*

'You could be the making of him, Eliza!'

She wanted to explain that she didn't trust Nev, or even like him. How could she tell his father that? when he added quietly:

'Think of Cora and Dede, eh?'

She came to a sudden decision: she couldn't worry about something that wasn't going to happen! She said aloud; 'Oh, you know I do, all the time!'

'I won't tell Nev I spoke to you,' Mr Norton assured her.

Following the solemn pronouncement on the wireless two days later that the country was now at war, after all the preparations, the mass exodus during the state of emergency which had led up to this confirmation, there was a definite feeling of an anticlimax. No bombs rained down on London or the industrial cities; the threat of invasion no longer seemed imminent. Those frantically employed on coastal defence had apparently been granted a reprieve. However, they remained wary and watchful.

Cora had lately discovered the novels of

the veteran American writer Zane Grey, who, the librarian told her, had died just this year, and she'd developed a passion for his stirring stories of how the wild West was won towards the end of the last century. She fancied they too were living now in a ghost town, not unlike the ones the cowboy heroes sometimes rode through. This eerie feeling was enhanced by the sight of sandbagged entrances to shops, with stoutly boarded windows to protect against shards of glass, should the windows be shattered in a blast during an air-raid. This was particularly important at the bakery. No crusty loaves on view, no enticing cakes, already trade was considerably affected. The newly trained bakery assistant had departed for the army, and Nev was left with an old chap coming up to retirement age. Less wages to pay, as he said sourly to his father, with a glance at Eliza; goodness knows if the business would survive in the long run.

The windows at home were criss-crossed with strong adhesive tape, and the cretonne curtains had been replaced with ugly blackout material. The streetlights no longer glowed at night; those who had no necessity to venture out stayed indoors. The few cars still on the road crawled along with drastically dimmed headlights. Nev put his motor in a lock-up garage for the duration of the war, and rode an old bicycle once used by an errand boy. The shop stopped deliveries. Petrol was already scarce.

Within a couple of months some of the evacuees returned and Cora's school re-opened on a limited basis. There was no talk now of taking the scholarship in the spring.

Ginny wrote that things were surprisingly quiet on the farm, too.

Particularly so, with young Jimmy in the army. He was determined to join up the minute the war began. Mal, of course, has been exempted from the call-up. He is needed on the farm, and with all food now to be home-grown, we will soon require extra hands to help.
We have enquired about the new Women's Land Army – Mal is not too keen, I must say! I don't suppose I can persuade you to join us after all? We could do our bit on the farm and look after Dede between us, and Cora enjoyed life here when she was younger and I'm sure would do, again...

When Eliza passed this letter to Cora to read, her face lit up with excitement.

'Oh, *can* we go, Eliza? I bet they still have fried bacon and plenty of butter for breakfast, because the rationing won't affect them like it does us – and if you keep bees you're allowed extra sugar, so I don't suppose they've given *that* up in their tea! Of course, it wouldn't be quite the same without Jimmy, but I did love it there!'

'I know you did. But I promised Mr Norton I wouldn't desert him, didn't I?'

Cora sighed. 'We *will* go back to California one day, won't we?'

'We will! Californy, here we come! We'll sing it, loud and clear then, eh?'

Christmas that year was a subdued occasion. The country was still playing a waiting game. Morale was very low after the British battleship *Royal Oak* was sunk by the enemy in Scapa Flow in November, with such a shocking loss of life.

There was little to buy in the shops. The newspapers dwindled to a few pages, church bells were silenced, and grated carrots added bulk and sweetness to the traditional plum pudding. Left-over food and peelings were consigned to pigswill bins provided by the council, another contribution to the war effort.

Cora received an unexpected parcel from her father. A *Rupert Bear Annual!* She sighed to herself, he doesn't realize I'm not a little girl any more, that I read grown-up books now, that I'll be eleven years old in May.

Then she saw Dede's beaming face when she unwrapped the book. 'Oh good, one for us to read together!' she exclaimed, smiling. She thought, well, if me dad knew the truth about Dede, it would have been meant for her, too.

The girls cuddled up together in the big bed, that special morning, with their Christmas presents and paper spread all over the covers. Cora opened the book and as she read aloud the rhymes specially written for younger children, rather than the text, she realized – and it was a lovely, warm feeling – that she was thoroughly enjoying it, too. Nut Wood, where Rupert and his friends explored, sounded like paradise.

The dawning of 1940 was icy-cold and full of snow. Cora slipslided her way to school, she wore thick socks inside her wellington boots, plus mittens she'd knitted herself on two needles – gloves needed four, and she wasn't that proficient yet – but her toes and fingers were numb by the time she reached the playground. She dodged the snowballs thrown by a couple of whooping small boys and joined a solitary girl waiting under the porch for the door to be opened. Not that it would be much warmer inside, as a notice warned pupils that the pipes were frozen, and that school would close at midday.

Her companion was smaller, slighter than Cora. She was a newcomer, for her own school had been evacuated. Naomi had left with her classmates, but returned after a brief stay in the country. The few local schools which remained open were secular.

Naomi was Jewish, her European grandparents, like Cora's had arrived in the area many years ago, and like Cora, she was a real little Londoner. Naomi's father was in the tailoring business, and it was he who had provided work for Biddy, Cora's mother. The girls immediately formed a bond on discovering this. Cora was protective where Naomi was concerned, because in appearance she was different from the other children, with dark hair braided round her head, olive skin and good, but old-fashioned clothes, including thick, ribbed, black stockings. Naomi was reserved in manner, but what she did say often made Cora laugh, as now, when Naomi observed drily:

'See how the wild and woolly enjoy the snow.'

Woollen hats pulled down to protect chilblained ears; scarves wound round the lower halves of faces, the dashing about to keep the circulation going, wild and woolly indeed, Cora agreed.

In class they shivered, despite keeping on their outer clothing. Their teacher had come out of retirement, was rather deaf, irascible, and shouted to keep order.

Naomi blotted a stray blob of spittle which had landed on her exercise book while Miss Puddefoot was at full throttle.

'This is the penalty we pay for being in the front line,' she whispered to Cora.

61

'Cora Kelly,' Miss Puddefoot cried, 'control yourself! Stand up and share the joke!' The cords stood out in her stringy neck in her agitation.

'Please, Miss Puddefoot, I was laughing at nothing—'

'You *stupid girl!* What are you?'

'A stupid girl, Miss Puddefoot.'

'Then sit down and *shut up,*' the teacher said sternly. 'The rest of you, close those gaping mouths.'

'At least you don't have to write lines and waste paper,' Naomi whispered.

Miss Puddefoot turned from the blackboard, giant compasses in hand, for she had been executing a chalk circle for one of her favourite questions: 'What portion is left, after...' The points of the compasses quivered in a threatening manner. 'Did anyone say anything?' She glared and gestured at the first row of double desks.

There was a muted chorus of 'No, miss!'

'Very well. Now, hands up! What portion remains...'

At break-time, while they sucked the icicle protruding from the top of their free milk bottles, Cora said ruefully, 'It's a pity Miss Puddefoot's too old to join the army, eh?'

'Well, she'd defend the school and us with those compasses, I reckon, if it came to it, don't you reckon?' Naomi suggested.

As they were not expected home at lunchtime, the two girls went first to the busy thoroughfare where Naomi's parents' business was situated, just one of many similar family enterprises. They entered the workroom on the ground floor, below the flat where her family lived. Naomi's mother and her seventeen-year-old sister Sarah worked in the business with her father, and other relatives who were refugees from Hitler's regime who had arrived in London earlier in 1939. There was plenty of work, with government contracts to fulfil, but the living accommodation was crammed to the hilt.

'Despite my mother's good intentions, harmony doesn't always prevail,' Naomi confided. 'It's hard to find a place to be quiet in our flat. My mother reminds us that our cousins now have no home of their own, that their father is left behind in Germany. If he had come with them he would probably have faced internment as an enemy alien here, as men are treated differently from women, but who knows how he is faring now?'

Amid the whirr of sewing machines, scissors snipping, the slap of bolts of cloth being unrolled, only Naomi's father noticed their arrival. He came over, a short man, with bushy brows beetling, but he was obviously concerned rather than cross.

'Is something wrong? Why do you come home so early?'

'The pipes are frozen solid at school. We

can't flush the WCs or get water from the taps. We are to stay home until further notice. Is it all right, Pa, if I go to Cora's for the afternoon? Miss Quinn will be there, and Cora's little sister. I can eat my packed lunch with Cora,' Naomi asked.

Mr Levin smiled. 'You may go. Be back by the usual time, before it gets dark.'

A black-haired girl looked up from her machine, then waved at them.

'Sarah, my sister – there are just the two of us,' Naomi told Cora.

'Your sister is very pretty,' Cora observed, as they walked away.

'Yes, but she is also unhappy. We have to share our room with two of our cousins. They whisper to each other in their own language, and Sarah believes they are talking about us. Before they came, *she* was the princess in our family – she was hoping to study mathematics at university, but now she is helping to make uniforms for officers, and she says the only way she will escape is when she is eighteen and can transfer to *real* war work,' Naomi stated.

'Mathematics!' Cora exclaimed. 'She must be very clever, your sister.'

'Yes, she is. Pa says she takes after his sister who is in the Civil Service.'

'Here we are.' Cora opened the gate. 'This is our house.'

'It's rather grand,' Naomi remarked, but

she didn't sound as if she was in awe of it.

There was the same reaction from Eliza as there had been from Naomi's father.

'Is there something wrong?' She and Dede had recently eaten their sandwiches in the kitchen, while Mr Norton enjoyed his tomato soup in the study. The Foster-Clarke's soup cubes were a boon now rationing was biting hard. He believed the soup was still home-made. She put her finger to her lips. 'Shush! Both Mr Norton and Dede are having a nap – come in here, and tell me your news!'

While the girls opened their lunch boxes, Eliza finished washing up at the sink.

'Is it all right if Naomi stays here this afternoon, Eliza?' Cora asked.

'Yes, of course. But I have things still to do. Why not take your friend upstairs until Dede awakes? She's curled up on the settee in the living-room. You've plenty of books up there to read. Nev won't be back for a couple of hours. Oh,' she went to the dresser, picked up a letter, 'this came for you, Cora. From your father.'

Cora waited until they were sprawled on the bed before she opened the envelope. Her father's writing was untidy, as if he had written in a rush, or when tired.

My dear Cora,

I have been thinking of you a lot, and regretting the way I never kept in touch with

65

your mother and you all those yeas. I am settled here now, hard work, of course, and lonely at times. This is a pleasant part of the country.

I am glad things are still all right in London at the moment.

In case that changes shortly, I am hoping Eliza will allow you to visit me for a few days, as I am due for time off.

I would send a postal order for the fare, and if Eliza could put you on the train, I would meet you at Canterbury. I could borrow a motorcycle for that purpose.

Let me know what you think.

Yours, Dad.

PS. The widow next door, Mrs Titchley, does my cleaning and cooking. She has a son about your age, a nice lad.

'I didn't know you were in touch with your father,' Naomi ventured.

'I hardly know him really,' Cora returned. 'But lately he has been writing to me, and to Eliza, and apparently he wants to get to know me better. In fact, well, you can read the letter! Here.' She passed the sheet of paper to her friend.

'D'you *want* to go?' Naomi asked, when she'd read it.

'I suppose... Eliza says he was married before he was ready for it, although he was older than me mum. She says some men take a long time to grow up.'

'Well, if you do decide to go, make sure you come back, won't you?'

'You needn't worry about that! Eliza, Dede and me, we're a family now.'

Cora took an armful of books from the mantelshelf. 'Which one would you like to read? You can borrow it to finish at home.'

Some time later, they were startled by footsteps on the stairs.

'Blimey! *Old Nev.* What's *he* doing home already? We'd better go downstairs.'

As they emerged they saw Nev standing outside his room. He had obviously overhead what Cora said. He looked really riled.

'You're getting too cheeky for your own good,' he warned Cora. *'Watch it!'*

Later, Eliza said to Cora: 'I'm so glad you've found a soul mate. Naomi is a good friend for you. Biddy and I were like that, you know, we could tell each other anything.'

On an impulse Cora flung her arms round Eliza's waist. 'You've got me now, Eliza, and you always will have!'

'I like to think so,' Eliza hugged her in return. She'd read the letter and said if Cora would like to visit her father, then she should. But she felt a twinge of sadness: would Cora eventually decide to join Bertie for good? She couldn't guarantee, with Mr Norton's health as it was, that their days here would not end sooner than she'd hoped.

FOUR

March, 1940

Cora hadn't travelled by train since her stay in California, and today, because she was unaccompanied, and the carriages and corridors of the steam train were packed with service personnel, Eliza entrusted her to the care of the guard, in his van. She sat on a wooden box midst a clutter of bicycles and unwieldy articles for delivery at points further along the line.

The guard blew his whistle, the train got up a good head of steam, and they were off. Cora waved at Eliza, holding tight to Dede's hand, until they receded from sight, then she opened up her new comic.

'Don't distract the guard,' Eliza had warned.

Cora wasn't quite sure how she felt about spending a few days with her father, now that the time had actually come. There was the secret which Eliza had quietly reminded her to keep, regarding Dede, and the fact that she hardly knew Bertie at all.

The guard, an elderly chap, glanced at his charge. He saw a slim young girl in a navy gabardine mackintosh, with long hair in a single thick braid hanging over one shoulder, restrained by the strap of her gas-mask container. She was travelling light, with her luggage in a canvas carrier by her side. She sat there quietly, turning the pages of a comic, occasionally smiling at the cartoons.

'Going on holiday? Off school next week?' he ventured, when he caught her eye.

Cora shook her head. 'School's closed. Chickenpox,' she replied.

'Not you, though?'

'I had it when I was younger.'

'So you're having a holiday?' he persisted.

'Mmm.' Cora had taken in all the exhortations on the hoardings. KEEP MUM. CARELESS TALK COSTS LIVES. You never knew what you might let slip, she told herself, *don't talk to strangers*. Don't let on where you're going.

Rebuffed, the poor guard sighed. Kids were old beyond their years these days. Blithering war, he thought.

Cora stood there uncertainly on the long platform at journey's end, as her fellow passengers surged towards the exit. She wanted to clap her hands over her ears at the volume of noise, from the departing train, at the shouts from those trying to attract the attention of the depleted force of porters, bellowing, 'Over here!' However, she concentrated on finding her father, once the steam dispersed.

Eventually she spotted him, waving frantically at her from the other side of the barrier. Relieved, she hurried to relinquish her ticket, to emerge on to the station forecourt.

'Sorry, didn't like to leave the bike,' he greeted her. 'It belonged to my neighbour's late husband, bit of a family heirloom, it seems. Here we are, give me your bag, I'll strap it on the back. When I've started her up, climb on the pillion, put your feet on the rests, then hang on tight round my waist. Don't worry, it's only a two-stroke engine, a *phut-phut*, it makes a lot of noise, but it's not fast, and runs on very little petrol.'

The AJS engine rumbled into life, and Cora obeyed instructions. She'd already donned the soft leather cap that he'd passed to her, and fastened it under her chin.

'You'll have to wait to see the city sights, the great cathedral, another time,' he yelled over the roar. 'We've a few miles to travel yet. Off we go, then!'

They drove along winding rural roads. As names on signs were obliterated, a wartime precaution, Cora wondered where they were heading. They whizzed past some delightful weather-boarded properties; there were signs of spring in the hedgerows and ditches; clusters of yellow primroses and celandine. In the gardens, snowdrops and purple crocus. They cruised slowly past a tall graceful white windmill with sails turning.

Country! Cora thought, pleasantly reminded of California.

The miners' cottages were on higher ground, overlooking fields; the winding towers of the pit visible against a louring sky. In its way it was picturesque too, if stark.

'Not such a pretty place,' Bertie observed, as they cruised to a stop in the middle of the hamlet, 'but a close community. Everyone looks out for his neighbour.'

Cora dismounted carefully. 'You haven't said hello yet,' she observed solemnly.

'Oh dear, haven't I? Sorry. It's good to see you, Cora, I wondered–'

'If I would come? I keep my promises,' she stated.

'Still prickly?' He smiled at her disarmingly. 'Anyway, this is where I live.'

She persisted: 'You look different, you've shaved off your 'tash.'

'Round here they sport the walrus variety. I didn't fancy that! Many of the older miners migrated to this part of Kent to work in the new collieries, from the North, Scotland and Wales during the Depression. There's a real community of them here.

'And you, I *have* noticed this time, Cora, you've shot up again!'

The cottage was one of a terrace, with front doors opening on to the street. It was built of grey slabs, with poky windows. But

71

there were clean net curtains up, and a black cat lounging on the step, idly washing behind his ears, Cora bent to stroke him as her father opened the door.

'Leave old Horace outside, he's got fleas,' he warned. 'He belongs next door, to young Tim. I expect the cat heard you were coming, and well, curiosity...'

Me dad's fanciful like me, Cora realized. She warmed to that.

They stepped straight into the living-room, sparsely furnished with a table, four assorted chairs, a sideboard and two easy chairs with wooden arms. There was a welcoming fire glowing behind the hook-on fireguard round the red-brick fireplace, with a couple of pairs of socks drying on the rails.

'Through to the kitchen.' Bertie opened the latch door. He nodded at another door on the opposite side. 'That leads to the stairs, and the bedrooms.'

'No bathroom?' Cora queried. She'd got used to her comforts.

'I'm afraid not. Decent size kitchen though, as you can see: brick floor. The door on the left is kept locked, because it leads down to the cellar. Key on the hook. That's where we retreat if the siren goes. Safest place to be.

'There's a tin bath hanging on the wall in the yard outside. Things are easier in that respect than they were, as we have the luxury of pithead baths nowadays. I don't have to drag the bath in and out every evening when I get home. There's a washstand in your bedroom. Plenty of hot water, too. Back boiler does a good job. This here is a walk-in pantry; the stove is coal-fired too. One of the perks of the job. I'm afraid the lavvy is out the back, but it's not *too* primitive.'

Cora spotted a note on the kitchen table. 'Dinner keeping hot in oven,' she read. It didn't smell too promising, she thought.

She hung her mac and gas mask on the back of the kitchen door as Bertie suggested, then took his advice to 'freshen up' before they sat down to eat.

He looked at her quizzically as she toyed with the lumpy mashed potato, leathery greens, grey mince and coarse-chopped onions.

'Not up to Eliza's cooking?'

Cora shook her head, made a grimace, but ploughed gamely on. You mustn't waste food in wartime, she thought.

When Bertie collected the plates, she noted his hands – calloused, with broken nails, ingrained with coal dust round the quick.

He grinned ruefully. 'Had to harden 'em up, after years of pen-pushing. I've come full circle, back where I began, though conditions in the mines are better now. I'd got a bit too clever at juggling figures.' He didn't enlarge on that. 'Pudding?' he enquired.

'What is it?' she asked cautiously.

'Stewed bottled rhubarb – can't promise it'll be sweet.'

'Thank you, it'll do,' Cora said, glad of something sharp-tasting after the grease.

She was unpacking her few things in the small bedroom, when she heard voices below. Then her father called her to come down and meet Mrs Titchley.

Bertie's neighbour was tall and raw-boned, wrapped around in a sagging cardigan in an unattractive shade of puce. She wasn't as old as Cora had imagined, maybe around forty but her forehead was prematurely furrowed and her expression careworn.

'Here you are then.' She looked Cora up and down with narrowed eyes. 'You're bigger than I expected. Mr Kelly said you were a *little* girl. I hope you won't put your feet through the sheet on the bed, I didn't have a longer one to lend him. The company only furnished this place for *one*.'

'I'll try to keep me feet in order,' Cora responded. Out of the corner of her eye she saw Bertie trying to suppress a grin.

Mrs Titchley looked at her suspiciously, to see if she was poking fun.

'If you like, Tim, my son, can come over and keep you company for the afternoon. Not much to do round here on a Saturday. The corner shop closes at midday. It's a fair old walk to the village proper and the main shops. Did you bring your ration book?'

'Yes, do you want it?' Cora asked. 'I put it on the sideboard.'

'Can't feed you without it,' Mrs Titchley said, scooping it up into a puce pocket. 'Meat's rationed now. Going back Wednesday, are you? What can you do with one-and-ten-pence-worth each, a week? Luckily, Mr Kelly gets allowed extra being an essential worker.'

Cora shuddered slightly at the memory of the mince. 'Wednesday, yes. I've got my identity card, too,' she volunteered. These small documents had been issued last October and had facilitated the issue of ration books.

'Just as well,' Mrs Titchley returned enigmatically. 'Well, shall I send Tim over?'

'Please.' Is he like her, Cora wondered? Has the widow designs on Dad? She realized with a start that she hadn't actually thought of Bertie in that sense before.

Tim was undersized for his age, with a freckled face, prominent front teeth and an engaging disposition. He'd got the afternoon all planned. He produced a pack of rather dog-eared playing-cards, and found a small fold-up table with a moth-eaten green baize top. They sat down near the fire. He shuffled the cards with dexterity.

'What yer want to play?' he asked.

'I only know Patience, and Draw the Well Dry.' Cora played that with Dede.

'Pay three cards for a king, two for a

queen, one for a jack and–'

'Four for an ace. Yes. All right?'

'Yup.' Tim dealt the cards at lightning speed. 'Keep yer eyes skinned,' he said cheerfully. 'Me mates say I'm a demon at this!'

'I'll leave you to it,' Bertie said. He'd been worrying how to entertain Cora, but he could relax now, he thought. At some point during her stay he would have to try to explain how it was that he had neglected her for almost all her life.

They listened to the sombre news on the wireless while they drank their cocoa.

'Now the Finns have surrendered, Norway and Denmark could come under attack next,' Bertie observed. What they called the phoney war here was actually a test of nerves, not a cause for complacency; something must surely break before long.

Cora removed a lump of cocoa with her spoon into her saucer. It was becoming increasingly obvious that her father wasn't house-trained. Rather like Nev, she thought. I hope he isn't going on at Eliza about things, as he does. She missed Eliza, Dede and kind Mr Norton already. She became aware that Bertie was looking at her rather anxiously.

'I'm sorry, you know, I'm not the sort of father you'd like me to be,' he said.

'Dad...' she said helplessly.

'No, don't try to make excuses for me. I let

76

your mother down badly, we both know that. If it hadn't been for Eliza, well, you probably wouldn't be sitting here drinking cocoa with me this evening.'

'Dad, are you, well, *interested* in Mrs Titchley?'

'Whatever makes you think that? I pay her, you know, for what she does to help in the house. The poor soul has hardly two pennies to rub together, and a son to bring up.'

'You don't intend to get married again, then?'

'Who'd take *me* on?' he said wryly.

Cora thought of what Eliza had said, about what could happen if Mr Norton 'popped off'. A preposterous idea struck her. But this wasn't the time to talk about it.

'I'd better make tracks,' she said. 'Give me your cup and I'll wash up.'

He rose too. 'Fires to bank up. Coal to get in. I like a bit of a lie-in on Sunday mornings, is that all right with you? Alarm goes at eight, instead of five, then I get up.'

'Does ... does Mrs Titchley cook breakfast?'

'No, she and Tim go to chapel twice on Sundays. He won't be allowed to play tomorrow. She's left our share of a cold rabbit pie in the pantry, for dinner. I'll make breakfast for us, I scrounged some eggs from the farm down the road. You can help, I'm sure you're better at it than me, eh?'

'Goodnight, Dad.' He patted her on the

head, as if she was Dede's age.

'Goodnight. Sleep well. It's good to have you here,' he said gruffly. 'When I saw you two kids enjoying your game of cards I realized just how much I'd missed out on being part of my own family. Tim's the same as you, brought up without his father from a young age. The responsibility's made his mother middle-aged before her time. Still, *you're* lucky having a little sister, aren't you?'

She nodded, not trusting herself to speak. Then she took herself off to bed.

There were two single bedsteads in her room, only one made up. The skimpy sheets felt cold and a bit damp. Cora kept her socks on, in case her feet protruded out of the end of the bed in the night. There was a flock eiderdown. Sighing and yawning at the same time, she pulled it up round her ears.

I wonder if Eliza and Dede are missing me? she thought. Would Eliza be pleased to know I've realized I actually like me dad? We are flesh and blood, after all.

They went for a walk after breakfast, when Cora had boiled the eggs to perfection. You couldn't beat a new-laid egg, she thought, and bread toasted by the fire, even if you had to spread it with marge, not butter.

The chilly March wind buffeted them along, and when she stumbled Bertie took Cora's arm. 'Here, hang on to me.'

They heard the organ playing in the church as they passed by, and later, from the chapel, fervent singing. Most of the village was at worship this morning, it seemed.

'You don't go to church, Dad?' Cora ventured. She knew so little about her father.

'Not now. As a child, up North, I attended chapel with my mother, like Tim. That was during the first war. Mother was English. The only Irish thing about my father was his name. Like him, I went down the pit at fourteen, even before my voice had broken. I was forced to give up my grammar school place because my family were impoverished. I determined to change my way of life as soon as I could, to get away from that place...'

'Have you ever been back?'

'No. I headed south, for London, and soon discovered that pen-pushing in an office, while not as arduous, can be just as frustrating. Still, I had a thirst for further education so I attended evening classes. I haunted the library.'

'So do I!' Cora exclaimed. 'Then you met me mum, I suppose?'

'Oh, that was some years later. I'd travelled a bit by then, taking jobs as they came up, but not sticking to them. In 1928 I was a clerk in a small hotel where both Biddy and Eliza worked, in Islington.' He hesitated, wondering how much to reveal.

Cora butted in: 'And you fell in love with

me mum and got married!'

He looked at her quizzically. 'I see you've inherited Biddy's romantic side! It didn't come about quite like that. Shall I say we got carried away, we married in haste and repented at leisure. Well, Biddy did, but I didn't hang around to find out.'

'It was lucky she had Eliza to look after her then,' Cora said in her forthright way.

They had reached the outskirts of the hamlet where the road branched to the colliery, deserted today. The massive gates were closed. They retraced their steps.

After a while, Cora realized she was hungry, even the rabbit pie seemed attractive.

'Thank you for telling me all that,' she said to her father, after they had walked in companionable silence for some time. 'I brought something with me which you might like to see later...' This was her precious box with the gingerbread man inside. It was time to tell him the story behind that, she thought.

There were several enduring memories which Cora would take away with her from her brief stay with her father in Kent.

The first was of waking before first light on the Monday morning to hear the hooter at the mines summoning the workers. Then came the tramp of many feet. The men were marching past to the early shift. Cora parted the curtains at the window and peered out but could only make out bulky, greyish figures and an occasional flicker of torchlight, directed at the road they were following. She soon dived back into bed, unfortunately catching her foot in the sheet to hear an ominous tearing sound, as she freed it.

Tim called out as he went to school on Monday and Tuesday mornings. He came in to say goodbye on her last evening there, and to return her ration book.

'I split the sheet, but I managed to cobble it together,' she whispered to him.

'Maybe Mum won't notice...'

'Oh, I'm afraid she will! Please tell her I'm sorry about it.'

'All right. I hope you can come again; pick a time when I'm on holiday, too.' He produced a farewell gift. 'My best alley,' he said shyly. 'Hold it up to the light.'

Cora obeyed, marvelling at the myriad threads of blue within the marble.

'I'll keep it in my box of treasures,' she said solemnly.

They travelled by bus to the station, as the motorcycle was almost out of petrol. 'None left in the can, now,' Bertie told Cora ruefully.

However, this meant that he could accompany his daughter on to the platform, to request her safe carriage in the guard's van once more.

She was ready to climb aboard, her luggage

had already been handed up. Bertie held out his hand, to shake hers, to say goodbye.

Cora hadn't intended to do anything of the sort, but when she saw that he was looking as if he didn't want her to go, on an impulse, she hugged him.

'Goodbye, Dad.' Her voice was muffled with her face pressed against his coat.

'Oh, Cora...' he murmured softly, that was all, as he held her tight.

'I know, Dad, I know,' she assured him, as if she was the adult and he the child.

She waved to him as she had to Eliza and Dede when she left London.

That was the best memory of all.

FIVE

May to June, 1940

'Open your war-record books,' Miss Puddefoot commanded.

The entire school was now accommodated in the main hall following a second wave of evacuation. The threat of invasion and attack on home soil was much more real, with Norway and Denmark occupied by enemy troops, who were unlikely to halt their inexorable surge through Europe, despite the

Allies' continued fierce resistance.

Cora opened the small red-covered note-book and dipped her pen in the inkwell.

'Someone's watered it down again,' she whispered to Naomi, sitting alongside.

Miss Puddefoot had discovered the cache of notebooks when she had undertaken a recent stocktaking of stationery supplies. She bore them in triumph to the top juniors.

'You older children should record what's happening in the world for posterity. Keep your handwriting small but neat, and your own thoughts on the war brief, but telling.'

They had something important to report today. In anaemic blue ink the girls wrote, at their teacher's dictation:

We have a new prime minister, Mr Winston Churchill. He has formed a coalition government. In his first speech in the House of Commons he has promised the nation, BLOOD, TOIL TEARS AND SWEAT.

Cora chewed the end of the wooden pen-holder, then added the comment:

I think I know what he means by that, but I'm not sure. Mr Churchill is quite old but he has plenty of fire in his belly. (That's not rude because our friend Mr Norton, who is old himself, but very respectable, said it.)

On the same day as Churchill took over the Low Countries were invaded. Holland capitulated, followed almost two weeks later by Belgium. The Maginot Line was breached during this period, the flank of the Allied main force approaching Belgium was cut off and isolated. The retreat began to Dunkirk. The school notebooks would soon record some incredible events as the nation held its breath.

There was frequent air-raid practice. The children had it down to a fine art, lining up, clutching their tins of iron rations, with gas masks slung over shoulders. They filed into the big shelter in the school playground, and sat down on their allotted forms. No jolly sing-songs, Miss Puddefoot and a young colleague, fresh from college, had a sheaf of general knowledge questions ready to fire at them to keep the children on their toes. However, by the time the all-clear sounded some of them, including Cora, had surreptitiously dipped into their tins and nibbled a Horlicks tablet or a precious square of chocolate. In a siege, she thought guiltily, she would be without sustenance.

Naomi, who was the only one so far to read Cora's notes, made a sly comment of her own.

'It's more comforting to have a bellyful of chocolate than fire, I think.'

Miss Puddefoot was well aware of the

stealthy tin-opening while she herself sucked on the extra-strong peppermints which she took for the spasms of pain in her chest. She told herself that these were caused by indigestion. She did not permit herself to smile on overhearing Naomi's remark, but she thoroughly agreed.

Changes took place at home, too. Nev no longer did an early baking, but made a single batch of bread for distribution midmorning. The shop closed each day now at lunchtime. As one accustomed to night work, he had been conscripted as a warden. He patrolled the local area after dark, vigilant for the odd chink of light showing, and alert for the drone of enemy bombers, which must surely come.

'Suits him, being officious,' Eliza observed privately to Cora.

Amazingly, the Panzer thrust was temporarily halted, although the demarcation lines along the occupied territory were firmly held. This unexpected decision was taken by the Führer himself. Even as the British Expeditionary Force was ordered to make for the coast and evacuation, the *Luftwaffe,* under the command of Hermann Goering, proposed to encircle them, to finish the job off, to rival the glory of the crack troops on the ground.

There was an emergency meeting on 20

May in what was known as the Dynamo Room, within a warren of secret war apartments built into the East Cliff below Dover Castle. Vice-Admiral Ramsay, called back from retirement, was Flag Officer in Charge of the port and straits of Dover. Under his leadership, Operation Dynamo was about to be launched. It was determined that light vessels would be more manoeuvrable for evacuation purposes. An urgent rallying call alerted private owners of small craft of the nation's need for their services. The response was immediate and astounding.

Cora, Naomi and their classmates copied into their record books:

It is inspiring to hear what is happening on the beaches at Dunkirk. All those brave soldiers waiting to be rescued, our French comrades-in-arms as well as the British, while being dive-bombed by enemy Stukas. The sand helps to muffle the explosions, and the men are digging in too, into what are known as foxholes. More servicemen are constantly arriving. All the little ships are sailing back and forth across the Channel despite the danger from shelling to themselves. The wounded are taken off first...

Then Cora added in her own words:

I did not think I should tell the class, it is my

birthday today. I am eleven years old. It is a MIRACLE, what is happening in France but it is not over yet. We have a soldier of our own who could be involved. We do not know if he has reached Dunkirk, or if he has been captured, or injured. Eliza says we must not think the worst. When we pray for the men still waiting to be saved, I say one for PRIVATE JIMMY BROOKES. He is nineteen years old and comes from California. (That's in Norfolk, not America.) Are you listening, please, God?

They were sent home early again that day. The children were too excited to concentrate. Cora ran all the way up their street, eager to learn the latest news and also to see whether she had any more birthday post.

Eliza greeted her with a hug and kiss. Dede pulled at her skirt, feeling left out.

'You've got two cards,' she said. 'Here you are, open them *now!*'

'Oh, good, one from Dad! I wasn't sure he'd remember.'

Cora opened that one first. A card, with a lucky black cat on the front and a simple message inside, *Love from Dad. Happy Birthday* xxx. There was a note on the back of the card. *The Channel is, of course, not many miles from here. So far, so good. All being well, am looking forward to seeing you again in the summer.*

A flimsy piece of paper fluttered to the

floor. Dede pounced on it.

'Give it to me please!' Cora requested. Dede was pretending to read the paper.

It was a postal order for five shillings. Eliza could tell from her face that she would have preferred a present. Nowadays there was not much to choose from in the shops.

'I expect he thought you would rather pick something for yourself,' she said.

The other card was from Tim. Pictured was a bowl of roses.

'I bet his mum chose that one,' Cora thought, but she was pleased. She liked Tim. She hadn't received a card from Ginny at Westley Farm as usual, but she didn't say.

'You should have asked Naomi to tea,' Eliza said. 'I've made a special cake.'

'Well, it's a bit difficult, you see, because Naomi is what they call kosher. She only eats food prepared in the Jewish way.'

'I didn't think of that!' Eliza exclaimed.

'More cake for *me!*' Dede said hopefully.

'More cake for Cora; it's not your birthday!' Eliza reminded her.

Dede's face puckered. Instantly, Cora picked her up and whirled her round, until she began to giggle. 'I'll share the extra with you, don't worry, Dede!'

Tea in the dining-room on such a special occasion. Mr Norton joined them, smiling at the girls' excitement. Dede was slyly prodding the shiny green jelly to make it quiver.

'Trust Eliza,' he said, 'to provide a splendid spread, even in difficult times.'

'*Fruitcake*,' Cora marvelled. 'How did you manage that?'

'Half the usual amount of marge and sugar, no eggs, but a block of dates, from under the counter at the grocer's. Simmered those in hot water until soft, then added the flour and other ingredients, a generous spoonful of mixed spices plus something which made the mixture swell and bubble before baking ... can you guess what?' Eliza asked.

'No!' Cora told her, tucking into the largest slice of moist, dark cake. 'It's delicious!'

'Bi-carb,' Eliza said triumphantly. 'That did the trick.'

'It usually does.' Mr Norton smiled. 'Eliza took it from the medicine cabinet.'

'I bet if *Hitler* was coming to tea you'd have added arsenic as well!' Cora joked.

'Hooray to that,' Mr Norton said. 'Don't forget to save a piece for Nev, will you?'

Cora couldn't help laughing at the thought that the mention of Hitler had reminded his father of his increasingly tyrannical son.

'We hasn't sung Happy Birthday to Cora yet,' Dede put in.

'Not with a mouthful of cake – after tea. Maybe Mr Norton will play it on the piano.'

He obliged with more than just one tune: Cora and Dede danced round the room, while Eliza tapped her feet.

The door opened and in came Nev, to put a damper on their enjoyment.

'How am I supposed to have a kip before I go on duty tonight?' he grumbled. 'You know Dad's not allowed to get overexcited with his health as it is, and I thought you'd have supper organized by now, Eliza.'

'You'll have to wait until the party's over,' Eliza cried recklessly. 'Fill up on cake!'

Later in the evening, in their bedroom, Eliza produced another present. She went to the top cupboard and lifted it down, having cleared a space on the chest of drawers.

'Mum's sewing machine!' There were tears in Cora's eyes. She had recently stopped saying 'me mum', because she thought it was a childish expression.

'I think you're the right age now to use it, I'll show you how. Look in the paper bag. Naomi's father was kind enough to give me a remnant, when I asked.'

There was a bundle of beige taffeta, left over from lining a pre-war jacket.

'That would make a nice blouse, Eliza. D'you think I could...?'

'You can do anything, if you try,' Eliza said fondly. 'I'll help you.' She didn't have Biddy's magic touch with dressmaking, she thought, but she'd do her best.

Saturday matinée at the picture house. This was Mr Norton's treat. The place was jam-packed with folk eager to see not the main film or the Laurel and Hardy short but the latest newsreel. Dede had to sit on Eliza's lap.

First there were rather blurry pictures of what looked like a desert of sand, with tanks and other armaments upended and abandoned. Then wavery glimpses of small boats approaching the shore and men wading into the water to be hauled aboard.

These were taken out to sea and transferred to big vessels unable to risk coming closer. The battle still raging was described, but not shown.

The men who had safely arrived back from Dunkirk were depicted. A raggle-taggle army, some walking wounded, with arms in slings and bandaged heads. They had been transported by special trains from Dover, and captured by camera as they stopped *en route* to London at a station where the WVS provided refreshments, filled rolls and mugs of tea. The local populace crowded the platform, children waving flags, last used at the Coronation, with women leaning over the barrier to shake hands thrust through the open carriage windows, shouting, '*Well done! Good Luck!*'

At this stirring cry most of the cinema audience rose spontaneously to its feet. Dede perched on the tip-up seat, with Eliza's arm firmly around her. The final words of the commentator were drowned as a great cheer went up and reverberated round the picture palace. *'God Bless our brave boys!'*

As they walked home later Cora asked Eliza: 'What will happen to those who were left behind?'

Eliza guessed she was referring to Jimmy. 'No news is good news' was the only reassurance she could muster.

At the beginning of June the evacuation from Dunkirk was officially over. Shortly afterwards British troops withdrew from Norway. Italy joined the Axis powers against the Allies and Paris was now under enemy occupation.

After the euphoria of Dunkirk, the recording in the school notebooks resumed with the following:

On 18 June the Prime Minister made another stirring speech to the nation. This referred to our FINEST HOUR.

We copied it from the newspaper into our English books in our best handwriting. I got a B+.

General de Gaulle also broadcast to the French people.

She added:

Mr C and Gen. de G are very different in looks! Mr C has what people call a 'baby-face' but maybe he is liked more, because of it. He also has a poetical way of speaking so you remember what he said. The Gen. is very tall with a nose you can't help noticing. His speeches are probably rousing, if only you knew what he was saying, but I don't think he makes his listeners SEE, as well as hear, his words (if you know what I mean.)

Later, Miss Puddefoot would write her own comment below this, in red ink.

This is good. I can picture exactly what *you* mean. P.P.

Just a month later, the Battle of Britain, the war in the air, began.

SIX

It was a hot, steamy day; the schools had just closed for the summer. Invasion, which had seemed imminent after Dunkirk, was still a very real threat. The Channel Islands were now under enemy occupation. A call for Local Defence Volunteers had had an overwhelming response. Those too old, or too young to join up, were defiantly determined to play a role, even with pitch-forks or fairground rifles. The country was on full alert.

Cora was once more travelling in the

guard's van to Canterbury. The train was full of service personnel as usual, sweating in heavy uniforms, overflowing into the corridors, guarding kitbags and rifles.

A long weekend, no more, Eliza had decreed. She wasn't at all sure that it was safe for Cora to visit her father in Kent at this time, although it appeared from the guarded reports on the wireless and in the newspapers that our brave pilots, despite being outnumbered, were dealing effectively with the *Luftwaffe*. Aerial combat had been fierce during the evacuation from the beaches, providing cover for rescue vessels, but now the enemy was crossing the Channel in turn, to bombard the south-east, targeting the group of aerodromes.

There was a lot of stopping and starting during the journey. The guard motioned Cora to stay where she was, while he went to enquire what the latest problem was. Cora had a new book from the library. She read steadily on.

They were nearing their destination when the train gave an almighty lurch and Cora was precipitated across the piled goods in the guard's van, instinctively flinging up her arms to protect her face as she landed in an undignified heap on the far side. A loose parcel struck a glancing blow between her shoulder blades and she heard herself exclaim *'Ouch!'* before she realized that the real pain was coming from her left shin, which had connected with a metal toolbox.

'Are you injured?' The guard's anxious shout made her struggle to sit up.

'I-I'm not sure...' she managed.

Thank the Lord we're not derailed. Unconfirmed reports of a fire bomb down the track. Let me give you a hand. I've got your bags. Everyone's getting out here.'

'My ... book,' Cora remembered.

'Don't worry about that, I'll look for it later.'

'It's a *library* book,' she said faintly.

She couldn't stand on her left foot, but hopped gamely with his arm supporting her, before he handed her down to a railway official waiting on the tracks. An orderly line of khaki-clad men was already marching towards the station, led by a sergeant.

'Stretcher needed here,' her new escort called.

The rest was a blur to Cora. Along with other passengers, mostly suffering from only minor injuries and shock, she was taken by ambulance to the city hospital.

There was a high-pitched noise coming from somewhere outside. Rather like a furiously whistling kettle. She closed her eyes, aware of fragmented conversation.

'Busy today,' observed one voice. 'Skies are full of smoke trails.'

'Saw one come down, dunno how far away

95

it was.'

'What happened to the locomotive?'

'Dunno. No fatalities, just this lot...'

Later she came to in a hospital bed. For a moment, she panicked, believing herself back in the diphtheria ward. Someone was sitting by her bed.

'Mum?' she said uncertainly. Then her eyes focused. There was a pulley above the bed and her injured leg, now in plaster, was suspended from this. She felt exposed, trapped, but the pain was mercifully dulled.

'Cora, I arrived as they were taking you down to the operating theatre.' Her father's voice was thick with emotion. 'It was a shock to learn you'd been brought here. I had to wait ages for a bus. What *am* I to tell Eliza? I promised to look after you...'

'It's ... not your fault, Dad. How long must I stay in hospital?' she asked anxiously.

'We don't know yet. It was a compound fracture, a bad break.'

'Dad, please go and ring Eliza *now*. Tell her I'm all right, won't you?'

'But...' he began uncertainly.

She closed her eyes. 'I need another sleep,' she murmured.

Bertie hesitated, then bent over the bed. He kissed her forehead. 'I'll be back.'

He returned the next afternoon, with another visitor.

'Tim!' Cora exclaimed, pleased to see him.

'Brought the cards,' he said awkwardly. 'But as you're not sitting up, yet...'

'We'll manage. Fetch another chair; put it the other side of the bed from Dad.'

As Tim went to do her bidding she asked Bertie; 'How did Eliza take the news.'

'Oh, she didn't blame me, but she's worried sick about you, of course.'

'When do you think I'll be well enough to go home?'

'Well, I spoke to the doctor just now, he thinks another two weeks in hospital. You'll still be in plaster, though he hopes you'll be on crutches by then. There's no chance you can travel home by train like that. Eliza agrees, you'll have to stay with me, Tim will be around to keep you company while I'm at work and Mrs Titchley will look after you.'

While she was digesting this she suddenly realized that Tim had not returned.

'I'll go and find him,' Bertie said. He stood up, looked at her. 'D'you mind, too much, being with me longer than you expected?'

Cora detected the anxiety in his question. 'No, Dad. I don't mind. Honest. Lucky I brought my war-record book,' she added. 'I can keep that up to date.'

He took an envelope from his pocket. 'I thought you might like this. Only a snap.'

As he went through the swing doors Cora looked at the small photograph. It was of a young couple with a baby. Biddy, with the tiny Cora, swathed in a shawl, in her arms, and Bertie, looking proudly at his wife and child. The edges of the snap were curled, as if it had been much handled. Cora put it back in the envelope.

She said to herself, I'll keep it in my box.

Bertie discovered Tim out on the terrace with some patients who'd been enjoying the sunshine in wheelchairs or day-beds on wheels. Nurses who had hurried at the sound of the alert to urge them to return to the wards were rooted to the spot in fascination, too.

Overhead in the clear blue sky, two aeroplanes performed a deadly ballet, the Spitfire's duck-egg-blue belly gleaming silver in the brilliant sunlight; the other plane appearing black, in contrast. They were both spitting fire, until one spiralled out of control with flames erupting from the fuselage. It plummeted towards the earth far below. The watchers let out their breath in unison as they spotted a swaying figure suspended from a billowing parachute. There was an ear-splitting screech from the victor as it glided away for the next foray. This was the noise which had puzzled Cora when she was in the ambulance.

'That's the sound a Spitfire makes when its ports are open, after its guns have been fired,' Tim informed Bertie. 'Some of the boys from school who've got bikes go out looking for spent cartridge belts which have been chucked out of the planes. They sling 'em round their shoulders and pretend to be Mexican bandits.' He sounded wistful.

'You know more than I do, old chap. Take that spare chair. Come on.'

The Battle of Britain raged throughout August, with considerable losses on both sides. It would actually carry on until the end of October, but something very significant occurred on 25 August when the first bombs were jettisoned on London by an off-course enemy bomber. There was almost immediate retaliation. Berlin was bombed.

On Saturday afternoon, 7 September, the London Blitz began. The docks, the great warehouses, full of vital supplies, were set ablaze by a domino effect. At nightfall there was the illusion of a macabre sunset to rival the real one. The great river around the docks bubbled and heaved like a cauldron of boiling soup. However, the murky Thames water would prove a godsend to the firefighters.

After dark, when the bombers returned for a second attack, Eliza, Dede and Mr Norton huddled in their dank refuge, the Anderson shelter. There were folded blankets, old cushions on the benches on either side; a folding table which held supplies, including drinking water, a flask of tea and what Mr Norton called hard tack, a tin of biscuits and pre-war corned beef. The only light was a big torch, which had to be wound on, so was used sparingly. A covered pail in a corner was for emergencies.

Nev was out with his stirrup pump to extinguish minor blazes, and knocking up folk to make sure they had taken shelter. His duties in the days to come, especially when the night raids were at their worst, would become ever more onerous.

Mr Norton's breathing became increasingly laboured. Eliza made him as comfortable as possible on one of the benches. She cuddled little Dede on the other. It was claustrophobic in the dark, and she strained her ears for the sound of the all-clear. She couldn't help thinking about Cora, and praying that she was all right in Kent.

Eliza found it impossible to sleep. She was cramped from holding Dede in her arms, yet she couldn't bring herself to lay her gently down. Amazingly, after listening to several stories, the little girl slumbered peacefully until dawn.

'Mr Norton, are you awake?' Eliza called out. 'Would you like some tea, now?'

The only response came from Dede, yawning loudly and stretching.

'May I have a biscuit, Mum, please?'

They were suddenly almost blinded by a shaft of light. The shelter door opened. Nev, his uniform covered in a powdery dust, stood there looking at them. His eyes were bloodshot, his face and hands streaked with grime. The long fearful night was over. In other parts of the country orders had been given for vital bridges to be destroyed, church bells clanged a warning, but again, the invasion had not materialized.

'Time to get back in the house,' Nev said. 'At least the electric's on. Dad, you and the kid had best go to your beds for another hour or two. I need to do that myself.'

Eliza bit back the exclamation that he couldn't get into his bed in that state. She turned to Mr Norton. He was visibly shaking. She slipped her arm in his.

'Got your stick? Nev's got the right idea. I'll bring you breakfast in bed.'

'Me, too?' demanded Dede.

'You, too. Off you go!'

Later, when she realized that those upstairs must have drifted back to sleep, she remembered that Nev was due at the bakery. Customers needed their daily bread.

She tapped on his door, stepped back as it opened. Nev, still fully clothed and unwashed, blinked at her.

'What time is it?' he asked.

'Time you got cleaned up and changed, to go to the bakery.'

'Could you give me a hand?' He sounded almost humble.

Warily, she followed him into his room.

'My shoulders are stiff, can you pull my jacket off?' He sat on the edge of his bed, and held out his arms like a child. Eliza was aware of a new emotion, compassion.

When he was undressed to his vest, she thought it was time to go.

'I'll run you a bath. The water's not very hot yet, but it'll do. You can deal with your trousers yourself. I'll sponge your uniform ready for tonight. Take your tin hat with you to work, as well as your gas mask, in case there's another daylight raid.'

He caught at her arm. 'Eliza.'

'Yes?'

'Come here...'

She stiffened. 'No fear, remember what happened last time you said that?'

'Dad said you'd make me a good wife. I don't suppose...?'

'*No.* It wouldn't work, Nev, you and me. We both know that. There's Cora and Dede to think of, too. You wouldn't want *them.*'

'I wouldn't object to the little 'un. Cora could stay with her father.'

She removed his hand, walked away. She was the one shaking now. She glanced up. *Let me be strong, oh Lord, for the sake of my girls. I've never shared a bed with any man and Nev's certainly not the one to make me break that rule.*

Cora received a letter from Naomi, telling

her about the bombing.

Dear Cora.
Every night now we go down to the street shelter as a matter of course. People are permitted to sleep on the platforms in the Tube when the trains aren't running, but they have to buy halfpenny platform tickets first. I wouldn't mind that, there is plenty of entertainment! Some have left London for Epping Forest, it's safer there. School meets in a local hall in the mornings only. How about you? What are you doing about your education? Sarah has got her wish. She is eighteen now and has been accepted for some TOP SECRET training, because she is so brilliant. We are not even allowed to know where she is staying. Have you heard any good news about your cousin Jimmy yet? I hope to see you soon, how is your leg?
Shalom.
Your friend Naomi.

PS. My family and Miss Puddefoot send kind regards.
PPS. I have found out Miss P's first name. It is PRUDENCE! I dared to ask her, and she told me! She said it was a virtue we should all strive to possess.

There was indeed news at last of Jimmy. To the family's relief he was alive, although a prisoner of war in Germany. A brief message came to his mother via the Red Cross.

I AM WELL. DON'T WORRY. YOUR LOVING SON JAMES BROOKES.

Eliza passed on the good news to Cora. 'Now we can all get on with our lives! Helen, Jimmy's fiancée is working and living at Westley Farm. Her brother and his family have taken over from her father. Ginny says Helen and Mal make a good team.'

Cora's mobility was improving, but Eliza decided that it was best for Cora to stay put at present, while London was under siege. The other great cities were now coming under attack. Cora was enrolled temporarily at the school Tim attended. Junior classes were single-sex, likewise the playgrounds. Cora missed her good friend Naomi, and her other classmates. Fortunately, her London accent was not out of place in Kent, where many Londoners had migrated between the wars.

To her surprise, the reticent Mrs Titchley had obviously warmed towards her. When Cora told her she was sorry she'd had to leave her mother's sewing machine behind, she suggested; 'You may come over and use mine when you want to. It was a wedding present from my husband to me, maybe your mother's was the same.' She paused.

'Has your mother been gone long, Cora? I didn't like to ask your dad.'

'She died when I was seven, soon after my sister was born.' Immediately, Cora realized she shouldn't have said that.

Mrs Titchley's eyes flickered as she considered this statement. She said merely, 'So there are just the two of you, looked after by a relative?'

Cora wasn't caught out this time. 'Mmm,' she agreed. She thought: Dad must have put it like that. He'd be ashamed to admit that he'd deserted us. Yet Mum loved him, I know she did, and in his way, I believe he loved her.

When the plaster was removed from her leg, and her father no longer had to help her upstairs at night, she saw, for the first time, the livid scar on her shin. In time, it would become less noticeable, but it would be a permanent reminder of this time and place. She was now sure Bertie would always be part of her life.

SEVEN

The face of London was changing, there were great gaps and ruins where fine buildings and mean streets alike had been obliterated by the bombing. Where the slums were concerned, some would look on it as a cleansing like the aftermath of the Great Fire. Most folk clung to the hope of better housing, a welfare state, when the conflict was over; but many Londoners would be sad at the end of an era.

You aren't safe anywhere, Eliza thought. She worried about Cora in Kent, but things were more stable in the countryside than here, so, although nothing was said, Cora was allowed to stay on with Bertie. At least she was able to attend school regularly. Dede was coming up to five; would Eliza have to send her away, too?

Every night for months the bombers came. The guns on the ground roared their defiance, adding to the cacophony. The bakery was a casualty during one attack. Along with the adjacent businesses, Naomi's father's workshop was blasted almost to oblivion. Her family emerged from the street shelter next morning to find their home, possessions, their living gone overnight. For them it was time to leave. What had they to stay for, to fight for now?

The family travelled north to stay with other relatives. The refugee cousins clung together, said little. Naomi's mother hung on grimly to her large black handbag, which she'd taken with her every night to the shelter. She'd been prepared: it contained the essentials for their new start. Ration books, identity cards, insurance documents, a roll of banknotes secured with a rubber band, a bag of coins, and her jewel case. Also a reel of cotton thread, dressmaking scissors and a packet of assorted needles. Naomi would tell Cora later, when they were in touch once more; 'My mother, you see, practises prudence. It is something I still have to learn.'

Eliza couldn't help admiring Nev's dedication to his ARP duties. She made sure he ate properly, that he rested during the day. Once when she tiptoed past his door she heard harsh sobbing. He'd arrived back that morning with a ghostly face coated with thick dust and scorch marks on his sleeves. The soles of his boots were blackened and gluey with melted tarmac from roads pitted with craters and still smouldering. She cleaned his hands with the special liquid soap provided, and he'd winced with pain as great ballooning blisters were revealed.

She could not draw out of him what had happened, but she guessed it was bad.

The bakery, the source of the Nortons' income, was no more; Eliza wondered how long it would be before they were in straitened circumstances.

One day Mr Norton called her into his study. 'A word with you, Eliza, please.'

She noted his grave expression, the way he clasped his hands together to conceal the shaking. He managed a brief smile.

'Don't look so alarmed, Eliza. Sit down. Where's Dede?'

'Cutting out shapes of left-over pastry on the kitchen table,' she said.

'I've had to come to a painful decision, I'm afraid. The business – well, I accept that's gone. Nev doesn't want to return to that line of work after the war.

'The insurance could take a long time to come through. I have an unmarried sister in Hereford, a retired hospital matron. I have been invited to join her. Nev is now eligible for call-up. I will have to put the contents of the house in storage, and leave it for the duration. I imagine Nev will eventually sell up. I know that I will not be coming back.' He paused, wondering if she had taken all this in. 'My sister will look after me...'

'You won't need me any more, Mr Norton?' Eliza asked. 'Is that it?'

He shook his head. 'I'm sorry, I don't want to part with you, but–'

'But you *have* to. I understand. I suppose I should have expected it. When?'

'Next week, if it can be arranged. Where will you go, Eliza? To Norfolk?'

'I ... don't know. Ginny has a full house, with the land girls.'

Mr Norton opened a desk drawer, took out a buff envelope. 'Don't open it now. Don't refuse it, please. This is to help keep you going until you find another job, a new home. My way of thanking you for your devoted care of me. Nev needn't know.'

'Thank you. I shall miss you,' she said simply.

She didn't look inside the envelope until that evening, when she was upstairs collecting the eiderdown from her bed. It was perishing cold in the shelter at nights now. What else could you expect, she thought, for it was November.

Eliza counted the white five-pound notes twice, thinking she must have been mistaken the first time. There were twenty. One hundred pounds!

'I'm a woman of independent means,' she said aloud. She concealed the money in the bottom of her old clutch bag, which like all mothers, she took with her everywhere.

She'd already made her mind up what course to follow. She'd take Dede to Kent, ask Bertie to find a place near him where she could stay, so Cora could join them.

'You took your time getting here.' The old lady, still in her bed amid the rubble of her ground-floor flat, reproved Nev. He and his colleague, a youth who'd arrived on his bicycle, had wielded an axe to get through to the sole survivor of a bomb which had destroyed the top two storeys of the house.

'Are you all right?' he managed, his throat

constricted with dust rising from the gaps gouged in the plaster ceiling.

'Don't be ridiculous. My legs are trapped. Aren't you going to get me out?'

They struggled with the heavy door which had been blasted across the end of the iron-framed bed. Luckily, this had protected her from the falling masonry. They could even improvise a stretcher from it. She lay there motionless, her lips firmly compressed because she had removed her dentures when she went to bed.

'Why weren't you in the shelter?' the boy asked her, as they lifted her up.

'I was too tired last night,' she said perversely. 'What would have been the point?'

There was another strong smell mingling with the soot and explosive odours. Nev suddenly identified it. She's sucking a peppermint, he thought. She'll need more than that for the pain when she realizes her poor old legs are in a right mess.

'Cover me up,' came the order. 'I don't want the world to see me in my *déshabillé*.'

Out in the street, the fire hoses were trained on sporadic flames. The man and boy were relieved of their burden. An ambulance had managed to get through.

'Thank you,' the old lady called, as they carried her inside.

Minutes later, as Nev wondered why the ambulance had not driven off, the medical orderly re-emerged from the back of the vehicle.

'She's gone, I'm afraid ... heart gave out, I reckon. You know who she was?'

Nev shook his head, shocked.

His companion answered: 'Miss Puddefoot, from the school. She retired while I was there, but she was back, doing her bit. Kids called her Prue, I expect she knew.'

Nev had heard Cora and Naomi prattling on about their teacher.

'Quite a character, I believe,' one of the firemen observed.

Those girls won't forget her, Nev thought. Nor will I. *Blood, sweat and tears,* isn't that what old Churchill said? Reckon it can't be any worse in the bloody Army.

My dear Eliza,
You must come to us! We have plenty of room, if lacking adequate bed linen, as Cora will have told you. Can you help in that direction? I will arrange for you to be met at Canterbury. The city has been bombarded by incendiary devices, but the firefighters at the cathedral have been very vigilant and by a miracle it is still there.

Cora is very excited to be seeing you both again. Stay as long as you like and welcome.

Take care meanwhile,
Yours, Bertie.

'There is a cabin trunk you can have, please take anything you need,' Mr Norton offered immediately he heard the news.

'Thank you,' Eliza replied gratefully.

'That eiderdown you're so fond of, eh, too. Mind you leave room for Cora's sewing machine! I'll book a taxi for you to the station.' He patted Eliza's hand. 'My advice is, tell Kelly the truth about Dede. People *do* change for the better sometimes.'

'Nev certainly has. Oh, I shouldn't have said that!' she exclaimed.

'I'm glad you did. He's made me proud of him at last. I'm only sorry you wouldn't take him on. You must keep in touch, Eliza, promise me that.'

'That's a promise I'm happy to make!'

'Got the old hoss and cart outside. Pass me the heavy stuff, I'll wheel it on my trolley.'

As they followed the burly, middle-aged man along the platform, Dede, bewildered by all the noise and the jostling crowds, pleaded: 'Carry me!' to Eliza.

Eliza lifted her up, glad to be relieved of the trunk and suitcases.

'Why didn't me dad come?' the child complained.

Eliza straightened Dede's beret, which had slipped down over her forehead. It still gave her a bit of a jolt to hear Bertie thus referred to by Dede. 'He's at work,' she said.

There was chilling evidence of the destruction in the city, but out in the sticks, as the driver said, 'the bastards mostly pass over, on their way to London. That's if our boys don't get 'em, coming or going.'

As Dede was about to repeat the interesting new word, Eliza clapped her hand over her open mouth. 'Shush...' she warned her.

They sat alongside the driver on a plank seat with Eliza holding on to Dede. Eliza definitely felt precarious, as the cart was rather rickety and they swayed from side to side. It had begun to rain, so they turned up their collars.

'Almost there,' the driver said cheerfully. 'Put that cover over your legs.'

The blanket he indicated had obviously been used to keep the horse warm. Eliza told herself she mustn't complain, but she was wearing her best coat, with velvet trim on collar, cuffs and hem. She hoped his statement was accurate. How much further to go? It had been such a glorious summer, but would they have to endure another bitter winter, she wondered? The only good thing to be said about this chilly drizzle was that the damp made her hair and Dede's curl even more tightly, she thought wryly.

Mrs Titchley welcomed them in the house, where there was a splendid fire going.

'You been paid?' she asked the driver, who was still standing on the step.

'Mr Kelly said he'd see me right at the end of the week.'

'I'll settle with you now,' Eliza said quickly. Mr Norton had slipped her five shillings extra with that in mind.

'Thanks, ma'am.' The driver looked as if he couldn't believe his luck.

'We've got that in common,' Mrs Titchley observed. 'I can't abide being in debt either. Mr Kelly is a bit impulsive, shall I say. Not that he spends all his wages in the pub. Some folk seem to have a hole in their pockets, eh?

'Leave your baggage in the corner, Mr Kelly can carry that up for you when he gets in. I've got the kettle on and made some rock cakes to tide you over until supper-time. Cora and Tim will be back from school shortly. They're always hungry, so the cakes will keep 'em quiet. Take your coats off, they need shaking, out the back door.'

They sat down at the kitchen table to drink their tea.

'Best put you in the picture, Miss Quinn. Two women in one kitchen don't do. You've got the little one to look after, so you'll be in the house all day. I've had a good clean-up as you can see, and now I leave it to you. I'll be joining the war effort, factory work; my late husband wouldn't have approved, but I'm looking forward to it.'

Eliza sipped her tea. She couldn't very

114

well say she might not be living in Bertie's house for long, that she, too, had hoped to get a job when Dede started school in the spring.

'Thank you for looking after Cora as you have, Mrs Titchley.'

'My pleasure. You've brought her up well. Have another rock cake, do.'

Cora bubbled with excitement when she was reunited with Eliza and Dede.

'It's wonderful to see you! You two are sharing my bedroom. Dad's borrowed a camp-bed for Dede. If we have to go down in the cellar at nights there's a big mattress on the floor for us! Dad's got a saggy arm-chair to sit in.'

'It's a good thing I brought Mrs Norton's eiderdown, then. It's already been on shelter duty. If we lay it over the mattress, the floor won't strike so cold or hard, eh?'

'Well, Tim, let's get home. Mr Kelly will be back soon after five,' said Mrs Titchley.

'Thank you,' Eliza repeated. She saw them out. Time to explore the house!

'I'll help you make your bed up,' Bertie said, as he carried the partly emptied trunk up the stairs. Eliza had already transferred some of the contents to the airing cupboard in the kitchen. Biddy's sewing machine was set up on the folding table in the living-room, and Cora was demonstrating its use to a fascinated Dede, on scraps of material.

'I can manage.' Eliza felt flustered.

'Oh please – you must be weary.'

She subsided suddenly on the side of Cora's bed. 'Yes, I am.'

'Put your legs up,' he urged. As she did so, he gently removed her shoes.

'What little feet you have,' he said softly, holding and caressing them for a moment in his big hands. 'Not surprising, I suppose, for a small woman.'

'A small, plump woman...'

He looked at her appreciatively, at the tangle of bright hair spread on the pillow; her rueful expression. Then, fleetingly, at her relaxed voluptuous body, the innocent display of dimpled knee. She hadn't realized her skirt was rucked.

'I've always considered you attractive. I'm sure I'm not the only man to tell you that.' He stifled a sudden huge yawn.

'You've had a heavy day, too,' she murmured, ignoring the flattery.

'You need looking after, I can see, I'm getting better at that, since Cora came.'

'Been bossing you around, has she?'

He smiled as he tucked the sheets into place on the other bed. 'I needed it.'

'Bertie ... I don't know how long we'll be staying,' she began.

'Oh, why's that? It would be hard for me to part with Cora now, you know.'

'I'm aware of that. It's just that ... I'm not sure of my position here.'

He sat on the other bed, facing her. 'We could get married, become a real family.'

'A marriage of convenience, you mean?' she challenged him.

'I imagine that's all you'd permit,' he said drily.

'Being wed – it's not a part you've played well in the past, Bertie.'

'I can't deny that. Biddy and I – well I regret being irresponsible. But you are much stronger than she was, Eliza. Maybe it would help even, you not being exactly besotted with me. You'd bring me to heel if I went back to my old ways, wouldn't you?'

'A *proper* partnership, is that what you're offering?'

'I suppose it is,' he said simply.

'Bertie – there's something I must tell you,' Eliza blurted out.

'Is it ... that I have *two* daughters, not one?'

'You know?'

'I guessed. That Christmas I was home, well, Biddy and I shared her bed. The timing fits, more or less. I'm Dede's father, too, I believe.'

'You don't know how much I wish she *was* mine...'

'She is. They both are. Don't worry, I don't resent the fact that you didn't tell me before this. Well, how long do you need to

117

make your mind up?'

Eliza stretched out her hand to shake his. 'I will marry you, Bertie, but on my terms, and not immediately. Let me get used to the idea, first. Don't say anything to Cora.'

'I won't let you down, I promise.' His clasp was warm, reassuring.

They all retired to bed early, but were woken by the siren just after midnight. They trooped down to the cellar. Curled up on the mattress with its feather topping, Eliza and Cora had Dede's warm little body between them. Eliza kissed the top of her curly head.

The cellar smelled damp, of wizened apples in a box in a corner. However, it wasn't as claustrophobic as the Anderson shelter. By the light of a flickering candle stuck in an empty milk bottle, Eliza glanced at Bertie, dozing in the old chair.

He doesn't know, she mused, that Biddy wasn't the only one who fell for him that time. He was a real charmer, seemed so educated, compared to us working-class girls. We weren't aware of his background then, of course. I never told her how I felt; he didn't realize. I thought I'd had a lucky escape when I saw how things turned out. *Still. I have Mr Norton's money, if it doesn't work for us.*

EIGHT

Summer, 1941

The whole country had endured another harsh winter, with gales, snow and ice. Great clouds hung heavy in steel-grey skies, but the bombers on both sides no longer menaced at night. The grand finale had been when the House of Commons was destroyed in May and there was a predictable, merciless reprisal. Gradually, searchlights were switched off, gunfire silenced. Folk went upstairs to bed once more.

The war continued. Hitler's armies first attacked Soviet Russia in June; the Allied forces fought far away in the searing deserts of North Africa. There was lease-lend from the United States, which, later in the year, would become fully involved in the conflict.

Spring appeared to be in a state of suspension, not even a brief taste of it, as in the previous year. The unseasonable weather continued until June. Some blamed it on the disturbance of the atmosphere during the Blitz. But as in 1940, there was a scorching summer, reminiscent of the Edwardian era. By July, golden cornfields dazzled the eye in a heat haze. There was a profusion of scarlet poppies.

It was cooler by the river, although the flying insects were irritating. Cora, Tim and Dede were on a Saturday picnic. Cora spread a small rug under a willow. Dede balanced on a swaying branch, with foliage dipping in the water. Cora warned: 'Don't wriggle too far out. Hold tight!' Her sister was an adventurous child. Stubborn, too.

Tim had his fishing-rod, a tin of bait, and a jar of water in which to gloat over any fish he caught. He'd promised Cora he would return them to the river. 'You can't eat 'em anyway,' he said, sounding rather disappointed.

'Thank goodness! I prefer fishpaste sandwiches – are you hungry yet?'

The three of them were already sunburnt. Eliza had dabbed the sore patches on the girls with calamine lotion, which gave them a clownish appearance. Cora and Dede wore home-made gingham shorts and suntops, fashioned from triangles of material, with halter-neck and back ties. Eliza had devised the pattern, but Cora had machined it all.

When Tim joked, 'Did you cut up a table-cloth?' Cora responded with a grin: 'A kitchen curtain, actually!' They were becoming ingenious, now that they had to juggle clothing coupons, for clothes rationing had come in last month, and they had Cora's new school uniform in mind. Tim wore his usual shabby drill short trousers; at twelve years old he hadn't yet acquired his first long pair. His mother would decide when it was time. That didn't worry him. They were much better off now that she was working in the factory and he'd been promised a bike soon. She was buying it by instalments.

In September the older children were going on to high school. Tim would be able to cycle there, Cora would have to take the bus. More youngsters were back from evacuation, normal education was slowly resuming.

As Tim baited his hook, Cora asked: 'Are you looking forward to your new school?'

'Not quite sure. All boys, like yours is all girls, and I'm not much good at sport.'

There was a ripple on the water, dappled in the light and shade. Tim cast his line.

Dede shouted out: 'I can see a big fish! Over there!'

'Do shut up,' Tim said ungallantly. 'I need you to keep quiet when I'm fishing.'

Cora started on the sandwiches. That was a signal for Dede to join her. She arrived in a shower of leaves as the branch jerked back. Tim sighed reproachfully.

Tim and I seem to be growing apart, Cora thought regretfully. He'll make other pals in September. Still, I hope I do, too. But will I find another friend like Naomi?

Eliza had been ironing since the girls went

out. Bertie was working a Saturday morning shift. She had the house to herself. The neatly pressed clothes piled up on a chair. She unplugged the iron, tested it with a damp finger. It still sizzled. She thought, *steaming*, like me! On an impulse she stepped out of her skirt, slipped off her stockings, suspender belt, then her blouse. She consigned them to the washing basket.

Appreciating the coolness of the flagged floor to the soles of her feet, she applied the iron to a crumpled cotton dress. *Summer's here!* she told herself. She was unaware that Bertie had arrived home, was standing in the doorway, bemused by the sight of Eliza in her skimpy rayon petticoat, revealing her pale bare arms and legs.

He cleared his throat to alert her to his presence. She whirled round and glared at him accusingly. 'Why didn't you say you were here?'

'Sorry. I wondered where you all were, came to find you.'

'The girls have gone on a picnic with Tim.' She faltered, colour rising in her cheeks. Fancy being caught out like this! 'I was just ironing my frock...'

'I can see that,' Bertie said, patently unembarrassed. 'Carry on. I'll go upstairs and get changed. Then I'll put the kettle on. We've a chance to talk, eh, being on our own?'

A little later they sat opposite one another in the living-room, Eliza on the rather lumpy settee she had recently purchased second hand and Bertie on what Cora referred to accurately as one of the 'uneasy' chairs. They sipped the hot tea.

'It's funny how tea cools you down on a day like today,' Eliza said gratefully.

'It makes you sweat, I suppose.' Bertie mopped his brow. 'Well, Eliza, I've been waiting for you to say the word.'

'Oh, what word is that?'

'You know very well. Words, actually, like, you're ready to marry me now.'

'We needed some time to get to know each other properly...'

'And have you changed your opinion of me, I wonder?'

She hesitated, thinking of the right thing to say. 'Yes. Though I have wondered from time to time whether the real reason you deserted Biddy was because there was another woman in your life.' When he didn't respond, she continued: 'We all have to forgive and forget what happened in the past. Cora most of all. It's a big step for me, as I get older, I realize I value my independence – making decisions for myself.'

'I wouldn't ask you to give that up. An equal partnership, but on your terms, isn't that what you said? Tell me what you expect of me, Eliza.'

'I want you to promise you won't take off again and leave the girls without a father. They love you, Bertie. Cora trusts you now. I promise to be there for them always, too, and to continue to make a good home for them.'

He set down his cup in the saucer, came to sit next to her. 'What about *us?*'

'I ... promise to be a good, loyal wife.'

'Is that all?' He tilted her chin with his hand, looked at her searchingly.

'A marriage of convenience, Bertie, remember?'

'*You* said that, Eliza. I've grown attached to you. Wouldn't you like children of your own one day? Don't we both need something more?' He stroked her cheek. 'You've got such fine, peachy skin ... goes with the hair,' he added softly.

'Freckles! Go with the hair too,' she said ruefully, but she didn't push him away.

'I saw you in a different light today–'

'You certainly did!' She blushed again.

'Look, I won't go on about that side of it now, but can we decide on a date?'

'How about next month?' She surprised herself. 'We can get a special licence.'

'That sounds good to me.' He was very close to her now. Then his lips were on hers, she was enfolded in his arms. She put up a feeble resistance for a brief moment, then responded eagerly to his kiss. It was so different

124

from her reaction to Nev's overtures.

I love him, despite everything, she realized exultantly, I suppose I always have. But I won't tell him until – *unless* – he lets me know *he* feels the same way. *Dear Lord, please let it be so!*

'Something's up, I can tell!' Cora exclaimed. She and Dede had arrived home unexpectedly early because Dede had been stung on the leg by an insect.

Dede's face was tear-stained. She had obviously made a big fuss. In fact, Tim had uncharacteristically told them bluntly it was time they cleared off and left him in peace. 'I haven't had a single bite, because of *her*.'

So Cora had given her sister a piggy-back and thrown the last sandwich at him.

'We found a dock leaf, but it didn't help much,' Cora told Eliza.

Eliza fetched the vinegar bottle and some cotton wool. 'Here, let me dab it with this. Cora'll make you both a nice, cool drink. We've got some lemonade powder.'

Later, Cora repeated: 'What's up, Eliza?'

Eliza glanced at Bertie, sitting in his chair, rustling the pages of the newspaper.

'You want me to tell her?' he asked. 'Well, Eliza and I have set a date. We're getting married soon. We hope you both approve.'

'Of course we do!' Cora squealed. 'I've been praying you would!'

'Cora!' Eliza said, then like Bertie she began to giggle. 'I'm so glad you're pleased.'

'Better say it now, before you get the wrong idea,' Bertie said. 'It's to be a quiet wedding, we don't want – we can't afford – a big do. Things won't change much.'

'But they *will*.' Cora was always truthful. 'You'll be moving into Dad's room, Eliza, and Dede can have your bed! *We* won't be so crowded. That's good. I need more space to do all the homework that's coming up when I go to the new school.'

When Eliza went upstairs to say goodnight to the girls and to turn the lamp off, she discovered Dede hiding in her bed, with the sheet pulled over her face.

'I just wanted to try the bed out!' she said, coming up for air, all rosy cheeked.

Downstairs again, Eliza told Bertie: 'Well, they've taken the news very well.'

'That's because it's what they were hoping for,' he observed.

'Bertie...' she hesitated, then: 'You didn't say earlier, when I asked if there had been any one other than Biddy. Not that it's any of my business.'

'Biddy obviously didn't say anything to you, but she guessed. Yes, there *was* some-one, but we never lived together. She was a nurse, over here from Canada for a time. When I made that stupid mistake, and had to pay for it, she went back home. I heard from a colleague of hers that she'd married an old friend and didn't want any further contact with me. D'you need to know more than that?'

'No, that's enough. Thank you for being honest with me.'

'And you, Eliza – is there something you want to reveal about your past?'

'I once had a lucky ... escape, that's all. Nothing I'm ashamed of.'

'I believe that,' he said softly. 'I think we'll be very comfortable together.'

Ginny was thrilled at Eliza's news. She wrote:

We have some news of our own! Mal and Helen are getting married later this year. Jimmy said in his second letter home from the prison camp, that Helen was not to wait for him, that he released her from their engagement. She was very upset but Mal then felt free to talk of his feelings for her. It now seems as if they were meant for each other, all along. Of course, we all miss dear Jimmy terribly, but at least he is out of the fighting.

'Out of the fighting,' Eliza repeated to Cora, after reading the letter aloud at breakfast-time. 'I think Jimmy would prefer that, to where he is, don't you?'

Cora nodded. She remembered Jimmy as he was, when she stayed at Westley Farm.

He was still her hero, but she kept this to herself.

'You must have a new dress for the wedding,' Bertie told Eliza. 'I've got a suit I've hardly worn, so you can have my coupons.' He didn't say that the suit in question dated from his first wedding day nearly thirteen years ago. He quickly suppressed the thought that Biddy had worn a loose dress to disguise her pregnancy. Eliza had no need of subterfuge: there had only been that single kiss to seal their commitment to marry.

'Thanks.' Eliza beamed. 'Cora can help me choose something pretty.'

'Tim's mum is making you a wedding cake – I don't know if I'm supposed to say! A sponge, she says, but she'll do the proper glace icing and decorations!' Cora said.

'Well, I'm grateful for that, because I have other things to do. Like whitewashing the walls in the big bedroom. Yellow, particularly nicotine, is not to my taste.'

'Not all due to my smoking: others lived here before,' Bertie said equably.

When she was on her own, after the children had gone to school, Eliza prepared for a day of decorating. She didn't actually use whitewash, but distemper, mixed in a bucket. She found a big brush, gave it a good soak in turps. Eliza donned an old overall, tied a scarf over her hair. Don't want it to turn white before time, she told herself!

She had cleaned the bedroom regularly of course, since her arrival. She usually left Bertie's clean laundry on a chair for him to put away himself. There was a pile of it today. She couldn't risk it being splatted by distemper. She'd shrouded the bed with newspaper, but now she opened the chest of drawers. She felt rather as if she was being nosy, invading Bertie's private space, but she smiled at the untidy contents. She said aloud: 'Might as well get these sorted out right now, eh, Eliza?' She didn't mind handling Bertie's clothes, as she had minded handling Nev's in the past.

The deep bottom drawer was difficult to open. She gave it a further pull. At first she thought it was full of old discarded jumpers, some motheaten, obviously not in current use. When she removed the top layer she discovered that they were a cover-up. Neatly piled beneath were Penguin paperbacks, in the familiar orange and green jackets. Mysteries and adventures were the main types; some of the books were well-thumbed, some obviously recent purchases.

'So this is where the money goes!' she exclaimed, but she was relieved. This was nothing for Bertie to be ashamed of, she thought. He must have been very lonely, living here on his own, until first Cora, then Dede and herself arrived. The books had been his companions. However, she carefully replaced the woollens. After all, she had her secret too: the bundle of notes in her handbag.

She realized she could still have quite a lot to learn about her husband-to-be.

Eliza and Bertie stood side by side in the register office, flanked by their witnesses, Mrs Titchley and Jack, a friend of Bertie's from the colliery. Cora sat between Tim and Dede. Cora looked quite grown up, with her glossy hair newly trimmed to shoulder-length and centre-parted. She wore a pretty blouse and a neat, short skirt, which showed off her burgeoning figure. Dede had a pink party-dress in shiny taffeta, worn once by her sister at her age and saved for a special occasion by Eliza.

Outside, it was unexpectedly raining, and they could see rivulets coursing down the windows. It might be August, but the lights were switched on in that austere room with the plain table and chairs, smelling of furniture polish. A vase of roses and maidenhair fern was the only concession for weddings, of which several were booked that day.

Eliza had dipped into her hoard for her outfit. Cora had wanted her to have a pink costume, but Eliza said, 'Not with my hair!' She banished the thought that green was considered unlucky, and chose a pistachio shade: not really a two-piece, but with the peplum at the front, it appeared so. Tiny chocolate-coloured buttons fastened the bodice: the collar and three-quarter length sleeves were banded with matching brown. She too had visited the local hairdresser, who had a talent for styling hair, and the resulting bubble-cut suited her round face.

She glanced at Bertie. Rather late, he'd discovered that his suit jacket was on the tight side. 'You've been feeding me too well!' he told Eliza. He could only fasten the middle button. She wondered what he was thinking. She gave a mental jerk, the ceremony had commenced. In ten minutes time she would be Eliza Kelly, not Quinn. She would have liked to be married in church, but she'd been brought up a Catholic, and Bertie, she'd learned from Cora, was the son of a devout chapel-going mother.

Her mother's wedding ring, her sole inheritance as the youngest daughter, slid easily on to her finger. She'd preferred this to an inferior, cheap, new band.

'You may kiss the bride,' the registrar repeated to Bertie. He inclined his head, hair shiny with brilliantine, and somewhat bashfully obeyed.

The girls were on their feet and hugging them both then, while the Titchleys and Jack waited to shake hands and congratulate the newly married couple.

The shower of rain was over: the paving stones outside the register office glistened dark and wet, but the sun had emerged through the clouds, and it now seemed it would be a hot day after all. Jack took some snapshots, and Bertie kept his arm firmly round Eliza's waist, gave her a little encouraging squeeze and whispered: 'Smile!'

They caught the bus back home, where a meal was set out on the table covered with a tablecloth. Sausage rolls, spam sandwiches, jam tarts, chocolate biscuits (one apiece) and the splendid wedding cake on Mrs Titchley's best gold-rimmed plate.

Dede, naturally, managed to get jam and chocolate smears on her new dress, but Eliza sponged it clean and hoped for the best.

The cake was cut, the sponge pronounced perfect, bouncy and soft, split and oozing raspberry jam. Eliza and Bertie were toasted in elderberry cordial (Mrs Titchley did not approve of alcohol) and after a final cup of tea, the party broke up.

It was a signal for the family to change their clothes, then to clear the table, wash up and listen to the wireless. The Force's Favourite, Vera Lynn, had them singing fervently along to the latest morale booster, 'The White Cliffs of Dover'.

Eliza, cuddling Dede on her lap, had tears in her eyes. She wondered; when will the war end? I don't want to bring another child into the world until it does. I really am the girls' stepmother now, not just their guardian. I don't suppose Bertie realizes that when we share a bed tonight, it will be the first time for me.

It was after ten before they were on their own. She busied herself with the usual evening chores, filling the water jug, adding a second glass to the tray. She couldn't put it off any longer. 'I'm going up now,' she told Bertie. He smiled, patted her arm. 'I'll be along shortly.' He added: 'It was a good day, wasn't it?'

Eliza nodded, then made her way upstairs. She undressed swiftly. She had a new nightdress, a generous gift from Ginny. Nothing too exciting, she thought, demure white sprigged lawn with thin shoulder straps. But then, they weren't having a honeymoon.

Bertie slipped into bed beside her. She already had her head on the pillow, turned on her side away from him. He asked: 'Mind if I turn my lamp on – read for a bit?'

'If that's what you usually do...'

She had actually relaxed, had closed her eyes, when he put the light out, tucked his book under his pillow. After a moment, he gently touched her shoulder. 'Goodnight then, Eliza.'

She turned towards him. 'Goodnight, Bertie.' She waited. His warm hands caressed her bare shoulders as he drew her close, kissed her. Unexpectedly he released her.

Impulsively she exclaimed before she

could stop herself: 'Is that all?'

'D'you mean...? I wasn't sure,' he whispered.

'I wouldn't have married you, Bertie, if I didn't intend to be a proper wife to you.'

'Oh, Eliza.' He sighed. 'Do I really know you at all?'

'That's how I feel about you!' she admitted.

'Then we must do something about that, eh?'

'That's what I was hoping for,' Eliza said. She mustn't think of Biddy tonight, she told herself, except, she believed Biddy would have approved.

NINE

By mid-September Cora was settling down in her new school. Her early fears, that she would lose her way in the maze of echoing corridors, were soon allayed. The first-year pupils were in the classrooms numbered '1A' or '1B', it was as easy as that. Finding the science laboratory, the art room, the gymnasium and the domestic science block was simple too: Cora hung back and followed the crowd. Morning assembly was held in the big hall, where music lessons and singing also took place.

She was proud of her new uniform. She didn't know that Eliza had dipped into her reserves to buy it. She wore a serviceable serge gymslip with a firmly tied girdle in the school colours of navy and gold. She wasn't skilful yet at knotting the matching tie, but Eliza often helped out in that respect. She was conscious of Eliza's warning: 'Don't put your fountain pen in your blouse pocket in case it leaks!' Cora wasn't enamoured of the voluminous navy interlock bloomers, which were on display in the gym, if you were not fortunate enough to have had an elder sister at the school to pass on a Grecian tunic. These garments were no longer obligatory, but shorts were not yet de rigueur.

Cora was glad she had a shorter hairstyle which was easier to keep tidy, although the girls' hair had to be tied back during school hours. The teachers were sticklers for neatness and politeness: sloppy speech was swiftly corrected. *Shades of the Great Miss Puddefoot,* as Naomi put it, in a recent letter. Cora agreed. She smiled at the PS: 'Bet our bloomers are baggier than yours!'

Being a tall, apparently confident girl, Cora found it easy to fit in. Her companion on the bus to school was not so fortunate. This was Dorothy, Bertie's friend Jack's daughter. Dorothy was timid, afflicted by extreme myopia, which was corrected by unflattering thick glasses. She lived with her grandmother, who sounded like a martinet. Cora soon took on the role of Dorothy's protector against the more pushy girls, who called Dorothy a swot.

'I'm a swot, too – there's nothing wrong with that! Stick with me, and I'll see they don't tease you,' she told Dorothy, who was too often in tears.

One day Dorothy had something important to impart. 'Dad and I are moving in next door to you! My mum and Tim's mum used to come down here from London every summer with their families when they were children, for the hop-picking. They were best friends, like us, but Dad and Lena hadn't seen each other for years until your mum and dad's wedding. Gran says she's done her bit by us! Dad's going to share Tim's room, they're rigging up a curtain down the middle! I'll be in with Lena: we're not bothering with a partition! It'll be nice to be like a family again, I lost my mum when I was only seven.'

'So did I!' Cora exclaimed. She couldn't help feeling a little envious that Dorothy would see more of Tim than she did. She added, 'I can't think of Mrs Titchley as *Lena!*'

'Well, you know more than I do,' Eliza said wryly, when Cora told her the news. 'I wonder if Jack told Bertie? If so, he hasn't said.'

She asked Bertie at supper time. He put his hand on his heart, grinned. 'No, he didn't confide in me – honest!'

136

'You're supposed to be best mates!' Eliza reminded him.

'We got thrown together, I suppose, because we're neither of us politically minded – me, despite my Irish roots. Of course, we follow what the Association decrees, or we'd be out of a job. Did you know that before I arrived there was a miners strike, in 1938? They were out for *weeks*. Many of the chaps were laid off, though there were some places available in another colliery. They weren't allowed to ballot among themselves, as they demanded, to decide who should take these up.

'Thank goodness, the outbreak of war meant plenty of work, even for a reluctant coalface worker like myself. Just last year the Ministry of Labour banned all industrial strikes and lockouts. That's not to say they *can't* happen, if enough of the workforce get together to defy the order. Don't forget, some of our chaps have been involved in a go-slow campaign, following a pay dispute, since before Christmas. There's always been a tough faction in Kent, where the majority of miners originated from other regions.'

'You should find another job where you don't get your hands dirty,' Cora exclaimed.

Bertie and Eliza exchanged glances. 'References are hard to come by,' he said. 'It's mining, or the armed forces, for me.'

Cora was about to say she didn't see why,

regarding references, but decided not to. It was obvious her father was not going to enlighten her.

Although she'd longed for her father and Eliza to marry, she hadn't realized that there was bound to be a subtle change in her own relationship with Eliza. This wasn't the case with Dede, because she was so much younger, she thought. Cora missed those cosy conversations with Eliza when they had shared a room. Now the door to the other bedroom was firmly closed after Eliza called out goodnight each evening. Nothing was said, but she knew instinctively that she shouldn't burst in on Bertie and Eliza when they were in bed. Cora couldn't help feeling jealous when she observed her father greeting Eliza first on his return from work. She was spared the embarrassment of seeing them kiss, but Bertie would give Eliza's waist a squeeze, or he would ruffle her curls as she bent over the stove to see how supper was progressing. Eliza would straighten up, her face flushed from the heat, and exclaim fondly: 'Oh, you!' It seemed too intimate. Cora worried how she would react if they announced they were expecting a baby. The school nurse had given her class the obligatory talk on the facts of life. She comforted herself with the thought that surely Eliza and Bertie were rather old for *that*. Another small sister or brother was not something she looked forward to. Dede was quite a handful!

Less than three weeks before Christmas 1941 there was the surprise attack by the Japanese on Pearl Harbor. The United States was now officially involved in the war. The first American troops would arrive at their British bases in the New Year, 1942. There were other big changes coming up, which would affect the Kelly family personally.

The first of these was Eliza's decision to work part-time at the factory with Lena Titchley. It was clean work, fitting together electrical parts for bigger aircraft components. She'd be taught to use a soldering iron. It was piecework and nimble-fingered women could earn a decent wage. Eliza's shift was from ten until two, so she'd be able to see the children off to school, and be there to meet Dede in the afternoons.

'What if Dede is ill?' Bertie asked her cautiously. He wasn't keen on her working. He earned more than some of the miners, being skilled enough to tackle the more difficult seams of coal. Eliza wasn't being forced into war work, with a young child to care for.

'We'll cross that bridge when we come to it!' Eliza retorted. 'Cora can look after her in the school holidays, of course, starting next week.'

Cora gave a reproachful little sigh, but didn't say anything. Dorothy would no doubt be willing to help, she thought. They weren't due back at school for another week or so.

That first morning they waved Eliza off. She'd caught her hair back in the regulation snood, and would be provided with a dark-green overall and headscarf to fix in a neat turban when she arrived at the factory.

'Keep the fires going!' Eliza called, as she crossed the road to catch the bus. In fact, the girls enjoyed their morning because they seized the chance to do some cooking, as Eliza had suggested.

There were plenty of potatoes, grown by Jack on his allotment and kept in a clamp over the winter months. They decided to make potato pastry. This required much less fat than for shortcrust. Dorothy peeled the potatoes because, as she reminded Cora, 'You don't peel 'em thin enough! My grandma says you waste a lot of the good-ness if you cut the skins too thick – you mustn't be in such a hurry, she says!'

'She's not here – fortunately!' Cora retorted, but she rubbed the knob of marge carefully into the plain flour which was not pure white, like pre-war, being wheatmeal, and added a pinch of salt and a small teaspoon of baking powder. No need to add water, because later, the cooked potatoes would be well mashed before being added to the mixture to bind it together.

Dede demanded: 'Give me a lump of pastry!'

'Wash your hands first, then you can make jam tarts, not play with it like Plasticine!' Cora told her firmly.

Now they had to decide how to fill the pie. More potato and other vegetables to cook. They diced the carrot, swede and onions first to speed the process. Then the mixture, which they grandly called *macedoine,* was spread over a bottom layer of pastry, together with a small amount of grated cheese, a touch here and there of marmite to add extra flavour, plus pepper and salt. The filling was moistened with a dash of the vegetable water, then the top crust was laid in place. The girls decorated it with pastry leaves, fashioned by Dede, and brushed the pie over with a little milk.

'There'll be plenty for Eliza and Dad tonight as well,' Cora said with satisfaction.

'You're very lucky your Eliza trusts you to do some cooking when she's not around,' Dorothy observed. 'Lena says our rations are too limited for me to muck around with...' She removed her glasses. 'I can't see through them, with all the flour Dede's spreading around!' She rubbed the lenses with her hanky.

'You've got beautiful eyes, you know,' Cora exclaimed, as her friend looked at her in that dreamy wide-eyed fashion peculiar to the very short-sighted. Dorothy's lustrous green eyes were fringed by long, curling lashes.

141

'The glasses are an old pair of my grand-ma's, fitted with my prescription lenses. Lena told Dad he should treat me to a new pair.'

'She's right! There you are, she may be strict on some things, but she's very kind in lots of ways, isn't she? Are you hoping she and your Dad'll get married?'

'I don't know about that. I'm not sure Tim would approve either! They're friends, of course, but not madly in love like your Dad and Eliza are.'

'Oh,' Cora said, colouring up. 'How do you know that?'

'Don't be daft,' Dede interrupted. 'Mums and dads *always* love each other. That's how they get babies, isn't it?' She sprinkled more flour on the table top. The remaining pastry was greyish, despite her perfunctory hand-washing.

Cora looked at Dorothy. They both grinned sheepishly. 'We'll have to watch what we say to each other in future, I think,' Cora said ruefully.

Eliza wasn't in the mood for making love one January night. She was tired, possibly she thought, because she'd never worked away from home since she'd taken on the children. She wasn't yet established in a smooth routine. She realized she'd hurt Bertie's feelings when he rolled over to the other side of the bed and lit a cigarette, a

142

habit she hoped he'd given up for her sake, as she disapproved.

It was dark in the bedroom, just a red glow as he drew on the cigarette; a curl of smoke as he exhaled. She wrinkled her nose in distaste. 'Do you have to?'

For the first time since she'd known him, he made an angry reply. This was a shock. She'd been resigned to the fact that he liked a quiet life, no arguments.

'Yes, I *do!*' he hissed vehemently.

'You ... you're cross with me because I didn't want to,' she began, hurt.

'I *needed* to be sure you loved me tonight, Eliza, before I told you some bad news.'

She sat up then, alarmed. 'I'm sorry, Bertie, honestly. Well, tell me, then.'

'We're all out on strike. That's it! We're in breach of Defence Regulations. There'll be compulsory arbitration. Suppose I go back to prison? At the least, we'll be fined. The men say they won't pay up. How can they, on the pittance most earn? They're planning mass demonstrations. I don't want to be involved, nor does Jack, but we've got no choice...' He stubbed out his cigarette in a little tin, kept for that purpose.

'*Come here,*' Eliza said softly. She drew him close, rocked him in her arms. In the cold weather they both wore warm flannel pyjamas. His face was pressed against her jacket buttons. 'Let me make you more comfortable,' she murmured, unfastening them.

'But you're too tired.' His voice was muffled by her full breasts.

'Not now. I want you to know I'll back you all the way – like you, I don't *want* to be involved, but needs must. You ... you said you needed to be sure I love you. Surely you know that, haven't I proved it often enough?'

'Of course I do. It's time to tell you, as if you hadn't guessed, that I feel the same way about you, Eliza. I don't want to be disloyal to Biddy's memory, but it was never like *this.*' His lips caressed her soft skin. 'You're a passionate woman...'

'And the Canadian nurse?' she asked tentatively.

'She fulfilled a need in my life, and I in hers,' he admitted. 'Does it worry you?'

'No. There's no need to say any more,' she said.

Cora had become immune to the thud of the miners' boots as they passed the row of houses on their way to the colliery each working day at dawn. This morning, however, she was awake and feeling fearful, waiting for the single rap on the front door for her father. The men were off to picket the mine. Bertie had taken her to one side when she arrived home from school yesterday, and told her, as simply as possible, why he had been at home all day.

'We're on strike, Cora. Jack and I. Well, we have to go along with the rest, though we hope it can be sorted out without too much trouble. No need to tell Dede, eh?'

'Dad, strikes *always* cause trouble. Ever since the Industrial Revolution...'

'I'm not a leader of men, Cora. I like to keep my head down.'

'Sometimes you have to stick up for your rights! Or other people's.' Cora had recently received a reprimand, rather than praise, at school, for standing up to a clique of bigger girls who were teasing Dorothy at break-time. They had snatched away her glasses and the poor girl was groping around in a vain attempt to find them. Cora had vented her wrath, retrieved the spectacles and was telling the bullies exactly what she thought of them, when a teacher's hand descended heavily on her shoulder.

'Is it time to get up?' Dede enquired sleepily from her bed.

'No, go back to sleep! I am.' But Cora knew she wouldn't.

Eliza opened the door, peeped round at the girls. 'Anyone fancy a cup of tea? I couldn't sleep, either.'

'I'll come and help you.' Cora climbed out of bed and joined her.

Downstairs, she asked: 'Isn't Dad going with the rest of them?'

Eliza shook her head. 'Not today. They say

the leaders will be prosecuted. You have to admire them for standing up for what they believe. But their poor wives and families... I know I did the right thing now, taking on the factory work. At least we'll have *some* money coming in.' She poured out two cups of tea. 'We'll drink it here. Your father's still asleep.'

'How can he be!' Cora exclaimed. She stirred half a teaspoon of sugar in her cup.

'Bertie has learned over the years to put unpleasant things out of his mind. I suppose he was like that with your mother. He didn't want to think about how his absence affected her... I'm sorry, Cora, I shouldn't say that to you, I know.'

'Why not? I'm not a baby any more, like Dede.'

'No, you're not! I ... hadn't realized, you see.'

'Dorothy said you and Dad were madly in love,' Cora confided.

Eliza smiled. 'Do we make it that obvious? He's not, never will be, the perfect husband, but then I'm not the perfect wife. I'm far too strong-willed!'

'Someone has to be! I want to be like you!'

'I hope your life runs more smoothly than mine, my dear.'

'Oh, it will! One day I'll go back to California and...'

'Meet Jimmy again. I know,' Eliza said, smiling.

The entire colliery was involved in the strike. Their spokesmen were sentenced to hard labour. The rest were fined, but stood firm, refused to work or to meet their fines until the men in jail were released. The government was forced to act after some weeks of disruption; the prisoners came home to a heroes' welcome.

The unrest continued until the following May, by which time only a handful of the fines had been paid by the miners. At Eliza's insistence Bertie was among the few. He gained a black eye and a bloody nose from his mate Jack when he found out, for Jack had been swayed by the militants. The confrontation took place with the two of them facing each other, encircled by Jack's new comrades, egging him on. Bertie had never been involved in a fight before in his life. He stood there, shaking his head in disbelief at the much shorter Jack, as he bunched his fists.

But the strike, which had seen other local collieries come out in sympathy, was officially declared over. A disaster had been averted, the war effort was stepped up.

Around this time Eliza suffered a miscarriage. She was three months pregnant. She and Bertie had been about to tell the girls what they hoped they would consider good news. Eliza, despite her distress, was back at work after two weeks. The factory was working flat out too. She had made a commitment which she was determined to honour. Trying to look at her loss objectively, she came to the conclusion that it had not been the right time for them to have a baby. She must have conceived, she thought, the night Bertie told her about the strike. She'd been so anxious and preoccupied with all that that entailed she hadn't had time to be excited about this unexpected event. She was thirty-four years old; she pushed away the thought that she might be too old to have a baby when this awful war was at an end.

Also in May Cora celebrated her thirteenth birthday. She'd guessed Eliza's secret, but they didn't discuss it. There was continuing bad feeling between them and the neighbours. Bertie and Jack ignored each other, Eliza and Lena only communicated at work. Tim avoided Cora, which she found very hurtful, but she and Dorothy were quietly determined to carry on with their friendship.

TEN

July, 1944

'We're going back to California! Eliza's taking us. First thing on Saturday,' Cora cried joyfully. 'An early summer holiday from school, hooray!' She'd called to Dorothy over the back fence to impart the news.

'I wish I could come with you, instead of being sent with Tim to Yorkshire. His uncle is collecting us in his lorry in a couple of days, on his way back from making a delivery at the docks.' Dorothy sighed dolefully. 'Tim and I hardly communicate these days, he's become a misogynist. My dad and his mum know we're not compatible.'

'You're too brainy, boys don't like that,' Cora said candidly. 'You're going to be a scientist, aren't you?' Dorothy was much more confident these days. New glasses with attractive frames had certainly boosted her morale.

'My dad says the young men who had to miss university because of the war will be given priority when the fighting's over. I'll be at the end of the queue!'

'Well, we'll sit our school certificate next

149

year, won't we, and then I'll probably leave and start work after I'm sixteen, because of Dad not being too well. But you'll be definitely staying on, to take your higher certificate.' Cora tried not to sound regretful.

Cora's little red-covered school diary, instigated by Miss Puddefoot, but long neglected, now recorded some important events. The Second Front had begun a month earlier, with the thrilling news of D-Day. Operation Overlord was launched, under a supreme Allied commander, the US General Eisenhower. The landings in France would come to be regarded as the climax of the war: retribution for the desperate retreat from Dunkirk four years ago. Russia was playing a vital role in the East, having taken 100,000 enemy prisoners at Minsk in July. For the people of occupied Europe, there was at last real hope of an end to the conflict.

However, a week after D-Day the Germans launched a terrible new weapon, the V1 flying bomb, targeting London from across the Channel. The defiant Londoners and those along the route, already dubbed Bomb Alley, where a number of the pilotless planes 'cut-out' prematurely, had their own appellations. *Buzz bombs, doodlebugs* were the printable ones. The RAF did their utmost to deflect the menace; pilots learned to tip the wings of the buzz bombs as they approached the coast, to turn them back over the sea.

However, they came in such droves, that a great number inevitably remained on course.

The morning before the authorities decreed that the schools should close Cora and Dorothy had rushed among a crowd of other girls from the bus toward the school gates. Directly overhead there was a sputtering buzz bomb. They flattened themselves *en masse* on the pavement as the engine stopped abruptly. The bomb careered towards the earth. When they heard the explosion, they lifted their heads fearfully. A couple of hundred yards on there was a plume of black smoke from a crater in the road.

A teacher suddenly yelled at them from the school. 'Get up, you girls – *immediately!* Run for the shelter!' The girls were galvanized into action. They were all sent home at lunch time during a lull between raids.

Later, over the garden fence, Cora said to Dorothy in a low voice, because the bedroom window in her house was open: 'We don't like leaving Dad. Doctor says it's chronic bronchitis, he must rest up. He's had to sign on. Eliza's made him promise to sleep in the cellar, just in case. She's made it more comfortable for him down there. She's only staying one night with Ginny.'

They both looked up as they heard yet another explosion – of harsh coughing, this time, from Bertie in the bedroom. Then Eliza

151

poked her head out of the window. 'You're supposed to be packing, Cora, remember? Dede's filling the case with her toys!'

''Bye, Dorothy. Have a good time tramping on the moors!'

''Bye Cora. Watch where you're treading on the farm.' Dorothy pinched her nose.

There was the disturbing drone of a lone buzz bomb. Even as they instinctively ducked, it passed low over their heads. A quick wave, then both scurried indoors, as Eliza shouted *'Cora!'* and slammed the window shut. Belatedly, the siren blared.

Bertie came downstairs in his dressing-gown to see them leave. He was wan and unshaven, but managed a grin. 'Looking forward to some peace and quiet with no chattering females around. Have a good time, girls, don't forget to write.'

There was a knock on the door. 'Who's that?' Eliza exclaimed. 'We don't want to miss the bus.'

Her eyes widened in surprise when she saw Jack standing on the step.

He said diffidently; 'Dorothy told me you were going to Norfolk. Lena said it was high time I helped an old friend in need. I'll be glad to keep an eye on Bertie for you.'

'Thank you.' Eliza sounded hesitant. She added: 'It's been so long, Jack. I've never understood it. Come in. We're just off. No

152

trouble, mind. Bertie's not up to it.'

'I understand.' Jack waited while Cora and Dede, then Eliza embraced Bertie.

As they clambered aboard the bus, heaving their suitcases before them, Eliza murmured to Cora, 'Oh, I *do* hope I did the right thing...'

''Course you did. You always do,' Cora said stoutly. She had a funny feeling inside her about leaving her dad: he'd hugged them in turn as if he didn't want them to go. The rattling of his chest was alarming. But she was glad he and Jack had made up.

'Fares, please,' said the conductor. 'We're running late already and I've heard part of the approach to the railway has been cordoned off due to flying-bomb damage.' They left the bus before the station stop and ran the rest of the way, arriving out of breath.

When they reached Liverpool Street station they heard the sinister dying notes of the siren. Their train was already alongside the platform. The last-minute travellers were not allowed aboard, but urged to the waiting-room. Eliza and the girls crammed inside with other families. Dede, usually so confident and bouncy, gave a little, hiccupy sob and clung to Eliza's jacket sleeve. Then they heard the thunder of anti-aircraft guns.

'Gone over,' an old porter told them laconically. 'One after another. Like a flock of giant, ugly birds. Get on the train now, the all-clear's sounding.'

Their carriage was so packed, with civilians and military personnel that they couldn't sing out, as Cora and Dede had intended, *Californy, here we come.* Instead, Cora whispered the words to her sister as she sat her on her lap, holding her tight, because she was aware that eight-year-old Dede was still shaking from their recent experience. Cora thought, I'm terrified, too. And Dad's likely worrying about us, coming into London. How *can* the great city recover, when this blooming war is finally over?

They travelled from the station, not as Cora and Eliza had – was it really so long ago? – in the pony-trap, but bundled in the back of a utilitarian vehicle which Mal, who was driving, told them was a Jeep. It was littered with straw and smelled strongly of pigs. As they bowled along they saw that the gaps down to the sea were barred by barbed-wire coils.

At first sight Westley Farm looked much the same as it had before. Mal came round to help them out of the Jeep. He took off his checked cap. Eliza and Cora were surprised to see that his once blond thatch of hair had receded at the temples and darkened. Mal had lost his boyish look.

He's a married man now – he always was serious, but now he looks impatient to get back to the evening chores, Eliza thought.

'Here comes Ginny,' she said aloud, with relief. 'Helen, too...'

After all the hugging they followed Ginny and her daughter-in-law indoors.

'Supper in fifteen minutes.' Ginny smiled. 'Helen will take you upstairs. Did I tell you the land girls have recently departed? One became pregnant, and the other married another local farmer. So for now we have plenty of room, if more to do.'

Helen, in khaki shorts and faded shirt, untied, then discarded her heavy farm boots. She padded ahead of them, in her thick socks.

'You and Dede are in the room you slept in last time you were here,' she told Cora. 'It's been called Cora's room ever since.' The girls disappeared eagerly inside.

Helen and Eliza climbed the next flight of stairs. 'My old room, too,' Eliza exclaimed, pleased.

'I'm often next door in Jimmy's bedroom when I can't sleep at nights,' Helen said in a matter-of-fact way. 'It's where I wanted to be, among all his books, when I came here to help out before Mal and I were married.' She moved away. 'I'll leave you to it.'

'Don't go, I won't take a minute, just a quick tidy-up.'

Helen closed the door. She pulled off the elastic band restraining her thick brown hair, shaking her head as if to hide her expression.

'What's up?' Eliza asked softly.

'Mal and I ... don't sleep together. We never have. I was prepared to be a proper wife to him. However, when he found out–'

'Sit down. Tell me, if you want to.'

'Ginny doesn't know – she mustn't! Jimmy and I, well, we couldn't help ourselves you see, before he went away, joined up.'

'You mean, you made love?'

'Yes. Luckily, there were no consequences, no baby. Just as well, he's been a prisoner of war now for four years. Maybe he won't even remember what happened.'

'Oh, I think he will. You do. But it's not Mal's fault, is it? He never said how he felt about you until Jimmy ended the engagement, did he? You're fond of Mal, aren't you?'

'Of course I am. We're a good team on the farm. We've actually got more in common than Jimmy and I had. But when Mal challenged me on our wedding night, said he had to know, I told him the truth.'

'That was probably unwise,' Eliza told her. 'I had to accept, you know, that my Bertie had plenty of experience before we married. Not just with dear Biddy, the girls' mother, but another woman, maybe more than one. We've made a good life together, and put the past behind us. I had to make the first move. That's what you must do.'

'I'm not sure I know what you mean...'

Eliza put a hand on her shoulder, gave her

a little squeeze. 'When, on our first night to-gether, all we did was kiss goodnight, well...'

'I still don't understand,' Helen admitted.

'I got my courage up and asked him: "Is that all?"'

'Was it?'

'I'm happy to tell you, it wasn't.'

'Oh, *I see.* I'm sorry to tell you my troubles so soon after your arrival, but you're the first person I've been able to confide in, Eliza.'

'My dear – don't you imagine Ginny guessed long ago?'

Cora tapped on the door. 'Ginny sent me to tell you, "come and get it!"'

The supper table was laden with good home cooking. Dede was already tucking in, sitting alongside Ginny.

'I don't know where Mal's got to,' Ginny said. 'Dede couldn't hold out any longer.' She looked fondly at the little girl. 'We're best pals already: fancy, we had to wait all this time to meet! Reminds me what I'm missing, with no grandchildren as yet.'

Eliza and Helen exchanged a brief glance. Mal took his place at the head of the table. He was well-scrubbed and had changed his clothes. Surely he had overheard.

'I should have put a dress on.' Helen, flustered, stood up. 'Excuse me..' She had a lot to think about.

The light switch clicked on next door. Eliza

sighed. Was Helen about to spend another lonely night in Jimmy's room? She turned over in her single bed, missing Bertie. Should she have given the advice she had earlier? Ten minutes later she heard footsteps retreating. *Help them to come together,* was her prayer that night.

Mal didn't acknowledge her return, but Helen guessed he was awake. In the dark, she addressed his rigid back. 'Mal, I won't be leaving our bed at night again, I promise you. I've closed the door on Jimmy's room. I ... need you to give me another chance, to forget what happened before we were wed – haven't I been punished enough?'

He answered then. 'I don't blame you, Helen. Jimmy was irresponsible. He always did what he wanted to do. I had to knuckle down on the farm at an early age.'

'Oh, Mal, Jimmy and I were engaged, only nineteen years old; he was going away. I can't regret what occurred. He won't be the same person when he comes back, after all he's been through. I know I've changed, too, grown up. You're the right one for me, Mal. I've never doubted your feelings for me, but unless they are consummated–'

'Our marriage will remain a sham, and Mother won't have the chance of those grandchildren she's on about,' Mal said gruffly. He slid his arms round her tentatively, then tightened his clasp convulsively.

'Don't let's waste any more time, eh?'

After breakfast, Cora asked Ginny: 'Can I show Dede round the farm – could we collect the eggs? She wants to see the beehives, where this jar of honey came from, too.'

'So long as you don't worry Helen in the dairy – or Mal – he hasn't had his breakfast yet, and he doesn't say a lot until he has,' Ginny advised. 'The basket's in the kitchen.'

'I'll have to leave here by ten,' Eliza reminded them.

'You must take some eggs and honey back with you for Bertie,' Ginny said. Letting the girls explore for a bit would give them time to talk about the problems in Kent.

Mal wasn't dour at all, but greeted them with a wide grin. He lifted Dede up to look over into the pig pen, and he told her about the bees. 'I'll maybe get you some honeycomb later, the sweetest thing you'll ever taste.' Then they went to find the eggs.

'The cats!' Cora exclaimed, when she placed the basket of brown eggs on the table. 'Can we give them their milk?'

Ginny filled the jug which Cora recalled from before. 'The old ginger tom's still around, believe it or not. He lost half his ear in a fight. He's a survivor, all right.'

The barn door was ajar; they blinked in the half-light. There was sacking nailed across the cracked windows. It was a few moments before they realized they were not on their own. They saw Helen first, in a creased cotton dress, sitting on a straw bale. Kneeling behind her, gently brushing chaff from her long, loose hair, was Mal, with his shirt unbuttoned as if it was the middle of the day. Both had flushed faces.

They've been kissing! Cora realized. They didn't want anyone to see them. She emptied the jug into the dishes. 'Come on. Dede – no telling tales, now!'

'Thanks!' Mal called after them. 'Catch!' A bright coin flashed through the air.

The sixpence landed by Cora's feet. She picked it up. 'Look, Dede – a tanner to keep mum!' She closed the barn door carefully behind them. It's nice, she thought, Mal and Helen can still be romantic when they've been married some years...

'Did you see Ginger?' Ginny enquired.

'Not today,' Cora replied, giving Dede a warning little pinch. Big sisters were expected to be responsible: to put smaller fry in their place.

'*Ow!* I found sixpence,' Dede said. 'Cora's keeping it safe for me!' She whistled a popular ditty through the gap in her teeth: *I've got sixpence, jolly, jolly sixpence....*

Eliza brushed the tears from her eyes as she watched from the open train window; the waving figures on the platform receded as the London train steamed away. So much travelling, she thought, for such a brief stay on the farm. Some of that spent worrying whether Helen and Mal had begun to sort things out. At least the girls were removed from danger, for a while, she hoped. Ginny had wept too, when they talked, confessing her fears for Jimmy at present, now that the invasion of Europe was under way. Maybe, Eliza hoped, Ginny will have something else to think about if Helen has taken my advice! If only *we* hadn't decided to wait so long before having a baby. Too late now, with Bertie being ill. The doctor hasn't said, but please God it's not the miners' lung disease.

Fortunately the passengers were able to disembark at Liverpool Street without incident. Eliza arrived, relieved, at Canterbury, and spotted a lone taxi waiting for a woman she knew. The two women walked along together.

'Just back from taking my children somewhere safer for the summer, like you,' the woman told her. 'Would you like a lift?'

'Would I! Thanks!' Eliza agreed.

She was home. Even as she groped in her bag for her keys the door opened and Jack ushered her in. Eliza could tell from his face that something had happened.

Her legs suddenly buckled, she sat on the nearest chair. 'Where's Bertie?'

'He had ... a bit of a turn.'

161

'What does that mean?' she demanded.

'I found him this morning. He was still down the cellar, he slept there last night. There was blood on the blankets, Eliza. He was too poorly to rise. I called Lena, and she sent Tim on his bike for the doctor. He went by ambulance to the hospital.'

'Did the doctor say – what?'

Jack shook his head. 'Not to me. Better come and see Lena. Our kids were picked up earlier. You'll be able to talk to her.'

'I had a feeling I shouldn't have gone away!' Eliza was sobbing in earnest now.

ELEVEN

The wards were full: there had been casualties from the bombing taken there all weekend. However, the following morning Eliza discovered, after hurrying down several different corridors and not finding Bertie, that he was isolated in a private room away from the busy part of the hospital. The sister in charge was non-committal, telling Eliza that a doctor would explain things to her later. It was best she wait in the day-room because Bertie was still undergoing tests. Eliza was merely permitted to wave at him through the glass panel on the door, but she wasn't sure that he saw her.

'A nice cup of tea,' a young nurse said, bringing her a tray. 'Biscuits? I don't suppose you stopped for breakfast, did you?'

'No. I had to call in at work, and explain I needed to take a day or two off.'

The nurse looked at her sympathetically. 'Prepare yourself for rather longer than that. Mr Kelly is very ill.'

The cup clattered lopsidedly in the saucer, tea puddled the small table. Eliza mopped at it ineffectually with her clean handkerchief.

'Are *you* all right?' the nurse queried. 'Leave that, I'll get someone to deal with it.'

'This ... has all been a terrible shock,' Eliza managed.

'Yes, of course it has. Try not to worry too much.'

The morning wore on, and Eliza still sat there, twisting the damp handkerchief in her hands, trying not to look at the clock on the wall. People came and went, smiled at her, made a cheerful comment or two. She could only bring herself to give a brief nod, to show she was aware of their presence. It was almost midday before the sister came in. 'Will you follow me, please, Mrs Kelly? The doctor can talk to you now.'

'I would like to show you something,' the doctor began without further preamble. Eliza gazed at the X-ray plates, with the light illuminating each one. The doctor added:

'Your husband has pulmonary tuberculosis. Both lungs are affected, one not as badly as the other. He must be moved to a sanatorium.'

'Sanatorium...' Eliza repeated faintly. She sank down on the proffered chair. 'But I thought...'

'You thought, as did your doctor, who sent Mr Kelly here, that your husband was suffering from pneumoconiosis, because of his work as a miner? The inhalation of coal dust was no doubt a contributing factor.'

'Is that what you call it? Yes.' *Sanatorium*, she thought, full of fear. The Swiss Alps, that's where those who could afford it went before the war. Exposure to cold, fresh air helped in the long road to recovery.

'I can guess what you are thinking,' the doctor said. 'Your husband will have to go away; he cannot be nursed at home, especially as you have children to consider. The disease is contagious. It is more prevalent again, the overcrowding in public air-raid shelters is possibly one of the causes.'

'We've never used those. Where will he go? Doctor, is treatment very expensive?' The only savings they had, she thought, was a mere twenty pounds or so, all that was left from the money generously given to her by her former employer.

'Before the war we could have sent Mr Kelly to the Royal Sea Bathing hospital in

Margate. Patients suffering from TB who need prolonged nursing care now have to travel further afield. There are sanatoria endowed by charities. One of these is in Scotland. A lovely setting, within a pine forest. We have contacted them. They are willing to take him and two other patients. The Red Cross will arrange transport.'

'*Scotland!*' It might just as well be Switzerland, Eliza thought.

'I'm afraid there has to be a means test, but, of course, as your husband is unable to work...' he paused. 'I am sorry to give you further cause for worry, but you, your children, and anyone who has come into close contact with Mr Kelly, will have to attend the hospital for chest X-rays and have samples of blood taken. There is also a procedure called a Mantoux test, which Sister will explain to you.'

'Our daughters are away,' Eliza explained. 'Staying with my aunt in Norfolk. They seem to be perfectly well. They are there because of the flying bombs...'

'A sensible precaution. Your aunt will be informed, and instructed to take the children to a designated hospital for the tests. In the meantime, your house will be fumigated by the local authority, before their return home.'

'When will I be able to go back to work?' she asked. 'My husband is on the panel at the doctor's, and I imagine the union will help, but–'

'That will depend on the results of your medical. How many children have you?'

'Two. They are fifteen and eight years old.'

'You are fortunate to have such a small family. I must ask you, is there any possibility that you might be pregnant now?'

'No,' Eliza said flatly, 'no possibility at all.' Not now, or in the future, she thought.

'You should go home, for you have arrangements to make. Your husband is in good hands here, I assure you. There is no miracle cure for tuberculosis, but there is a lot the patient can do to help himself. Complete bed-rest is essential. The recovery rate is much improved. But you must still expect him to be away for at least a year.'

The doctor shook hands with her. 'Goodbye for now, and good luck, Mrs Kelly.'

Eliza knocked on her neighbour's door before going into her own house. She retreated down the short path as the door opened. Lena was drying her hands on her apron. She waited apprehensively for Eliza to speak first.

'Bertie has TB,' Eliza stated.

'I'm sorry to hear that. Is that why you're keeping your distance?'

Eliza nodded.

'I had a feeling … that's why I left the soiled blankets. I lost my mother, you see,

166

and two of my sisters to it.' Lena had never spoken of her loss before.

'My dad died of it, too.' Why did I shut my eyes to the signs? she thought; the notches Bertie made in his belt because he lost weight; his flushed face, the sweating, the pains in his chest he put down to indigestion. He had, at her insistence, been treated by the doctor for the cough which refused to go away.

'What's going to happen?' Lena asked.

Eliza gave her a brief résumé of the doctor's talk.

'I wish I could ask you in, make you a cup of tea, but...' Lena looked worried.

'D'you know what I need most, Lena? Sleep. To blot it all out for a few hours.'

'You do that, my dear. Call us if you need us.'

'I will. Lena...'

'Yes?'

'It's good to be back, you know, the way we were, before our men fell out.'

Eliza went upstairs, hesitated by her bedroom door, then turned and went into the girls' room. The beds were neatly made up. She pulled the curtains, took off her top clothes, then curled up in Dede's smaller bed. There was a bulge under the pillow. She pulled out a little rag doll, which had been inadvertently left behind. It was something to hold on to. She was too exhausted

167

to pray for anything except oblivion.

'Thank God,' Ginny said fervently as they left the hospital after hearing the results of their tests. 'You two are all right, and so is Eliza. So make the most of your holiday here, won't you? Though I sometimes wonder if it's as safe here as Eliza believes. Old Lowestoft has been bombed quite a lot, but then it's only twenty miles across the North Sea from Germany. They've had their share of them doodlebuggers!'

'Aunty Ginny!' Young Dede was scandalized. 'Bugs, not–' Cora clapped her hand over her sister's mouth, to prevent her saying it.

'It's so nice here,' Cora said. 'But Eliza must be lonely. She can't even visit Dad. She sends letters to him, but he's not allowed to write back yet.'

Ginny put an arm round each of them and hugged them to her. 'Why don't you ask if she wants you back with her, Cora? You could leave Dede with us, eh? You're just the age to be a good support to Eliza.'

'Eliza's cared for Dede and me all these years; I'd really like to look after her now.'

The following Saturday Eliza arrived, and agreed to take Cora home with her.

There was a letter at last from Bertie.

'Baked, no doubt, before posting.' Eliza's lips quivered. She read aloud:

168

It's much colder here, quite a shock to the system.

Every day all us chaps (we are strictly segregated!) are wheeled out in our beds into the grounds. We shiver away and breathe in the country air, with the heady scent of pine, but we can only look up and see the treetops against the sky, while lying flat on our backs.

Our beds are so close we are packed like sardines in our ward. I am still undergoing tests, but no treatment as yet. It is a case of wait and see.

The staff are kind, the food is good, if not very hot, but the RULES! 'Thou shalt not ... talk, spit, read, sit up or be ungrateful, for you are lucky to be here.'

I miss you, and the girls more than I can say. My love, Bertie.

PS. If they are not too motheaten please send me a couple of my old jerseys. I need them to keep warm in bed!

Eliza added: 'He writes a good letter, that's where you get it from, Cora.'

Ginny said: 'He doesn't ask how you are, or how you are managing.'

Eliza immediately rose to his defence. 'I'm back at work, he knows that.'

'I didn't mean... I just wish you could stay on here with me.'

169

'I didn't like the bit about spitting,' Dede put in, making a face.

'Dad's got good manners, he'd never do that!' Cora told her primly.

'Thank goodness! That's how the disease is mostly spread,' said Eliza, adding: 'Cora's school will be reopening soon. In another week it will be September. The buzz bombs are easing off now that so many of the launching sites have been destroyed by the Allies. We have to believe this is the beginning of the end of the war in Europe.'

'I do hope you're right,' said Ginny. 'In the meantime, Dede can attend our local school while she's here. I'm glad to have my honorary granddaughter a bit longer!'

Cora and Eliza returned to Kent, fortunately unaware that a new wave of terror was about to begin. At the beginning of September, the V2, a rocket, not a pilotless plane like its predecessor, hit London, causing devastation. There was another mass evacuation from the capital, for the V2 was a silent weapon which could not be foiled in the same way as the V1. Winter was approaching as the Allies advanced to attack the new rocket bases, and Bertie endured his first bout of surgery, artificial pneumothorax, the collapsing of one lung to rest it and encourage healing. He could not even pass the time in reading, for the ward sister had confiscated the paperback books Eliza had concealed in

170

the sleeves of the woollens she had sent him.

Anyone would think you had sent me a hacksaw to make my escape! Nothing escapes Sister's eagle eye.

Eliza smiled wryly as she read these words. Bertie's writing was uneven, faint in places. How long would it be before they were reunited? Could married life – love – ever be the same, she wondered. Would Bertie ever be able to work again? Would they have to move away from here?

Tim and Dorothy were back, next door. Tim cast covert glances at the almost grown-up Cora, at her trim figure, her shining fall of hair and pretty face. However, the old rapport had long gone. He was aware that Dorothy was jealous because he did not look at her in the same way. For his part, he envied the close friendship between the two girls, the whispering whenever he came upon them together, the giggling, which he suspected was directed at himself. He agonized over the acne on his face, unaware that Cora and Dorothy also regarded the appearance of any angry spots with despair. They learned to disguise the blemishes with calamine lotion; Tim was told by his mother to scrub his skin with carbolic soap.

Eliza reassured Cora with plenty of hugs. 'You're so tall and beautiful! And clever too.

Your dad will be so proud of you. As I am.'

They were sitting by the fire when she said that, Eliza still with her hair in a snood, looking pale and tired. She hadn't been in long from work. Cora lit the fire when she arrived home from school, and started cooking the evening meal. After they washed up, she settled down to her homework. She was still catching up after the summer break on the farm, and the school certificate was looming next spring. They missed Dede, of course, but it seemed best to leave her with Ginny, Mal and Helen while Bertie was away. The war still dragged on, and the V2 rocket menace continued.

Now, Cora asked: 'D'you think my mum would have been proud too?'

Eliza had a lump in her throat. She said huskily: 'I know she would.'

'Eliza – did you really marry Dad for my sake and for Dede? Do you sometimes wonder if it would have been better if the three of us had stayed as we were? I know, you see, that Dad might not get better. Meanwhile you're wearing yourself out trying to manage, I know that, too...'

'I married your dad, Cora, because I fell in love with him. Oh, not when we moved here, long before that. Biddy and I – well, she was the one he chose, of course.'

'Is that why you didn't marry anyone else? Old Nev was keen, I think.'

'I'd have been a widow soon enough, he was killed in action, after all. I do have respect for his memory, but I would never have married him.'

'Well, I'm glad you didn't,' Cora said vehemently. 'Dad needs you, we all do.'

'As I need you.' Eliza yawned. 'I've toffees in my bag. Let's share them, eh?'

There was a new nurse on duty in Bertie's ward that night. She moved silently between the beds, tucking in a sheet here and lightly placing a cool hand on a fevered brow, there. She shone her torch on the signs above each patient. SILENCE was requested for the patients on either side of Bertie. This was because tuberculosis had affected the throat and larynx.

Bertie gave a plaintive little cough, to show he was awake and required attention.

'Water?' the nurse whispered. 'Are you allowed to sit up?' The torch illuminated his face as he whispered back: 'Yes.' The nurse's own face was shadowed.

She didn't chink the glass against his teeth, or let water drip down his chin, as she held the tumbler to his lips.

'Thank you,' he said, slipping down in the bed. Something was puzzling him. The nurse was about to move on, when he plucked at her arm. 'Do I ... do I know you?'

'Well, I believe I know you. Your chart

names you as Albert Kelly. Are you called Bertie?' He nodded. 'This is the last place I expected to see you,' she said.

'I heard you went back to Canada, got married.'

'It didn't work out. I returned here, just before war broke out. My son stayed in Ontario, with my parents. And you, what happened after you left – that place?'

'I was sent to a Kent coalmine. My first wife died, I married again. My children are with my second wife, Eliza.'

'I must get on,' she said. 'We will catch up with each other later.'

'Goodnight, Lindy,' he said.

TWELVE

May, 1945

There was dancing in the streets, beacons were lit at high points all over the country; there was a cacophony of bells and packed churches on VE Day, following Winston Churchill's broadcast to the nation proclaiming victory in Europe. The joyful celebrations continued throughout the night. Crowds gathered outside Buckingham Palace when the Royal Family were joined by the Prime

Minister on the balcony. The cheers were deafening; London was literally lit up once more.

There were many street parties to come. Trestle-tables were laden with hoarded food. Dede was reunited with Cora and Eliza in time to join in the festivities. However, Bertie remained in the sanatorium, with no definite news of his release.

It was not yet the end of the conflict with Japan. Troops fought on in Burma, while Allied prisoners of war awaited repatriation. Jimmy was among the first to come home.

Ginny was careful not to say too much about the reasons for this, aware of how much the Kelly family missed Bertie. She wrote to Eliza:

I know how keen you are to see Jimmy, and I hope it will be possible for you and the girls to visit us later in the summer. I am feeding him up, but he doesn't have much appetite.

He sends his best to you all. I pray Bertie will be home soon, too. I have some exciting news! Helen and Mal are expecting a baby in the new year. All well in that respect...

Eliza was happy that her advice to Helen had obviously worked, but she felt a twinge of regret that her own hopes had been cruelly dashed.

Bertie was now up and about most of the day, permitted to walk to the bathroom, although still clad in hospital pyjamas and dressing gown. He wondered wryly if this was to discourage escape. The doctors expressed cautious optimism; he had endured several more sessions of pneumothorax and was responding well to treatment. Wheelchair excursions to the occupational therapy centre were the highlight of his week. Here the sexes mingled: the women were more industrious than the men at craftwork. Knitting needles clicked, crochet hooks clipped in and out of woollen knee-blankets, fine hems were sewn. Bertie wrestled with basket-weaving. He half-listened to the gossip around him, but preferred to retreat into his own private thoughts. World events seemed of little importance compared to his longing to be with his family.

It was Lindy's last week at the sanatorium. She was returning to her homeland, to the young son she had been parted from for six long years. Over the past year she and Bertie had not referred to their previous relationship.

'D'you fancy a detour among the pines?' she suggested, on her last morning. Without waiting for his answer she pushed the wheelchair along a winding path, which veered to the left of the route to the craft centre.

It was always breezy on the slopes and the

scent from the shivering pines was invigorating. Lindy paused to tuck the blanket firmly round Bertie's waist. If it slipped it could tangle in the wheels.

He couldn't control the sudden impulse to touch the neat coil of pale hair in the nape of her neck, as she bent to adjust the cover. She straightened up instantly, her face as flushed as his own, her eyes betraying mixed emotion.

'Perhaps this wasn't such a good idea,' she said, applying the brake. She stood for a moment, looking down at him, incredibly slender in her uniform. Very different from his little, curvaceous Eliza. 'I still have feelings for you, Bertie,' she stated baldly.

'I ... I'm sorry,' he mumbled.

'I know. You're a reformed character these days. I never saw you as a family man. You and your Eliza – you obviously have something we never had.' She paused. Then: 'Did you ever love me?'

'Your friendship meant a lot to me...'

'It went further than friendship.'

'Yes. I don't regret that. If we'd met again, somewhere other than here, perhaps I would have been tempted... There is something I have to ask you. Your son...?'

'Was born a year after we parted. There, you can stop feeling guilty,' she said.

Lindy released the brake, turned the chair. 'You'll be on your way home soon, too. I shouldn't be telling you that, it's the doctor's place to do so. Go back to your Eliza and the children and do the very best you can for them. That's all I ask of you.'

'I won't forget you, Lindy,' he promised. 'I'm sorry I can't kiss you goodbye.'

'Just as well, eh?' She managed a smile. She had lied, for the sake of a woman she had never met, but whom she felt she knew: Eliza.

The war with Japan ended in August, though the actual surrender was on 2 September. Cora found the atom bomb too terrible to contemplate. She recorded only:

There is great relief that VJ Day is here at
  last.
We are going to California to celebrate.
Best of all, Jimmy will be there.

'Keep an eye on Dede,' Eliza reminded Cora.

The girls were accompanying Mal, Helen and other young people to a special ceremony. At midnight bonfires blazed all along the cliffs at California, sparks flew; the beach below and the rolling sea were illuminated by the reflected light. Potatoes roasted in the embers, to be split when cooked; precious butter melted on the floury halves, running down chins to spot clothes with grease. A simple feast, but one never to be forgotten. Thermos flasks of milky tea and Bakelite cups were produced from rucksacks; a couple of hip flasks containing something stronger were secretively passed around. Courting couples lurked among the scrubby bushes; children danced about, singing, and waved improvised 'sparklers' – thin, dry sticks with smouldering tips.

Helen rested against a hummock of grass, with Mal's arm round her shoulders.

He scooped out some potato and fed her with it from a spoon.

'You're spoiling me,' she said.

'They're still too hot to handle.'

'My hands are as tough as yours after doing the same jobs as you on the farm.'

'Maybe,' he conceded. He took a quick look round, then gave her a quick kiss on the lips. He lightly caressed the slight swell of her stomach. 'Think they've guessed?'

'Of course they – if you mean the crowd here – have.'

'Has Jimmy realized?'

'Like you, I haven't spoken much to him since he came home He ... he's turned in on himself. Who knows what he's thinking?'

'He could be wondering why you didn't wait – why you married me, Helen.'

'You know what he wrote...'

'Yes, but did he really mean it?'

Helen stood up. 'We'd better see where

179

Cora and Dede have got to. It's getting on for two a.m. – time to drive home, I reckon.'

Eliza and Ginny stayed up until the early hours too, at the farm, stirring a cauldron of soup to warm the revellers on their return. Jimmy remained in his room. The Kelly family had arrived the day before for a long weekend, but had not yet seen him.

A sleepy Dede was carried off to her bed in her little room. Now that Cora was older, she shared with Eliza.

She yawned, carried her empty soup plate to the sink. 'Mind if I go up?'

Ginny patted her arm. 'Sweet dreams, Cora. We'll try not to wake you later.'

They want to talk, I reckon, Cora said to herself, about the baby and that. Ginny doesn't realize I'm sixteen years old, and know it all.

There was a light showing under Jimmy's door, next to the guest bedroom. Cora couldn't help herself: she tapped on the door. She didn't expect an answer, certainly not the invitation: 'Come in!'

Slowly, she turned the handle, ventured inside. Jimmy was sitting, still fully clothed, on top of the covers, hunched against the pillows piled on his bed.

'I guessed it was you,' he said. 'Well, take a seat, and let me look at you. How many years is it since we last met?' His voice was low, husky. He cleared his throat.

'Nine,' she calculated swiftly.

'How old are you now?'

'Sixteen.'

'Almost grown up.'

'Not almost, I am! And you – you must be twenty-five?'

'Not quite. But I feel much older than that.'

She mustn't say it wasn't surprising. They both remained silent.

Cora was aware that he was staring at her. She wished she wasn't wearing the old clothes recommended for the picnic on the cliffs. She'd donned a pair of Helen's dungarees, rolled the legs up to her bare calves, put sandals on grubby feet, and was wearing a cotton top she'd made last summer, which had split under the arms since she'd grown proper bosoms, as Eliza put it. She folded her arms across her front instinctively.

In turn, Cora took in Jimmy's altered appearance. He was painfully thin. His face was unhealthily pale, the freckles prominent. But his hair, she noted with relief, had not receded like his brother's; Jimmy still had his mop of cropped, sandy curls.

When he opened his mouth to speak again, she was shocked to see that some of his teeth were in urgent need of dental attention. He guessed at her reaction.

'Prison-camp diet,' he said matter-of-factly. '*You* look well on wartime rations. Well, Cora Kelly, time to say goodnight, I think.'

181

'We haven't said hello properly, yet.' This wasn't the reunion she'd dreamed of.

'Not too old for a hug, are you? I'm glad to see you, Cora.' He smiled at her.

Cora rose in a rush, almost knocking the chair over. She crossed to the bed. He took her hands in his, pulled her close, kissed the top of her head.

'You smell of bonfire smoke, Cora Kelly. Well, aren't you going to repeat those words I've waited to hear again?'

'I ... I don't know what you mean,' she prevaricated. He loosened his clasp, and she sank down on the edge of the bed beside him.

'Of course you do,' he teased.

'I was a silly little girl then.'

'You were nothing of the sort. You were brave, funny – and honest. I thought of you while I was incarcerated – does that surprise you? You'd come through some awful things too – losing your mother after being desperately ill yourself, when you were so young. You were sort of my inspiration, Cora. If you could make it, so could I.'

Cora put her hand on his shoulder, stretched up to whisper in his ear. 'When I grow up I'm going to marry you, Jimmy Brookes! There, satisfied?'

He smiled. 'You'd better go. Goodnight, Cora.'

Disappointed, she made her way to the

door. Then she turned to say: 'Will I see you tomorrow? D'you know how much every-one is worrying about you?'

He nodded. 'Time, that's what I need most. Too much time wasted...'

She closed the door behind her. She thought, at least he didn't respond, when I said what I did: *Some hope, Cora Kelly.*

Ginny helped Mal with the necessary early-morning chores, while Eliza cooked break-fast for the workers, and for the rest of the household, who appeared at intervals, lured downstairs by the smell of frying bacon. Helen came into the kitchen in her dressing-gown. All she could manage, she said rue-fully, was: 'A large mug of tea. No milk.'

Cora and Dede tucked in happily; double-yoked eggs – what a treat! They were just on the toast and honey when Jimmy came in. The family tried to conceal their surprise. Dede vacated her chair. 'You can sit here, Jimmy, I'm so full I could bust!'

'Not for me, thanks,' Jimmy said, as his mother was wondering whether there was enough bacon for another breakfast. 'Any toast going?'

'I'll make some more,' Cora offered. She felt embarrassed, sitting next to Jimmy who looked rumpled as if he'd slept in his clothes, after their encounter last night.

'No, I'll do it,' Helen said. She felt relieved

that Mal had already come and gone. She speared a thick piece of bread with the toasting fork, held it out to the glowing coals in the stove, as she sat on the old milking stool. Her pale face flushed from the heat.

'Excuse us,' Ginny said, collecting the empty plates. 'Any volunteers to wash up?' She looked at Cora and Dede.

Helen and Jimmy sat on opposite sides of the big table, Helen sipping her tea while Jimmy spread a thick layer of the farm butter on his toast.

When he had finished eating he expressed his satisfaction. 'That was good.'

'I'm glad you enjoyed it,' Helen said. 'Well, I must make a move, get back to work.'

'Don't go. We haven't had a chance to talk, since I came home.'

'I ... suppose not.'

'Helen, I can see that you and Mal, well, you're very close. Are you fretting I might be bitter about that? What we had, you and I, was youthful passion, we would probably have outgrown that in time anyway, without the wartime separation. I want you to believe I'm happy for you, especially now.'

'You noticed?'

He smiled. 'Of course I have. Uncle Jimmy – I look forward to that.'

'Oh, Jimmy – thank you!'

'And I thank you, all of you, for your forbearance since my return to the fold. Not

expecting me to talk about life in the camp...'
He paused, then added softly: 'I did realize,
you know, that you'd spent time alone in my
room at times. You always turned down a corner on a page when you were reading a book.'

'You always said it was an irritating habit.'
She didn't deny his supposition.

Cora reappeared, to enquire: 'Finished
with your plate, Jimmy?'

'Mmm. Another cup of tea would be nice.
Any chance of that?'

'Of course,' she replied.

He caught at her arm, 'This is the girl I'm
going to marry one day, Helen. She's already
popped the question!'

'Stop teasing!' Cora cried, in another echo
from the past, making her escape.

The weekend passed far too swiftly. Cora
realized that Jimmy wasn't anywhere near
back to his old self. Perhaps he never would
be. It was a sombre thought.

No doubt he'd been joking about marrying her in the future, but Cora had made her
mind up; others might think she was far too
young, but she *knew* she was in love.

Bertie was home. He'd come by ambulance.
He walked unaided to the front door of the
house, then realized he no longer had his
key. He lifted the knocker, then waved as the
vehicle drove off with two other patients

anxious to be reunited with their families.

It was a chill November afternoon. There were leaves on the path. He realized that Eliza must still be at work. The travellers had stopped off half-way yesterday, stayed overnight at a hostel, then resumed their journey after an early breakfast.

'Dad!' Arms were flung around him in an excited embrace. Cora was back from school. Then Dede rushed out from next door, where she had been waiting for her sister, and it was her turn for a hug.

There were tears in Bertie's eyes. They hadn't hesitated to embrace him, he was no longer a pariah, he thought, though he was still unsteady on his pins.

Lena called out, before ushering Dorothy inside her house; 'Good to see you! Eliza'll be home in about an hour's time – she wasn't expecting you 'til tomorrow!'

'I'll take your case up, I must get changed,' Cora said. 'Sit down, Dad, and I'll soon get the fire going. Dede, prove to Dad that you can now make a good cup of tea, eh?'

Bertie sat down on the settee and looked at his daughters. Cora was now a young woman; he hadn't envisaged what a change there would be after a year apart. Dede was still a little girl with that cheeky grin, singing: 'I like a nice cup of tea in the morning, I like a nice cup of tea at night!' She could hold a tune now.

He continued, accepting it gratefully: 'My idea of heaven is – a nice cup of tea!'

'I must get on with the supper,' Cora said, dusting her hands on her apron after handling the lumps of coal. 'Fishcakes – is that all right?'

'Coley, not cod,' Dede informed him.

'You won't be able to tell the difference,' Cora told him confidently. 'Onion and bottled tomatoes disguise the taste. I'll open up another jar of blackberry and apple and make a turnover.'

'You'll make someone a good wife.' Bertie was bemused by her confidence. 'How's young Tim?'

'Oh, it's his night at the Cadets. Why did you mention him in the same breath?'

'Sorry, I'm sure! You and he – well, you were always good pals, Cora.'

'Not any more, Dad. He's still a callow youth.'

'Well, when you put it like that... Any chance of a biscuit?'

'You'll spoil your appetite,' Cora reproved him, but she fetched the biscuit barrel.

Eliza opened the door, unsuspecting, then let out a shriek when she saw Bertie.

'Come here!' he said, not getting up.

'Let me just take my hat off first!' She threw it on top of her coat, which she'd flung on the nearest chair.

'Dede!' Cora hissed, beckoning her sister

to join her in the kitchen, then closing the door firmly, so that Eliza and Bertie could be reunited in relative privacy.

'It's all right for us to kiss,' he whispered, holding her tight. 'I got the all-clear. Oh, Eliza, I thought this moment would never arrive—'

'Me, too. You must be so weary, my darling, after all that travelling...'

'If you're hinting at an early night...'

'Is – is that permitted – you know,' she asked anxiously. 'It doesn't matter, of course, if it isn't...'

'No hurry. But they did say, Eliza, it would best if we didn't add to our family. I'm sorry because I know you were hoping—'

'Shush. I won't say that doesn't matter, but the most important thing is, we're together again.'

'It's not going to be easy, I can't go back to my old job. I'm not allowed to work anyway, yet. Life will continue to be a struggle,' he said.

'Saturday tomorrow, you timed it nicely.'

'Don't I always?' he said.

PART TWO

1947-1950

THIRTEEN

It was exactly a year since Cora had become a working girl. In 1946 she had her school certificate safely under her belt, as Eliza put it; she didn't have the choice of continuing her studies, with her father not yet fit and still unemployed, and Eliza leaving the factory for part-time work in the village shop, nearer home, so she could look after him.

Cora was well aware that she was fortunate to get a job, particularly one with prospects, in the post-war upheaval. The school had advised her to write to the head postmaster in Canterbury, asking to be considered for a position as a telephonist. Many others had had the same idea. It was some time before she heard she had been selected for an interview.

She was very nervous when this important day arrived. She was relieved when the bus to Canterbury was on time. She paid her fare and sat down on the edge of the seat. She was glad she wasn't travelling on the school bus, with Dorothy in her gymslip and panama hat, braided hair and sensible laced shoes, prattling away. Cora wanted to concentrate on rehearsing answers to possible questions!

191

The other passengers glanced at the girl with eyes closed to shut out her surroundings. Cora wore the clothes she and Eliza had decided were suitable for this momentous occasion. A demure white blouse; shiny rayon stockings which Cora hated because they were an ugly shade of tan and needed a girdle to hold them up; a pleated grey skirt; a short, boxy jacket and Cuban-heeled shoes from Dolcis. She wasn't too sure about her hair, which, with Eliza's help, she'd pulled back from her face and pinned firmly into a french pleat at the back. Looking at her reflection earlier, she had bitten her lip, thinking: I look at least forty, despite my lack of make-up! Fortunately, she had managed to convince Eliza that any hat, however small, would look ridiculous perched on that hair-do. Short cotton gloves clung tightly to her damp hands. Would she be able to shed them without a struggle?

Time for one of Eliza's private exhortations: a habit she too had adopted in times of stress. *Please don't let me wobble on these darn heels, or ladder my stockings!*

The main post office was an imposing edifice. It was with trepidation that Cora presented herself at the reception desk with her letter. She followed a friendly girl along an echoing corridor to a large office where the panel of interviewers was waiting. They weren't as formidable as she had feared; she removed the gloves without too much trouble, then her hand was firmly shaken by each member in turn. They introduced themselves as Miss Taylor, Miss Wood and Mr Clarke.

'Please sit down.' Mr Clarke wore a sober, pin-striped suit with a gold watch-chain looped across his waistcoat. He had a pleasant, deep voice, a reassuring smile. He was flanked by the two middle-aged ladies, also intent on putting Cora at her ease.

They went through the application form, noting her educational achievements. Then came questions on general knowledge, geography and arithmetic. Cora's self-assurance grew as she answered these without faltering. The panel had to assess her suitability, her general intelligence, before she could be recommended for the six-weeks training course. They explained gravely that failure to complete the course would be considered a waste of time and of the money invested in her by her prospective employers.

After an hour of skilful probing Cora realized she'd actually enjoyed the experience. Mr Clarke glanced at his pocket-watch, snapped the case shut. He rose, indicating that the interview was at an end. His colleagues each passed him a folded paper. He studied these, then told Cora: 'It gives me much pleasure to inform you that you have passed the test with flying colours. You will be advised by letter later when your course begins. Good luck!'

The ladies added their good wishes. Miss Wood, whom Cora was to meet again in her role as supervisor, added: 'Your elocution is excellent. *Exactly* what is required.'

Cora's cheeks were rosy as she thought of those constant reminders about slipshod speech from the redoubtable Miss Puddefoot, and later, by the high-school staff. These strictures had seemed tiresome at the time, but now, worthwhile.

The course proved challenging but help and encouragement was always at hand. At the end there was the knowledge that she could now take her place on the switchboard alongside experienced telephonists with a supervisor on hand to iron out any difficulties.

Her first day at work was nerve-racking, although her course had included practical work on the switchboard handling live calls. Her fellow workers were friendly. She got to know them more during tea-breaks in the communal rest room where she was allocated a locker for her belongings and her headset when it was not in use. The relaxed atmosphere and the girlish chatter, mostly about boyfriends, visits to the pictures or to dances, was entertaining and enlightening to a lively girl who, because of her family circumstances, led a restricted social life.

On Saturday evenings at home they listened to the wireless: the Palm Court Orchestra with Max Jaffa, a *juicy* name as Dee giggled, followed by Saturday Night Theatre, which held Cora enthralled. To Kim – Miss Kimber – a kind, older telephonist, who had had the distinction of helping to maintain vital telephone links during the war, Cora confided that she really missed Children's Hour at 5 p.m. each day.

Cora's hours of work varied between 8 a.m. to 6 p.m. Monday to Saturday. The night staff also covered Sundays. Connecting calls to all parts of the country was exciting. Cora selected the appropriate dialing codes. If the line was engaged the call could be kept in hand on request and tried again later. She was proud that subscribers in the Canterbury district were reliant on her and her fellow telephonists to connect with other subscribers in distant places. After several months Cora was capable of dealing with most enquiries on her own. Any difficult requests would be passed to her supervisor, or referred to a special enquiry point. She soon excelled in having more cords and plugs connecting and in progress than other operators nearby. The days passed very quickly, because she was enjoying her work, unlike some of her less fortunate friends, who had left school at the same time as she had.

This year, 1947, had opened with terrible

weather. There was flooding countrywide, coal was in short supply despite the nation-alization of the industry in January and rationing including bread, was made even more stringent. Many offices reverted to a Dickensian atmosphere, with staff working by candlelight. The big freeze-up lasted until March. Life actually seemed harder than it had during the war, because of all the cuts and bitter strike action.

Now it was September: there was a Royal wedding on the horizon, and Cora was about to embark on her first real holiday for years. She was off to California for two whole weeks. She was eighteen: surely *romance* was a real possibility?

The afternoon sun streamed through the kitchen windows at Westley farm.

'Stir yourself, Jimmy,' Helen demanded. He was sitting at the table with a book open before him. At least, she thought, this was an improvement on shutting himself away in his room. She nudged the book aside and put down the bowls of windfall apples, green tomatoes, a trug of onions. 'I need your help with this lot.'

'Why now?' he queried mildly.

'Well, when Mal and Ginny arrive back with Cora in an hour or so, she'll be greeted by a real farmhouse special, the wonderful smell of cooking chutney! You can deal with the apples, watch out for the grubs, and discard any badly bruised bits. Cut 'em in quarters and chuck in the pot.'

They chopped in silence for a while; then Helen, who was tackling the onions, exclaimed ruefully: 'My eyes are streaming.' She went to the sink to splash cold water on her face. Looking out of the window, eyes still smarting, she observed that Barry, her eighteen-month-old baby was still asleep in his pram in the yard. He was fractious if he didn't have his afternoon nap, but it meant he would be reluctant to go up into his cot until late evening. She sighed. The pram would bounce when he woke, and he'd yell for attention. Fortunately, he was securely strapped in. Mal had been a placid child, his grandmother said wryly; Barry reminded her of Jimmy at that age, a little live wire.

'Stopped weeping?' Jimmy asked. He'd come up beside her, slipped his arm around her pinafored waist, in a casual fashion. 'You're more rounded, it suits you.'

Helen stiffened. She found this brotherly contact a little disturbing.

'You reek of onions,' he teased

'Finish slicing the apples.'

When the big saucepan was brimming, and set on the hotplate, Helen asked: 'When are you going to get a job, Jimmy? You're much better now, aren't you, and–'

'I'm a burden, am I? I would remind you

197

that this is the only home I've got.'

'You know that's not what I meant. We all understand why it's taken you so long to get over what happened to you in that dreadful place.'

Unexpectedly, he moved closer, so that she could feel his breath fanning her upturned face, as they stood by the stove: 'I'd have done so quicker, if you'd waited for me.'

'Oh Jimmy – please! You seemed to accept that things had changed.'

'My feelings were so mixed up, Helen. After all, I'd told you to get on with your life, without me. Now, I'm getting back to normal, in all respects. I can't help thinking what it would have been like if you had married me, not my brother.'

'Don't!' in an anguished whisper.

Then his arms were tight around her; they were kissing in feverish excitement. They were backing towards the door when the spell was broken by the sounds of the pot boiling over and hissing on the stove and the noisy arrival of the Jeep; followed immediately by cries from the baby and barking from the dog.

They sprang apart. Looked at each other. Then Helen went out to lift her little son from the pram. She buried her burning face in his sandy curls to hide her guilt, before hurrying to welcome Cora.

Cora and Jimmy had discovered the old bicycles in the barn, cleaned off the mud, tested the brakes and oiled the chain.

'Last time I came to the cliffs,' she said, as she wobbled along on the near side with Jimmy on the outside to protect her from passing traffic, 'it was the VJ bonfire night. We couldn't go down on the beach, then.'

'Well, you can today. The holidaymakers have mostly gone, after a busy season; the donkeys will have stopped giving rides on the green, and the tea hut will be closed, but Mum's packed us a picnic and a half, it's a lovely day and the sea looks perfect for bathing. Got your costume, and a towel?'

She nodded. They dismounted and propped their bikes in the bushes. No need to padlock them, they were too decrepit for anyone to pinch, she thought.

They went down the wooden steps to the sands. It was midday, and the beach was indeed deserted.

'Let's get changed and have a swim before we eat, otherwise we'd have to wait, and then the tide will have turned,' Jimmy said.

'Where?' she enquired, looking in vain for somewhere she could disrobe privately.

'You turn one way, and I'll turn the other,' he suggested cheerfully. 'You do swim, I suppose?'

'Yes. My school used the local swimming-baths. I can only do the breaststroke.' She was glad he couldn't see her blush at her mention of that part of the anatomy.

'I can only manage a dog-paddle. Mal and I learned here, when we were kids.'

'I'm ready...' Cora allowed the big towel to drop. She'd made the two-piece white terry-towelling swim suit herself. It really was quite discreet – high-waisted shorts, a brief inch or two of pale midriff, with a simple bra-top with wide straps. This went on over her head, with a band of elastic at the back to hold it snugly in place.

'You certainly fill that out very nicely,' he said approvingly. 'Goodness, you really have grown up! I'm relieved the moth hasn't got at my ancient trunks.'

They piled their belongings together and covered the mound with one of the towels.

'I should have brought a swimming-cap,' Cora remembered belatedly, as they waded out to deeper water, and then plunged into an oncoming wave. Her long black hair, worn down for the holiday, floated out around her shoulders as she swam.

The water was much colder than they had expected. They employed some vigorous strokes to combat the goosepimples. With no one about to care, they indulged in horse-play, splashing, ducking and diving, shouting with glee.

As Cora emerged from the sea and paddled the last few yards to the beach, she squeezed the water from her hair, unaware that her underwater antics had displaced her top and that she was innocently revealing more than she'd intended.

Jimmy naturally noticed, but suppressed an appreciative grin. He called merely: 'Time for lunch, I think. The sun will soon dry you off.'

Cheese-and-tomato sandwiches were soon wolfed down, apple turnovers likewise. Cora bent over the beakers, pouring tea. Jimmy, lounging replete on his towel, was treated to an even more revealing display as he looked up at her.

'Oh!' Cora exclaimed, suddenly realizing. 'You might have told me!'

'Oh!' He mocked her. 'Come here, Cora Kelly...'

'What for?'

'Can't you guess? I'm going to kiss you. You're beautiful and desirable. I'm sure I'm not the first young man to tell you that?'

'We-ell. You are, actually.'

'You're always so honest, Cora. I love you for that.'

'Do you? Do you really?' She couldn't help herself. She shifted near enough for him to catch hold of her, and pull her down beside him.

'Don't worry,' he whispered. 'I'm not going to take advantage of you. Just one kiss, I promise. I'm a bit rusty in that respect...'

It didn't feel that way to Cora as she felt the warmth of his body against hers, his hands twining in her damp locks, his lips seeking a response from her trembling mouth. She came abruptly to her senses, pushed him away.

'I–I'm not sure you intend to keep your promise, Jimmy Brookes!'

He sat up. 'You're right. Mind if I have a cigarette?'

Cora slipped her cotton dress on over her costume. She felt in control now.

'You'll have to marry me, Jimmy, if, you know... Shall we walk along the beach?'

'You know what? That's not a bad idea. Marrying you. But first I need to sort myself out properly, find a job, and be able to provide for you.'

They walked along hand in hand, barefooted.

If Eliza could be happy with Dad and accept him as he was, being aware of his reputation with women, and also as he is now, still a sick man, Cora thought, so can I, with Jimmy. I'll need to be strong for both of us.

FOURTEEN

'You obviously did rather too much sunbathing yesterday,' Ginny observed shrewdly, as she spooned soft scrambled egg on buttery toast, then passed a plate to Cora.

Cora glanced ruefully at her lobster-red arms. 'Thanks. Eliza says it comes of having such a fair skin, despite having dark hair. My Irish heritage, I suppose.' Gingerly, she patted her chest; even the fine cotton of her blouse added to the discomfort.

Ginny noted the gesture. 'Best to keep covered up, I reckon, Cora.' She paused. 'You're a young lady now. You don't want to give Jimmy any ideas, eh?'

They were the last ones at the breakfast table. Mal was busy with the stock, and Helen was bathing Barry upstairs. Jimmy hadn't appeared so far this morning.

Ginny was like Eliza, Cora thought. No subject was taboo. She finished her mouthful, took a gulp of tea, then said casually; 'Oh, he's already got those.'

'Oh, has he! In a way it's good, because it means he's getting back to normal.'

'Don't worry, Ginny. Eliza's always dinned it into me, save yourself for marriage.'

203

'Good. Remember, the spirit's willing, but the flesh is weak. I don't want you walking down the aisle with a large bouquet as a cover-up.'

Cora giggled. 'There's a lot I intend to achieve before I settle down to be a housewife, Ginny. I've a career to consider for a start. But I don't want to miss out on the courting bit!'

'Oh, don't you?' Jimmy said cheerfully, as he came in the kitchen. 'I'll see what I can do about that. Now, Cora, how do you fancy a day in town? Haven't you noticed the suit? Excuse the whiff of camphor, this is its first outing since 1939. You can shop, while I visit the labour exchange. Don't look so startled, Mum, I intend to take whatever's going. Then, if I'm paying my way here, I'll feel free to consider my future, too.'

Ginny looked thoughtfully from one to the other. She guessed that Cora was falling in love, whether she realized it or not, and after all, the girl was already dear to their family, because of Eliza. She could be just what Jimmy needed, to speed his recovery.

'I'd rather tag along with you,' Cora told Jimmy later. 'Don't worry, I won't hover about and say anything out of place. I haven't much spending money: I give most of my wages to Eliza, the rest goes on fares, lunches and clothes.'

'Well, I don't mind, unless you're thinking

of holding my hand, like yesterday.'

They had parked the Jeep in a sideroad, and now began the walk into town.

Later, they sat on a seat overlooking the wide stretch of the beach at Yarmouth. Everything was on a bigger scale here, she thought, than at Californy. There were still holidaymakers here. They'd treated themselves to another picnic lunch, on account of Jimmy actually having the chance of a job. His interview was booked for late afternoon.

Cora had taken the precaution of buying a newspaper. She spread this out on Jimmy's lap. 'You mustn't get food on your suit. Take your tie off and tuck your handkerchief in your collar. Maybe cockles in a jar wasn't such a good idea...'

'I can rinse my hands in the sea. You sound like my mum, Cora.'

'I know. Tim always said I was too bossy.'

'Who's Tim?'

'Oh, the boy next door. We used to be real pals but he was later maturing than me. Maybe he'll grow up quickly, now he's off to do his National Service.'

'You prefer older men, do you?' Jimmy teased, easing the top off the little pot.

'Here – have a stale bread-roll. Not baked today, I suspect. Milk? Could curdle with the cockles. D'you know, I'm not sure I like 'em – they're *rubbery*, well, chewy.'

'You didn't answer my question. We'll get

a cup of tea at the kiosk.'

'You know the answer, don't you? I intend to marry you, *one day*, Jimmy Brookes.'

'And that's that, is it?' He looked bemused.

'That's it, Jimmy,' she said. 'I haven't changed my mind since I was seven.'

Helen found Mal feeding the pigs. He turned. 'Mum said you weren't feeling too good, that you were having a lie-down,' he said. Then, as she flung her arms round him and hugged him tight: 'Whatever's up?' he added, concerned. He patted her back with his grubby hands, leaving smears on her clean shirt.

'There's something I have to tell you, Mal...'

He stiffened, disengaged himself, looked at her searchingly. 'Is it something I'd rather not hear?' he said slowly.

She shook her head vehemently. The words spilled out. 'No! I think I'm pregnant again, and we said we'd wait until Barry was more off-hand, but–'

His relief was palpable. 'Why ever didn't you say? What grand news! Our young rascal Barry is being spoiled rotten by his doting grandma. He needs some competition. Helen, you're a lovely mother, and – you're a wonderful wife. It's just that sometimes–'

'Sometimes ... you wonder ... if things had worked out differently ... I know. I love *you*

Mal. Jimmy, well, Cora obviously intends to sort *him* out.'

It was his turn to hold her close. 'Now, you'll smell of the pigsty, too,' he murmured. 'We'll both need a long soak in the tub tonight.'

Laughter bubbled up inside her. 'Ginny's going to a whist drive, and–'

'Jimmy and Cora'll have the parlour to themselves. *We've* earned an early night.'

'Branch library assistant!' Ginny exclaimed. 'That's usually a job for a school-leaver. Is that really what you want to do?'

They were tucking into a tasty cheese-and-potato pie, with homegrown salad stuff.

'I've always been a bookworm haven't I?' Jimmy said. 'It's the only working experience I have – I ran a lending library in the camp, with the books from the Red Cross. It's a temporary position, but it will give me a chance to study. You never know what it might lead to.'

'Oh, please wish him luck!' Cora put in.

'I do, my dear. Will you wash up? I must get my face on for the meeting tonight.'

'My heart used to sink, when I was a boy, whenever I saw you wearing lipstick,' Jimmy said. 'Knowing Mal would be in charge here while you were shuffling your cards. It always ended up with us having a wrestling match and a fierce argument.'

'I soon sorted you out, on my return. You're not too old now,' she warned him.

'I'll make sure he behaves,' Cora said demurely.

They shared the big armchair once they were on their own. The lights were low, there was electricity on the farm now, but they were always mindful of the cost.

Jimmy lightly traced with a finger the silvery scar on her leg which was a reminder of her traumatic journey on the train from London to Canterbury, all those years ago.

'How did that happen?' He placed his hand firmly over the blemish.

She couldn't suppress a shiver of anticipation. 'I imagine you've some scars, too.'

'Mental, rather than physical. But they're more difficult to live with.'

She laid her face against his, sighing. 'Let's make the most of this evening...'

'The last time you insisted on sharing this chair with me, it was so you could giggle in my ear, I was told to be patient with you because of the hard time you'd been through. I'd much rather have been playing table tennis at the church youth club, with Helen. It all seems so long ago,' he murmured. 'It's up to you to draw the line, Cora Kelly. You promised my mum you would, eh?'

'Don't worry, I will.'

Saying it was one thing, Cora discovered, implementing it was quite another.

Eliza was always wary of buff-coloured official communications. The long envelope remained on the table after she'd cleared the breakfast dishes.

'Aren't you going to open it?' Bertie asked, seeing her worried expression.

'I haven't got time...'

'You don't have to be in the shop until two today,' he reminded her.

She sat down abruptly, pulled down her rolled-up sleeves, rubbed her damp hands on her apron. She picked up the envelope as if it might burn her fingers, slowly eased open the gummed flap.

She perused the letter in silence. Bertie waited impatiently.

Slowly, a bemused smile lit up her face. She looked at him. 'You won't believe this, but it's from Mr Norton's solicitor. It's to inform me that the late Mr Norton's sister, who inherited his property after he passed away, died earlier this year. Following her brother's wishes, she has left his house in London, and the furnishings, to me!'

'Any money involved?' Bertie asked tentatively.

'Apparently not. That doesn't matter! Bertie, it's a dream come true! A house of our own, with the Coal Board pressing us to leave here to provide accommodation for a working miner, and not yet offering us anything in exchange half as convenient.'

'You mean – move to London?'

'Yes! Why not? It's a big house; apparently Miss Norton had it converted into two flats after the war. The top flat has a sitting tenant, so the rent would mean an income for us, from the start. Dear Mr Norton could be our salvation, as he was in the past.'

'What about the girls?'

'Dede's eleven. She's only just changed to senior school. She's self-confident, she'd adapt to a change. Oh, just think, maybe she could get in to the school Cora would have gone on to, if it hadn't been for the war.'

'Cora. She's doing well in the post office. She might not be keen to move.'

'She's not thinking much about her work right now, that's obvious.'

'Ginny's letter, you mean? Don't you think Jimmy's a bit old for her?'

'Of course he isn't! He went in the army before he gained much experience in that respect, and all those years in that dreadful prison camp...' Eliza paused, suddenly recalling Helen's confession. No need to tell Bertie that, she thought.

'A couple of innocents, then?'

'Mmm.' A silent plea. *Please don't let Cora follow in Biddy's footsteps.*

The second week of Cora's holiday was rather an anticlimax. Jimmy was preoccupied with his job at the library and, because the rest of the family were naturally busy on the farm, Cora seemed to spend most of her time amusing Barry, wheeling him along the lanes, which made her recall her perambulations with her sister when she was that age.

She sneaked into Jimmy's room to borrow a book to read, one rainy afternoon.

He hadn't made his bed, and on an impulse, she smoothed the sheets and pulled the covers into place, plumped the dented pillow. She folded his rumpled pyjamas neatly and tucked them beneath the pillow. She thought: Eliza wouldn't approve, but Jimmy's unaware I'm playing at being a dutiful little wife.

She thumbed through a book from the shelf, one which had attracted her because it was out of line with the rest, as if it had recently been replaced. She smoothed out a turned-down corner on a page half-way through the book. Poetry: she hadn't expected that somehow. Her face burned as she realized that it was powerful, erotic stuff. She closed the volume hastily, slotted it back into place on the bookshelf. Would Jimmy realize she'd discovered his secret?

Downstairs again, she was in time for a cup of tea. 'I was wondering where you were,' Ginny said, as she cut two thick slices of fruitcake. 'At a loose end? Sorry, it's not much fun for you, is it, with Jimmy away all day? Anyway, let's enjoy a chinwag together, you and I, as we did when you were a little girl.'

'I think I know what you're going to say. Not to get carried away by my feelings. Not to read too much into ... well, Jimmy and me...'

'I don't want you to be hurt, my dear. I'd be delighted for you both if I thought it could all be plain sailing. It's done Jimmy so much good, you being here, but–'

'You're not sure it will last?'

'What a wise girl you are! I believe *you've* made your mind up. You'll need to be very patient. Not expect too much.'

'I'm not sure about that. I expect a great deal. But I promise to be patient, Ginny.'

'You model yourself on Eliza, I can see that. She's so proud of you.'

'I know. I'll try not to let her, or you down.'

'Don't let yourself down, dearie, that's the most important thing.'

Cora was to silently reiterate her promise to Ginny on the evening before her departure. She packed her case before she retired for the night, for she would be leaving quite early next morning, Jimmy worked on Saturdays, he would be off before she came down to breakfast. So they had already said goodbye, after supper.

She lay in bed, thinking about the euphoria of the first week of her holiday, when she and Jimmy were really getting to know each other. It had been such a promising start. However, this past week he'd been preoccupied, concentrating on work. He'd said a general goodnight and made his way upstairs around nine o'clock. No more kissing, or embracing, or whispered endearments – it was as if he was distancing himself from that.

The handle turned slowly on her bedroom door. No knock. She guessed who it must be. 'Hello, Jimmy,' she said.

He came over to the bed. She sat up, the sheet pulled up beneath her chin. Her face was illuminated by the bedside lamp. He stood regarding her solemnly for a minute or two. Then: 'Can we talk?' he asked.

She nodded. He sat on the end of her bed. He was wearing pyjamas like the flannel pair she had tidied away for him the other day.

'Why are you looking so serious?' she enquired.

'I couldn't get to sleep. I knew you must feel hurt – about the offhand way I've treated you this week.'

'Jimmy, I understood. You had plenty of other things to think about.'

'Yes, but I couldn't put you out of my mind, Cora. Disturbing thoughts, which I shouldn't be entertaining about a lovely young innocent girl like you. I'm sorry–'

'For what? I was probably thinking exactly the same,' she admitted.

'The last thing I want to do is to upset you, but I have more personal sorting-out to do before I can make any commitment to you.'

'I can understand that, too. I can wait.'

'It wouldn't be fair of me to expect that. I don't want to tie you down, spoil what should be the best years of your life, being young and fancy-free. I intend to leave here when I finish my stint at the library. I'm aware that Mal resents my presence, the way our mother fusses over me since my release; oh, he's been decent enough not to say, but I'm not being fair to him, or Helen either, by staying.'

'You make it sound like you're the cuckoo in the nest!'

He smiled. 'Well, I am. I have to fly away, eh, and make my own way.'

'You'll keep in touch?' she asked anxiously.

He hesitated. 'Probably best not to. If we're meant to be together, I'm sure that one day we will be, dear Cora.'

'Aren't you even going to kiss me good-bye?' Her voice wavered.

'Yes, of course.'

A brief hug, a brushing of lips, then he was gone.

Someone was lurking in the shadows outside the bathroom. Helen had emerged to

214

see Jimmy entering his room. She waited a few moments, then tiptoed past his door and then the room next door where Cora slept. She heard the muffled sobbing, but thought, anguished, what can I do – did he come to his senses before it was too late?

FIFTEEN

A month later Eliza, Bertie and Dede alighted from a taxi outside their new home. Their belongings were following by carrier. They saw that the wrought-iron gate hadn't been replaced. Along with others along the street it had been contributed to the war effort 'to help build more planes' which had been more a propaganda exercise than a real requirement. The whole area appeared neglected; to be no longer a quiet place to live, judging by the noisy children whizzing up and down the pavement on scooters, shouting out: 'Mind yer ankles, missus!'

'Nev wouldn't have approved,' Eliza observed wryly.

Theirs was the ground-floor flat. The large reception room at the front of the house had been partitioned to make two good-sized bedrooms; the kitchen was unchanged: they could eat in there, as they had in the old days.

215

The smaller dining-room was furnished with the comfortable club chairs and settee that had once graced the sitting-room. The study had become a combined bathroom and WC.

'We'll be quite self-contained,' Eliza exclaimed. 'Plenty of room for us!'

They looked into the first bedroom. Dede pointed out the big bed where she, Cora and Eliza had slept, then, with a grin, the prim portrait of Mrs Norton.

'I'm not sure I can live with that,' Bertie said.

'You could have it in your room,' Eliza suggested to Dede, tongue in cheek.

'No fear!'

They moved on to the next bedroom. There were two beds in there, for they hoped Cora would join them most weekends. At the moment, she was lodging with Lena, their former neighbour. Lena and Jack had finally tied the knot. Their sleeping arrangements having conveniently changed, they could accommodate Cora. She was sharing with Dorothy in Tim's old room. He was serving with the army in Germany.

'I wish Cora'd decided to come with us. It's not the same without her.' Eliza sighed.

Bertie squeezed her hand. 'She's eighteen, Eliza. You and Biddy were independent at that age, remember? That's when we three met.'

'Now,' Eliza put in quickly, 'lunch. We'll

216

call on the sitting tenant upstairs later!'

'Home, sweet home,' Dede said blithely. 'I like it, don't you?'

They unpacked from Eliza's basket a large pork pie with more crust than meat, a jar of Ginny's dark-brown chutney, opened a packet of Smith's crisps to share, lit the gas under the kettle, and sliced a loaf.

It was familiar, yet unfamiliar, Eliza thought, gazing round the kitchen. The cupboards were bare, apart from the pots and pans; they must do some shopping.

'I'll go,' Dede offered cheerfully. 'Write me a list! The corner shop's still there.'

'I'll have to come with you, ration books to sort out, Dede. Bertie, you have a rest on our bed while we're gone, eh?' She looked anxiously at her husband. He was still thin and tired easily.

'Turn that picture to the wall then!' he said.

The sitting tenant was at home. Eliza and Dede could contain their curiosity no longer. When they had unloaded their shopping and packed it away, they went upstairs.

'Hope he's not taking a nap, like Dad,' Dede whispered. 'He might be grumpy.'

'Allow me to do the formal introduction – don't butt in,' Eliza warned her.

She wondered, oh dear, which room is which?

The door to what had been the main bedroom opened, and a tall man stood, framed in the doorway. He was not as old as Eliza had imagined, being aware that he was a widower: probably he was not much more than thirty. He had a friendly face, untidy fair hair and owlish horn-rimmed glasses resting lopsidedly on a beaky nose. 'Mrs Kelly, I presume. I am Andrew Livingstone.'

Dede couldn't resist it: '*Dr* Livingstone, I presume!'

He smiled. 'Not doctor – but I suppose you could say I support the medical profession. I dispense medicines in Boots, the chemist. My Saturday off.'

'Now you know!' Eliza told Dede. 'This is my younger daughter, Deirdre.'

'Don't call me that – I prefer Dede!' she protested.

'So do I. Would you care to come in?' Mr Livingstone invited.

The solid dining-room suite had migrated upstairs, together with Mr Norton's bureau and writing desk. Eliza felt sorry for Mr Livingstone: she hadn't noticed in the past how gloomy the dark oak furniture appeared. Then she took in the bright, bold paintings on the wall, the Oriental rugs and an old bookcase, painted white and crammed with books.

Mr Livingstone observed her surprise. 'I frequent secondhand-furniture shops – it

218

makes all the difference to furnished flats if you add a few things of your own choice.' He indicated the desk, strewn with papers. 'I am following a correspondence course... Shall we have a cup of tea, while we discuss my tenancy?'

'He's very nice,' Eliza told Bertie later, when she looked in to see if he was awake.

'Good. I hope he didn't take too big a shine to his attractive landlady?'

'Bertie! I'm almost forty, remember, with all that goes with the age...'

'You're still alluring to me. Come and join me on the bed, eh?'

'Bertie!' she repeated. Dede had decided to walk round the block, to see if any of their old friends were still around. 'Five minutes, that's all, 'til Dede gets back.' She kicked off her shoes and slipped under the coverlet beside him.

He hugged her close, nuzzled her neck with his lips. 'I'm an old crock these days, Eliza, aren't I? I wish we could go back to how things were, before I got so ill.'

'It doesn't matter,' she comforted him. They hadn't made love since he returned from hospital. It matters, she thought, but she'd never say.

'Yes, it does.'

'I don't love you any the less, Bertie.'

'You're a wonderful woman.'

'We've the chance to make a fresh start

here, in all respects,' she said.

Cora was already having misgivings about her living arrangements. Lena, Mrs Jackson as she now was, had recited a list of house rules.

'She's like that,' Dorothy confided ruefully when Lena had departed, and Cora was unpacking her case in the bedroom. 'Stick to the rules, and you'll be all right.'

'D'you think,' Cora said slyly, 'she gave your dad a list of do's and don'ts, when they eventually got married?'

Dorothy giggled. 'I guess the reason they left it so long was because Lena wanted to be sure she was past having another baby! I think she'd have been more embarrassed than me, or Tim, if she *had* had one! She's very kind really, Cora.'

'Oh, I know! It's just that, well, if they'd got wed when your dad moved in with you, they might have had, you know, more *fun.*'

'You seem to know a lot about that sort of thing since you visited California! Did Jimmy have anything to do with that?'

Cora threw a pillow at her friend. 'I can't say – you're too young! You're still at school.'

'I'm only a few months younger than you, so there!'

'You'll make up for lost time, no doubt, when you go to university. Naomi hints as much in her letters. I always thought *she* was a bluestocking!'

'Oxford,' Dorothy said wistfully. 'I'm not sure I can aim that high.'

'Well, the undergraduates seem to go everywhere by bike, so ask Tim if you can borrow his and practise while he's away, eh?'

'I might. At least he's writing to me. I suppose he hasn't got a girlfriend like some of the lads, so he's pretending *I'm* the one he left behind, back home.'

'Well, you could do a bit of that, too; make the girls at school green with envy!'

'What I need,' Dorothy sounded pensive, 'is to be allowed to look more grown up.' She tweaked the end of her long plait. 'I haven't had my hair cut since I was seven. Dad followed what Grandma decreed. I wish–'

Cora put in impulsively: 'I fancy a new look too. Let's do it!'

'Without asking permission, you mean?'

'Why not? It takes me ages to put my hair up every morning. It would be a lot easier wearing a headset all day if I had shorter hair.'

'I'm not sure I've enough pocket money left–'

'My treat!' Cora said grandly. 'I've just had a pay rise of five bob a week!'

The hairdresser combed out Dorothy's long hair. 'Take a last look at the old you, dearie,' she said cheerfully, adjusting the mirror on the stand. She held a hand-mirror so that Dorothy could see the back of her head in the glass.

Cora, sitting beside her, waiting her turn with an identical pink bib protecting her clothes, saw the involuntary tremble of Dorothy's lips. She knew that without her glasses her friend could only discern a blurred image, but she wouldn't admit it.

'Now,' said the hairdresser, picking up her scissors, 'for the transformation!'

Fifteen minutes later, Dorothy, having replaced her glasses, gazed at her reflection. She'd requested: 'Nothing too drastic, please!' The result was all she'd hoped for. Her hair hung in a curved bob to her shoulders; Dorothy had hesitantly suggested a fringe, while adding: 'My grandma said you shouldn't have a fringe if you wear glasses, but I've always wanted one to cover my high forehead!'

'There's fringes and *fringes,*' the hairdresser said, snipping away. 'You don't want a flat, straight cut-across affair. A short, feathered fringe will suit you, I'm sure.' She turned to Cora, whom she had met before, but whose hair she had merely trimmed. 'What d'you think, Cora?'

'You look completely different, Dorothy. It really suits you! My turn?' she asked.

'Yes. Are you wanting a new style, too?'

'I am. What d'you suggest?'

'A *gamine* cut? All the rage in Hollywood, they say. You've got such thick hair, you can wear it short. We wet the hair and then layer it with a razor. It's an easy style to care for.'

'Sounds just what I'm looking for,' Cora said.

Later, back home, they sneaked upstairs before Lena realized they were back, and could comment. There was a washbasin in the newly installed lavatory. Grabbing towels, brush and comb, they locked the door, then turned on the hot tap.

'Drene shampoo,' Cora said, producing a bottle from her washbag. 'Makes your hair shine, it says. Better than that gritty powder you have to mix with water, eh? I'll do your hair, then you can wash mine. Bend over the basin, Dorothy!'

Within half an hour, they were sitting on their beds, heads wound round with towel turbans. They rubbed their hair vigorously.

'At least it won't take nearly as long to dry.' Dorothy said. She was beginning to feel apprehensive. How would her dad react?

'Look, all I have to do with mine is give my head a good shake, ruffle it, as the hairdresser said. Take the towel off, and I'll comb yours for you, fluff the fringe up.'

They grinned at each other. 'The deed is done,' as Cora said.

When they sat down at the supper table Lena took a long hard look, but said nothing. She nudged Jack. He noted the appeal in his daughter's eyes. He responded to that with: 'You look very smart, the pair of you.'

'Thanks, Dad.' Dorothy beamed her relief.

Lena gave him another poke in the ribs. 'Just so long as you don't appear at mealtimes with your lips painted bright red...' he mumbled.

Cora whispered to Dorothy: 'Mealtimes no; but other times, why not?'

Eliza certainly had something to say about the short hair and lipstick when Cora arrived the following Friday evening for the weekend.

'Oh, Cora, your lovely hair! You look like an – *urchin!*'

'Urchins don't wear nylons, or make-up, Eliza.' Cora had decided against letter-box red and had outlined her lips with a softer shade of coral pink.

'Nylon stockings! Wherever did you get those?'

'My friend at work, Kim, was sent some from America. She said she was getting too old to show off her legs, so she thought of me.'

'Show off your legs! Thank goodness for the New Look, and longer skirts, my girl.'

She doesn't realize, Cora thought, that I'm telling the world I'm all grown-up! If only Jimmy could see me now.

They were standing in the hall while this exchange took place, when Andrew, as they now called Mr Livingstone, came down the stairs.

'Sorry to intrude,' he apologized, holding out an envelope to Eliza. 'The rent. A month in advance, as you know.' He smiled at Cora. 'You must be Dede's big sister. She told me you were coming!' They shook hands. He added: 'Actually I was hoping to meet your husband, Eliza. I wondered if he would feel like a stroll down to the pub with me. I wouldn't lead him astray – promise! Half a pint of bitter's my limit.'

'Well,' Eliza said uncertainly, 'perhaps you'd better ask him yourself.'

'On second thoughts,' Andrew said, 'I should leave it until another time, eh?' He looked at Cora. 'You all have a lot to talk about, I'm sure. Good evening, then.'

The front door had hardly closed, before Dede came rushing out, in pyjamas and dressing gown. 'I've just had my bath! Dad restrained me, until Andrew had gone!'

She hugged her sister enthusiastically. 'Ooh! You smell lovely! What scent are you wearing? And your hair – I love it! And your lipstick – d'you think...?'

'Nope,' Cora said fondly. 'But you can have a squirt of eau-de-Cologne!'

Over supper, corned-beef hash and baked beans, Eliza told Cora: 'I'm going job-hunting next week.'

'Oh, do you have to? I thought you'd enjoy being a stay-at-home mum at last!'

'I'm sure she would,' Bertie put in unexpectedly. 'But there's not much chance of me getting a job, other than work I can do at home – folk are still wary of anyone who's had the old TB.'

'That's not fair, Dad! You've been clear of it for ages now.'

Eliza rested a hand on his shoulder. 'With you at home, my dear, I can work full time. You'll be here when Dede gets home from school in the afternoons. You know how to cook, don't you, from living on your own that time in Kent?'

'Cora will remember my culinary efforts, I'm sure,' Bertie said ruefully.

'And you, Cora?' Eliza asked. 'Is it working out for you at Lena's?'

'To be honest, they're very kind, but they treat both Dorothy and me like kids. Dorothy has piles of homework every evening, which she does in our room, so I lie on my bed and read mostly 'til lights out, prompt at nine thirty.'

'When I was your age, Biddy and I only had one night off a week. We went dancing, or to the pictures, and we made the most of our time off.'

'So should you, Cora,' Bertie said firmly.

'Well, you're making it easier for me, I

must say, to spring my surprise on you! You've heard me mention Kim—'

'The one who gets sent nylons from America?'

'Yes. You'd actually approve of her, if you met her. She's had an exciting war, she says, and now she's ready to settle down, although she hasn't found Mr Right! She's moved to a nice flat not far from work and she needs help with the rent. Kim's asked me if I'd like to share with her. What d'you think?'

'You're old enough to form your own opinion. She ... she sounds genuine.'

'Thanks!' Cora beamed. 'I suspect Lena will be relieved not to have the responsibility of me much longer!'

SIXTEEN

The flat at the top of the tall, narrow house, although in a good area, was not quite what Cora had visualized. There were two small bedrooms, but the kitchen area, with a gas ring, small cooker and sink with a single cold tap, was in an alcove off the living-room. They'd have to send linen to the laundry. The bathroom had a noisy geyser. The flat was up two flights of stairs, but as Kim said

227

breathlessly to Cora: 'Look at the view over the river!' At night, when the myriad city lights were reflected in the water, the Great Stour appeared mysterious and magical.

It was not a part of the city with which Cora was familiar. She would shortly enjoy her Sunday strolls with Kim past the ancient weavers' cottages, and along the grandly named St Radigund street.

The stove was temperamental, and two greedy gas fires were the only means of heating the rooms. They seemed to feed endless coins into the meter on the landing.

No wonder, Cora thought, that it was too expensive for one person to live on their own; two really could live – almost! – as cheaply as one. They drew up a rota: cooking the evening meal, shopping, cleaning. Each put a specified amount in the housekeeping purse, which covered the rent and all out-goings. At the end of the first week, Cora was left with ten shillings to herself. Her bus fare and lunches had to come out of that! But it was a good feeling, being independent.

Kim kept an unobtrusive eye on her young flatmate. She introduced Cora to the delights of the local theatre, where they viewed the stage from aloft in the cheapest seats; and to her first foreign film with subtitles.

On stay-at-home nights as winter set in, they 'toasted their toes' by the hissing fire, and knitted busily. Both were avid readers, and swapped their library books half-way through the week. Kim also subscribed to a book club, and although the books were cheaply produced and carelessly edited, all the latest titles were on the list. The girls were particularly impressed by a lively young American writer called Betty Macdonald, and her autobiographical books, like *The Egg and I*. 'Anybody can do anything!' Betty asserted, with which Cora and Kim certainly agreed.

They talked a great deal too. Cora confided her complex family history, and revealed the contents of Aunt Poll's box because she knew Kim would keep the details to herself. In turn, Kim opened up to Cora.

Elsie Kimber, always known as Kim, had been adopted as a baby by an elderly couple who loved her dearly, and encouraged their clever daughter throughout her schooling. Unfortunately, they had died within a few months of each other, when Kim was in her late teens.

At the outbreak of war, when she was twenty, Kim was selected for her intelligence and resourcefulness to join other young women in a secret location to maintain vital telephone links in times of national crisis. In 1940 she became engaged to a sergeant-pilot in the RAF. He had not survived a bombing raid on Germany. After the war, Kim joined the supervisory staff at the

Canterbury exchange.

'You have to get on with life,' Kim said firmly. She was small and slight, with soft brown hair in a simple bob. She probably looked much as she had when she left school, Cora thought, not conventionally pretty, but a strong character.

'I hope you'll meet someone else one day, Kim.' Cora didn't think that about herself. She firmly believed that she and Jimmy would be together in the future.

Kim shook her head. 'I'm happy being single. It has its compensations! Good friends mean a lot to me. *You* keep me in touch with the younger generation, Cora!'

Eliza had not yet had the offer of a suitable job. Too many better qualified folk had returned to the area and even the humblest forms of employment were at a premium. The only income they had coming in was the rent from the upstairs flat, and Bertie's small disability pension from the Coal Board.

In a way, she told herself, it was a good thing. With the onset of the colder weather Bertie's health had deteriorated. He didn't have the strength to help with the household chores. Eliza sat him down by a good fire, encouraging him to write regular letters to Cora, who couldn't afford to come home more than once a month.

She was shovelling coal into a bucket in

the basement store after lunch, wryly recalling the not so long ago days in Kent when coal was the one thing they were not short of, when Andrew appeared in the doorway.

'Here, let me do that,' he exclaimed, concerned.

'You're wearing your best suit...' He was home early, it being Wednesday.

'It doesn't matter.' He took the shovel from her. 'Eliza, how red and sore your hands are! I'll bring you a soothing cream from the shop tomorrow. I came to find you, because I have something to ask you.'

'Join us for a cup of tea,' Eliza said impulsively. 'Bertie's in the living-room.'

Bertie was pleased to see Andrew. He sat hunched in his chair, with a rug round his shoulders, and another tucked round his knees.

He looks so grey and drained today, Eliza thought, when she handed him his mug. 'I expect you can do with a nice hot drink, dear. Biscuit?'

Bertie shook his head. 'Just the tea.' His appetite was very poor.

Andrew made the fire up and took the chair opposite. 'Good cup of tea, Eliza.'

'Now, you wanted to say something?' She warmed her hands on her cup.

'I wondered if Cora would be home this weekend,' he said diffidently. 'You see, I won two tickets for *Annie Get Your Gun,* the

231

Irving Berlin musical at the Coliseum, in the Christmas draw at work. It seems a shame to waste them.'

'I'm afraid Cora won't be home until Christmas! Two weeks to go! Can you ask someone else to accompany you?' Eliza queried.

He shook his head. 'I've friends at work, yes, but they all have families and as you've probably realized, my social life is rather limited.' He paused, then confided: 'I'll go back a bit. I moved in here with my wife two years ago, when I was demobbed. This was our first home together. We'd married in 1940, when I left college to join the RAMC, and Joy, the ATS. I served overseas for the duration of the war.'

'You were studying medicine?' Eliza was curious.

'Chemistry. I was about to resume my course when Joy became desperately ill. I cared for her until she died, of cancer, six months later.'

'I'm so sorry. We didn't know.'

'Afterwards I had to work, of course, but I'd lost heart for my studies. However, I am now hoping to catch up through my correspondence course. Inevitably, I forget the cooking pots on the stove and I apologize for the frequent smell of burnt potatoes.'

'We had noticed!' Bertie said, with a smile. 'Look, I've an idea. Why don't you take

Eliza to the show? She deserves a night out, after waiting on me, hand and foot.'

'I couldn't leave you,' Eliza objected.

'Of course you could! Dede will keep me company. You can tell us all about it, when you get back.'

'If you're sure...' What will I wear, she worried.

As if reading her thoughts, Andrew assured her; 'Nowadays, you don't dress up for the theatre, I'm told, and anyway, these are modest seats in the upper circle. I look forward to your company, Eliza. Thank you for the tea. I'll leave you now.'

'Nice chap,' Bertie said, when he'd gone. 'Shame he lost his wife so young.'

On Saturday evening, as Eliza and Andrew hurried to catch the bus, Eliza stumbled but just managed to stop herself pitching forward. The streetlamps were lit, but they were in the dark patch between the pools of light.

'Here,' Andrew exclaimed, 'take my arm.'

'These darn shoes,' she said ruefully, 'I haven't worn them since my wedding.'

'That must be a long time ago – oh, sorry, that's tactless of me!'

'Actually, six years ago.'

'Oh...'

'You're thinking, of course, that Cora came along some years before that?'

'That's none of my business.'

'I don't usually feel I have to explain, but our friends know, of course.'

'Does that mean I'm in that category?' he teased.

'I suppose it does. Bertie's first wife Biddy was my great friend. When she died, soon after Dede was born, I took the children on. Bertie ... wasn't around at the time. Later, he got in touch, and eventually he and I decided to marry.'

'For the children's sake?'

'Yes. But it's been a very happy marriage, despite Bertie's illness.'

'That's good. Oh, look the bus is just drawing up to the stop. We must run!'

They arrived at the theatre in St Martin's Lane, just after 7 p.m. The show was due to begin in half an hour. Before the war, the scheduled start would have been an hour later. Public transport also had been affected by the blackout years so the last bus was earlier too.

There was a lengthy queue for the gallery and pit. The rival buskers were busy: there were a pair of jugglers and a virtuoso performer on a fiddle. It was a cold evening but fortunately dry. Eliza and Andrew enjoyed the extra entertainment as they shuffled forward in the shorter queue for the reserved seats. Pennies flew through the air, were caught neatly in a cap, and there was much cheerful badinage.

Inside the Coliseum there was a welcoming warmth, comfortable seats with an unobstructed view, and programmes to peruse. They read potted biographies of the stars: Dolores Gray as Annie Oakley, with Bill Johnson as Frank Butler. They learned that the show had opened on Broadway in May, 1946 and was still running there.

The buckskin costumes, the Davy Crockett caps, the colourful backdrops: Eliza stored all the details in her mind to share with Bertie and Dede when she got home. The music and the wonderful lyrics received exuberant applause. 'There's No Business Like Show Business', 'Doin' What Comes Natur'lly', and the tender ballad, 'The Girl That I Marry', which caused many of the female audience, including Eliza, to dab their eyes.

She wasn't aware of Andrew's frequent glances, his pleasure at her reaction. She had removed her shabby overcoat and even the sight of her in her well-worn blue velvet dress, with the artificial marguerite pinned on one shoulder, made his pulse quicken at the excited rise and fall of her generous bosom. At one point she turned to him to express her delight in the singing and inadvertently this part of her brushed against his arm. When the lights went up in the interval, the rich colour of her hair was accentuated. She really was a most attractive woman: he found that unexpectedly disturbing. He

235

reminded himself sternly that she had a sick husband at home, who trusted him with his wife.

Three hours later, as they walked back up their street, Eliza held his arm without his asking, and talked dreamily of what they had seen.

'Will you come in for coffee?' she asked, as they hung their coats in the hall.

'I won't, if you don't mind. Your family have obviously gone to bed.' They had glimpsed the light from the front bedroom window.

'Thanks Andrew, for a wonderful evening.' She stretched up, kissed his cheek.

He drew back as if he had been stung. 'Goodnight,' he said abruptly, as he turned to ascend the stairs.

Oh dear, did he think...? Eliza was embarrassed. It took her a minute or two to recover her equilibrium, then to go through into her own quarters.

'I'm back!' she called. 'Who wants to hear all about the show?'

When Dede had returned to her bed, Eliza undressed swiftly and switched the light off. Bertie had not said much, Dede had asked all the questions.

Eliza moved close to her husband under the covers. 'Miss me?' she ventured.

'Of course I did. But I'm glad you enjoyed yourself.'

'When you're better, Bertie, we'll go to a show together.'

'Is that a promise? I feel bad you know, that we've never gone out on our own.'

'We couldn't leave the children.'

'I'm tired. Well, goodnight, Eliza dear.'

'Goodnight my darling,' she whispered. She made a silent plea. *Please God, let us get back to the way we were.*

Upstairs, it was some time before Andrew retired. He was still wide awake, thinking of his first evening out with another woman since his wife died. They'd had only a few days together as a married couple before the war parted them. Fate had been cruel: there had been no happy outcome. Joy was already aware that it was unlikely she would survive from her cruel illness. He had performed intimate tasks for her with compassion and love; at least he had no regrets.

Some time during their last weeks together she had whispered: 'You must get married again, Andrew. You didn't deserve this.'

'I should say that to you,' he said, choked.

Tonight, he'd looked at Eliza – so different in looks from his slender, beautiful wife, but just as warm and womanly. She's a married woman, he told himself, he must resist temptation. He attempted to banish the errant thought of what it would be like to be with her right now, holding her in his arms.

'Don't be a fool, Andrew Livingstone,' he

said aloud to the emptiness all around.

'I'm sorry you won't come home with me tomorrow,' Cora told Kim, the night before Christmas Eve. 'You won't have much fun here on your own.'

'I'll be working, busy with all the festive telephone calls,' Kim reminded her.

'You didn't have to this year, as you worked last Christmas.'

'It's easier for me, without family ties. There are others in the same boat. We raise a glass or two to salute the season, you know. We eat the odd mince pie. There's plenty of good spirit, and we enjoy all the decorations the juniors have put up.'

'I'll make you a tinsel tiara, eh?'

'That sounds better than the bunch of mistletoe we try to dodge! The post boy seems determined to catch us, one by one.'

'Well, I shall be waiting for a Christmas call from you, remember. We try not to make too many outgoing calls, but we're lucky to be on the phone.'

She left work at lunchtime, and made her way to the station. Christmas with the family: she was eager to place her parcels round the little Christmas tree which Eliza had bought at the market.

The train was packed with others on their way home.

Jimmy, she thought, where are you now?

Not at the library, he had finished there after two months, Eliza had learned that from Ginny.

What's next, I asked him. He said he was going to travel around for a while, visiting old friends from the prison camp. He mentioned Liverpool. I had a card from there, that's all so far. I do worry, but he obviously feels he can cope with life better now...

He's restless, like Dad was, Cora was resigned to that. She closed her eyes as Eliza did, and offered a silent plea. *Please let him miss me, and come back soon.*

Dede rushed to meet her sister when she spied her coming up the road. 'You're loaded!' she said with satisfaction, relieving Cora of some of the parcels.

'All ready for tomorrow?' Cora asked.

Dede hesitated. 'Mum had to call the doctor out this morning, Andrew said he thought she ought to. Dad's not at all good, Cora.'

'Is it – his old trouble?'

'Not his lungs, doctor says, but maybe ... it can come out elsewhere. Don't say anything to Dad, will you? Mum'll tell you all about it later.'

'I won't,' Cora promised. Her excitement at coming home, the anticipation of Christmas, was fast evaporating.

Dede turned at the door. 'Dad's in bed, of course. Oh, it's so good to have you home! We *need* you, right now, we really do.' Her lips quivered.

Cora held out her arms. 'Come here, Dede. Let me give you a big hug.'

'Can I be next?' Eliza asked, coming up behind them.

'Of course you can – you're my mum, after all...' Cora had picked exactly the right time to say that.

From the bedroom, they heard a husky voice call out, 'Cora, is that you?'

'It's me, Dad. We're all together for Christmas,' she said.

SEVENTEEN

'Move your bed nearer mine,' Dede insisted. Together, she and Cora pushed the single bedsteads together.

'I missed our bedtime chats,' Cora said, when they lay companionably side by side.

'So did I. But you've got Kim to talk to now.' Dede was obviously a little jealous.

'Well, *you're* my sister, but she's older and wiser – as I am to you, eh?' Cora joked.

'Cora...'

'Yes?'

'Do you – do you think Dad's going to die?'

Cora reached out to hold her sister's hand. 'I don't know,' she said honestly. 'I can see how ill he is.'

'The doctor said Dad ought to go to hospital, but he wouldn't agree – not until after Christmas.' Dede suppressed a sob.

'He said not to kiss him, just in case – but Eliza's sharing his bed.'

'He said she should move in here with me, but she wouldn't.'

'Eliza believes Dad will get better, like last time.' Cora said.

'I know that. Cora, how can we make it a *proper* Christmas tomorrow?'

'We have to, and we will. Goodnight, dear Dede.'

'I wish... I wish I was grown up like you...'

'It's just as hard to bear, whatever age you are,' Cora said sadly.

'A cup of tea for my two beautiful girls. Happy Christmas!' Eliza brought in a tray of tea and three mince pies. 'I'll have mine with you. Bertie's still asleep. Shove up, Dede, make room for me.' She discarded her slippers and dressing-gown and slipped into the side of Dede's bed so that she was between them.

'Happy Christmas,' Cora echoed. 'When did you make these? They're still hot!'

241

'I was awake around four, so I thought, why not do a spot of baking?'

'They're delicious. You haven't lost your touch, Eliza.'

'Did you only make three?' Dede queried hopefully.

'No, but let the rest cool off for later, eh?'

'What's the time now?' Dede grabbed her sister's wrist, looked at her watch. 'Mum! It's only ten past five!'

'Don't you usually look in your stocking, round about now?' Eliza returned.

'That was when I was little. I'm eleven and a quarter now, remember!'

'Here.' Cora reached out and untwisted the pillowcase from the bed knob.

Until it was time to get up and face what the day ahead might hold, Dede laughed and exclaimed over the inexpensive Christmas novelties.

Eliza was in the kitchen, preparing breakfast, when there was a tap of the door. Andrew asked: 'How is Bertie this morning?' before he added: 'It's very good of you to invite me to spend the day with you. These are a little token of my appreciation.' He placed a carrier bag on the table. 'I'll come back later, eh?'

'No! Do stay. To be honest, I could do with your help with Bertie.'

'Of course, just say what needs to be done.'

'Well, he wants to wash and shave in the

bathroom. He had enough of blanket baths in the sanatorium, he said. The girls have finished in there, so...?'

'Glad to assist,' Andrew said. 'I'll go now.'

'I'm not getting back in bed,' Bertie insisted, after he had completed his ablutions. 'Not until I have to, anyway.' But he obviously did not have the strength to get dressed.

'I don't blame you,' Andrew told him. He saw Bertie wince as he instinctively pressed his lower back with his palms. 'Is that where the pain is?' he asked quietly.

Bertie nodded, but merely said: 'Are you joining us for breakfast?'

'Thank you, yes. Eliza kindly insisted.'

'That's good.' Bertie allowed Andrew to place a steadying hand on his shoulder, as they walked slowly towards the kitchen.

'Ham and eggs!' Andrew marvelled. 'How ever did you manage that, Eliza?'

She tapped the side of her nose. 'State secret, Mr Livingstone.'

The girls unwrapped their parcels. '4711 perfume – thanks, Andrew!' they chorused.

'Boots special,' he smiled ruefully. 'Not very imaginative.'

'I'm afraid we haven't got you anything,' Eliza apologized.

'You've given me something better: a real family Christmas.' He removed his glasses, rubbed the lenses with his handkerchief.

'See, I'm all misty eyed!'

Eliza fetched a cushion to support Bertie's bad back. As she bent over him, he whispered, 'You look very fetching today.'

'Thanks to Cora. I feel like a Christmas fairy!' She indicated the sequins Cora had painstakingly sewn on the yoke of her hand-knitted emerald-green jumper.

Cora had certainly been industrious. Dede wore a scarlet felt waistcoat, with flower-pot shaped pockets and embroidered sunflowers. Cora had run up a pretty blouse for herself in white muslin, material which didn't require coupons.

As Eliza straightened up, she became aware that Andrew was smiling at her. He must have overheard. She thought wryly: *a fairy who's fat and almost forty...*

'I made you gloves, Dad, can you wait until after breakfast for them?' Cora asked.

'Well, I don't think I can handle my knife and fork wearing 'em!' he joked.

They were all determined to enjoy the day ahead.

Christmas lunch was a modest affair, roast chicken with plenty of vegetables. The plum-pudding was short on dried fruit but had been darkened with gravy browning. Dede's custard was rather lumpy, but no one said anything. The remaining mince pies were reheated and Eliza was complimented on her rough-puff pastry. Dede's last-minute

244

crackers, fashioned from cardboard and red crêpe paper, stuck on with flour-and-water paste, contained comical paper hats, and were vigorously pulled with cries of *Bang!*.

Andrew rose from the table. 'Allow me to do the washing up!'

'I won't say no – thank you. Who'll give Andrew a hand?' Eliza looked at Cora.

Eliza's trying a little matchmaking, Cora thought. He's very nice, but he's too old for one thing – he's thirty-two; Dede found that out, so he's only seven years younger than Eliza, more her generation. Anyway, Eliza knows I've found my soulmate, although *he* hasn't even sent me a Christmas card. She said aloud: 'I'll help you, Andrew.'

The afternoon games were necessarily muted, with Bertie asleep in his chair. Even Dede managed to mouth the cry of 'Housey-Housey!' when she filled in her card as Andrew held up the numbers. Eliza had made some mock marzipan with almond essence and soya paste, colouring one half red and the other half green. She'd cut out festive shapes, like holly leaves with rolled berry balls, and tiny fir trees in red tubs. These were the prizes: most were won and eaten by a jubilant Dede.

Cora sat back when the game was finished and played cats-cradle with her sister.

'You're shutting your eyes – it's your turn, Cora!' Dede demanded.

They were all yawning by half past three, after their early start to the day. The sudden piercing cry from Bertie startled them.

Eliza was instantly on her feet, at her husband's side. He was mumbling incoherently now. She said urgently: 'What's up, my dear?'

Andrew, noting the alarm on the girls' faces, joined Eliza, shielding the sight of their father, obviously in a state of collapse, slumped in his chair. 'Cora,' he said urgently, 'Please telephone the doctor.'

'We can't do that on Christmas Day!'

'I'm afraid we must. Quick as you can, now. Dede – bring that small bottle of brandy your mum poured on the pudding, to set it alight – and a teaspoon – hurry!'

When they'd left the room, Andrew turned to Eliza. 'I don't think we should move him before the doctor comes. Have you another blanket? He's shaking, gone into shock – we must make sure he's warm enough.'

Dede returned with the whisky. 'Fetch the eiderdown from our bed, please,' Eliza said, then, to Andrew: 'Will you hold his head steady, while I give him the spirit?'

Cora opened the door to the doctor, unfamiliar in a patterned pullover, with a scarf hastily wound round his neck against the cold. He was still wearing his new Christmas slippers. Fortunately, he lived not far away, had come immediately. Eliza knew he had left his young family to attend Bertie, and was grateful.

'Will you girls make a pot of tea?' the doctor suggested tactfully. 'Don't hurry about it,' he added as they rushed to do his bidding.

'Would you like me to make myself scarce too?' Andrew asked.

'Stay within earshot, I shall need your help to carry Mr Kelly to my car.'

'You're going to take him to the hospital?' Eliza asked fearfully.

'I'm afraid so. Quicker than sending for an ambulance – fortunately, it's not far away. This is not a problem we can resolve here at home. I need a second opinion from a specialist, for a start.'

'He promised to go there tomorrow...'

'That could be too late. I'm sorry to have to put it like that, Mrs Kelly.'

'I understand,' Eliza said faintly.

The doctor glanced at her, concerned. 'I really feel we shouldn't waste time. Call your friend now. Will you pack a few things for your husband in an overnight bag? Bring it out to the car. You can accompany him, of course.'

She nodded, then found her voice. 'Andrew, can you come and give me a hand please?' Cora would look after Dede, she knew, but it was comforting that Andrew would be there to support them, *if...* Tears blinded her eyes as she went to the bedroom to pack Bertie's things.

The three left behind looked at each other when the phone rang after what had seemed an interminable wait. It was Cora's friend Kim, with Christmas greetings.

The days passed, Bertie remained in hospital, very poorly with renal failure but, as Eliza said stoutly, 'still here'. Cora returned to Canterbury, Dede to school, Andrew to dispensing medicines for customers' coughs and colds, and Eliza was at last offered a part-time job, at Blooms, the local news-agents and stationers. It was a godsend.

It was January, 1948. The war had been over getting on for three years, but bread was still rationed. The government was busy imple-menting nationalization of industry: the rail-ways were first on the list. The long-awaited National Health Service was about to become a reality. Eliza prayed it would not be too late for Bertie to benefit from it.

The Blooms were Jewish. They had been made homeless at the same time as Naomi's family, had returned to London after the war and set up in business again.

Mr Bloom was a little man, no taller than Eliza, who was not quite five feet tall. He was a man of few words. His wife, in contrast, towered above him, a raven-haired woman, still beautiful in late middle age. She was the matriarch of their extended family, even though they had no children of their own.

'My husband,' she told Eliza when they first met, 'is the brains of this enterprise. I am merely the figurehead.' She smiled as she said this, and Eliza couldn't help imagining her lovely face and fine torso adorning the prow of a sailing ship.

Eliza enjoyed every part of her job. Mr Bloom had already dispatched the newspapers on their early-morning round when she arrived. He would be upstairs in the flat above the shop, eating his breakfast. Mrs Bloom was at the helm, as she put it, in a black dress with immaculate white cuffs and collar. Her hair was elaborately braided round her head, gold-rimmed half-moon glasses dangled from a chain around her neck.

'Good morning Eliza. Icy out there today?' She had a warm, contralto voice.

'Good morning, Mrs Bloom. It certainly is. Where would you like me to start?'

It was a long shop, two rooms made into one. The far end was devoted to the stationery side of the business. Requisites for the aspiring writer; bookkeeping manuals; exercise books & scholastic equipment; notepaper & envelopes; brown paper, string & sealing wax; pencils & pens; everything for the artist – all these sections needed to be tidied and replenished at the start of each day.

Eliza made a neat pyramid of the bottles of ink in their cardboard boxes: blue-black, green and red. She counted the pencils – separated the 2B from the HB. A rubber band secured a dozen fine-nib mapping pens. There was a pleasant smell of cedar wood from the pencils. She rerolled the stiff cartridge paper. All these tasks took her mind off the fears which kept her awake at night. The hospital had warned her that Bertie's life was slowly slipping away. Sometimes she couldn't help thinking of the baby they had lost: the child would have been five and half years old if it had lived. It was some comfort to know that Cora and even Dede were old enough to understand what was going on.

'You look tired, my dear,' Mrs Bloom exclaimed one morning early in February. 'Here, take my seat behind the counter. I'll put the new magazines out.' She paused, then: 'How did you find Mr Kelly yesterday afternoon?'

'He ... didn't – couldn't – speak, but I'm sure he knew I was there. Dede caught the bus after school to the hospital. She's being very brave, I'm proud of her.'

'And your other daughter? Cora, will you send for her?'

'She'll be home this weekend, two days' time. I've warned her how things are.'

'If you need to take time off – we understand, my dear.'

'Mrs Bloom, thank you. But I need to carry on while I can. It helps, you see.'

'I see.' The shop bell pealed. 'Ah, a customer. I leave her to you.'

Eliza managed a smile. 'May I be of assistance?' she asked.

Bertie passed away quietly on Saturday evening. His wife and his daughters were with him, they had kept their vigil at his bedside all day. There were no final words from him, but they were comforted by the manner of his going.

It was almost eleven when the sister-in-charge ushered them out. 'Your friend is here to take you home. He has a cab waiting. Tomorrow is soon enough to make the arrangements. The almoner will see you then.'

Andrew came towards them. He took Eliza's cold hands in his, while Cora hugged her sister close. He had to bend his head to catch Eliza's whispered words: 'It's over.'

'I know,' he said gently. 'I understand.'

EIGHTEEN

It was more than two weeks after the funeral before Eliza could bring herself to open the envelope which, Bertie had told her when he first went into hospital, was in the inside pocket of his wedding suit. The letter was only to be read in the event of his death.

She had lost weight over the past two months, so kind Mrs Bloom had shortened and altered one of her own smart black dresses for Eliza to wear. She sat down in Bertie's chair. She was pale-faced: the only bright thing about her was her red hair.

The letter had been written in pencil over several days when he was already frail.

My dearest Eliza,

Perhaps you will never read this letter, for I may grow old in spite of everything and forget that I wrote it. If this is not the case, I want you to know that marrying you was not only the most sensible thing I ever did, but the happiest event of my life.

You have been both a wonderful wife to me, and loving mother to Cora and Dede. I am only sorry I was such an inadequate father in their early years. I hope they are aware how much they mean to me now.

I should have told you that when I was in the sanatorium, one of the nurses was Lindy Wright, the Canadian woman I was involved with before I met you again. I promise you, there was no 'reunion'. I told her about you, of course. She was glad to hear I was happily married, although her own marriage had failed, back in Canada. I believe she intended to return home after the war, but if you could bring yourself to write to tell her of my passing, I would be grateful. I am sure the sanatorium would forward the letter. She can then draw a line under the affair.

My darling, will you do this for me?

You are still young, I hope you will marry again; if you get the chance of happiness *don't hesitate* – take it!

I love you, Eliza.

Bertie.

For the first time since his death Eliza could at last really cry. Tears streamed down her face. She folded the letter, replaced it in the envelope, tucked it in her apron pocket. It would be a difficult letter to tackle – she wasn't a fluent writer like Bertie had been.

She had forgotten it was Wednesday afternoon, that Andrew would be home after one o'clock. Since the funeral he had taken to looking in on her on his return to make sure she was coping.

'Eliza,' she heard him exclaim, as if from a distance, 'What's happened?'

Her eyes focused on his concerned face then. He still wore his overcoat, with a powdering of fine snow on the shoulders. 'Oh, Andrew, I'm so sad...' she gulped.

He moved a chair opposite her, she was aware that their knees were touching, and that he was grasping her hands as he had the night Bertie died.

'Of course you are, but this is the release

you need, it's important to let your emotions out. You've had to be strong for Dede's sake. Cry all you like in front of me.'

'I need someone to hug me, to hold me tight...'

He hesitated for a split second, then he lifted her to her feet, folded his arms round her, rested his chilly face against the top of her head. 'There, did that help?' He released her, assisted her back into the chair. 'I'll make a cup of tea, shall I? Then if you feel like talking, well, I am willing to listen.'

It all spilled out: her happy, though impoverished childhood, her friendship with a girl from a similar background, Biddy, Cora and Dede's mother. She even told Andrew how she, too, had fallen in love with Bertie but kept it from him, and from Biddy. She emphasized that she had never considered it a burden, bringing up her friend's children.

'So, in a way, I have come full circle, returning to this house, where dear Mr Norton made us welcome. Cora was ten when Bertie came back into our lives.'

'You didn't feel resentful?'

'I was wary. He had to prove to me that he had changed.'

'You were still in love with him, though?'

She nodded. 'The surprising thing was, he grew to feel the same way about me.'

'Just think of that,' Andrew said slowly. 'It will be a comfort to you, I'm sure.'

Eliza sipped her tea. 'Thank you, Andrew, you're a real friend to us.'

Cora had a good listener, too, in Kim. Her colleagues at work were sympathetic, but the daily routine had to continue, and personal problems set aside.

One day she came in from work to find an airmail letter on the mat. She turned it over, wondering who it was from.

'Open it!' Kim urged, as curious as Cora.

'There's a name on the back – it's from an old friend – Tim Titchley. He's with the occupation forces in Berlin!' She opened the flimsy envelope carefully.

Dear Cora,

Dorothy wrote to tell me the news about your father. I thought I should send my condolences to you and your family. We were good pals in the early days in Kent. I think it is my fault we drifted apart. You grew up quicker than I did. However, the Army makes men of callow youths!

I would really like to resume our friendship. I have an ulterior motive of course – letters from home mean a great deal. Will you write to me please?

I will be back in England this summer. I hope to see you then. Another year to go before demob!

Yours, Tim.

PS I am naturally known as 'Titch' by my mates, even though I am now a six footer!

Cora passed the letter to Kim. 'There – what d'you think?'

'Let me *read* it first! He sounds nice. What does he look like?'

'Well, when I last saw him, he was spotty and obnoxious.'

'It seems you may well be pleasantly surprised when you meet again.'

'I'm not sure Dorothy will like me striking up a correspondence–'

'Rubbish! Dorothy's thoughts will all be on her final exams at school, and the hope of university to follow. But I should tell this Tim about Jimmy, eh?'

Jimmy...' Cora said, 'What is there to tell?'

Suddenly it was summer. Actually, it was May, but the long, hard winter was past. British troops were still needed in the trouble spots abroad, cinema newsreels depicted some shocking events, like the assassination of Mahatma Ghandi in January, but in the smaller world encompassed by London, there was cautious optimism.

'You should take a holiday,' Mrs Bloom advised Eliza as they sorted out the new greetings cards one morning and arranged them on a stand.

'The Whit week is coming up. Dede's been invited to stay with family in Norfolk.'

'Why don't you go with her?' Mrs Bloom suggested.

'I think she will enjoy it more on her own. We've been, well, so much together these past months.'

'That's only natural.'

'I know. Then there's Andrew to consider. He's more like family now than the sitting tenant, which is how we referred to him when we took him on with the house. He has his evening meal with us, and Sunday lunch. We appreciate his company, and the extra ration book means we can have a better spread.'

'You don't have to explain yourself to me, my dear. I'm sure there is nothing improper in the arrangement.' Mrs Bloom was studying a wedding card. The pictured bride in her sumptuous white dress was on the arm of a handsome groom. 'This reminds me of my first wedding day – I wore just such a gown – and my husband was so tall and handsome – I tell you, I was so proud!'

'I didn't know you'd been married before!' Eliza exclaimed. She thought, Mr Bloom could never have been described in that way.

'I was eighteen; young, I know, but my sweetheart was off to war, the Great War, of course. It was 1916. We married in a hurry, but my mother produced this wonderful

257

gown, because she said I must have a day to remember. Her eyes were red-rimmed with all that midnight stitching, I tell you. A few months later, I was a widow. I was expecting a baby; I had an unexpected proposal of marriage from one who had also loved me, but hadn't said, because I chose his friend.'

'Mr Bloom?'

'My dear Mr Bloom. He was turned down by the army because of his health – like your Bertie, he had suffered from TB, but as a child. It affected his spine, his growth. Yet, here he still is, and in good order, as you can see.'

'So you were married?' Eliza prompted.

'Three months only after my young husband's death. He wanted only to care for me, you see. You are wondering, no doubt, about the baby I was carrying. She was born prematurely, and I lost her when she was not even one week old.' Mrs Bloom added simply: 'That is how it was. Mr Bloom and I were not blessed with children, but we have been married for nearly thirty-two years, I grew to love him, and I can say we are still contented. I hope you will be as fortunate.'

'Thank you for telling me all that,' Eliza said. She had a sudden idea. 'Could we make a counter display – wedding invitations, boxes of confetti, cake decorations, those silver horseshoes and so on? There must be lots of weddings coming up this summer.'

'You do that, my dear. Don't forget the pretty wrapping paper!'

Dede was very excited at the thought of spending a week on the farm, especially as there was a new baby to meet: Helen's second little son, Laurie, was six weeks old. She was going by coach to Great Yarmouth, where Mal would meet her.

Eliza saw her off at Victoria coach station first thing on the Saturday morning. She was relieved that Dede's fellow travellers were, in the main, family parties. She wondered now how she could have let Cora travel on her own by train in wartime, but, she told herself, Cora was a responsible girl, not as scatterbrained as her sister! After the last minute admonitions she waved her daughter off: 'Have a safe journey!'

There was no reason to hurry home. Eliza had more money in her purse now she was working; she decided on an impulse to look round the shops, to buy a new dress; it was time to shed the black satin now that clothes coupons were no longer necessary.

Three hours later she rested her tired legs in a friendly little Italian café, and drank a welcome cup of frothy coffee. On a spare chair she carefully placed a carrier bag containing her purchases. Had she been rash? The dress, pale-yellow cotton, complimented her colouring, she had been fortunate to find one in her petite size, because the new length meant most hemlines were round her ankles, not her calves. She was not too sure about the full skirt, but the assistant had assured her that she could wear it because of her trim waist. Eliza also invested in new underwear: no one would see that, of course, but it would make her feel good. 'You're what they call a pocket Venus,' the young girl flattered her.

Losing weight, Eliza thought, despite the sad reason behind it, made her look, and feel younger.

When she arrived home she just had time for a bath and hair-wash before preparing a late lunch for herself and Andrew, who had this Saturday afternoon off. She told herself: 'I can't change into new clothes after all the rushing about, without freshening myself up!'

Fat sausages in flaky pastry, a green salad on the side, a shop-bought pink-and-white angel-cake sandwiched with synthetic cream, cups of Camp coffee – not as exotic as that which she had treated herself to this morning – she and Andrew sat chatting at the table, with the sun streaming in through the kitchen window.

'I sent my final course papers off today,' he said.

'Fingers crossed! What then?' She hoped he would not be moving on.

'If I get my degree, I can make plans – I mustn't assume I'll pass.'

'Of course you will – all that studying and writing every evening!' Eliza paused, removed her pinafore, feeling self-conscious in the bright dress. Also, she'd discarded her stockings and wore new Bata sandals to complete the summery look.

Andrew remarked appreciatively, 'You look very pretty today.'

She blushed. 'I thought it was time I shed the black. Bertie would have agreed.'

'Care to go for a walk? I can enjoy my afternoon off without feeling guilty now.'

'I'd love to,' she said.

Eliza hadn't been to the local park since just before the war, when Dede was a toddler in a pushchair. There had been colourful flower-beds then, lawns with railings around them and signs requesting politely: PLEASE KEEP OFF THE GRASS. She'd strolled along, nodding and passing the time of day with other young women with babies in prams, or energetic under-fives on reins. There was usually a queue of thirsty children at the drinking fountain on a hot day like this one.

Now, the railings long gone, youngsters kicked footballs on the balding greens, dogs rushed in their wake, barking; the play area was padlocked, the equipment had been dismantled. The tennis court was deserted, likewise the bandstand. But there were still flowers, straggling rose bushes, and seats to observe the changing scene.

Eliza and Andrew walked arm-in-arm round the perimeter of the park. She was disappointed to find it so neglected, not to see park attendants with their wheelbarrows, watching out for the occasional daring boy who'd climbed over the rails to retrieve a ball.

However, there was a new kiosk which sold soft drinks and packets of crisps. The man in charge deftly removed the bottle caps, then they sat on a nearby seat. Eliza could hardly believe she was drinking warm lemonade straight from the bottle, something she'd never permitted the children to do. Changing times, she thought.

Back home, it was actually a relief to sit in the cool of the living-room until it was time to make supper: baked beans on toast: 'You can trust me to cook something that simple!' Andrew said.

The phone shrilled, startling them. It was Dede ringing as promised, asking, 'Where were you? I tried earlier...'

'Now I can relax,' Eliza said ruefully, 'knowing she arrived safely.'

'Have you had enough of my company?' Andrew enquired, as he dried the plates.

'Oh no! Shall we listen to the wireless, or just chat?'

'Chat – seems a good idea.' He looked at her thoughtfully. 'I get the impression you're feeling more positive about things. The new clothes, for a start.'

'I suppose I've been in limbo since Bertie died. I wasn't sure I could carry on. Getting the job at Blooms was a turning point. Mrs Bloom, well, she helped me to see that things *would* get better, that time heals, that you mustn't give up...'

'It sounds trite, but life really does go on,' he said.

The evening passed uneventfully; they seemed to have said all they needed to; they sat together on the sofa, until it was time to switch off the wireless.

She was nodding off, when she felt his hand on her shoulder.

'I should leave you...' He rose, but remained standing there.

Eliza was suddenly wide awake. 'Don't go!' She scrambled to her feet.

Then she was in his arms, standing on tiptoe, her face pressed against his chest, where she could feel the drumming of his heart through the thin cotton shirt.

'Don't spurn me like you did after we'd been to the theatre,' she whispered.

'Spurn you?' His voice was muffled, too. 'I realized then, how I felt about you! I knew I mustn't betray Bertie's trust in me.'

She wouldn't tell him about Bertie's early

philandering, about the assurance, in his last letter, that he'd not renewed his association with the nurse called Lindy. He'd told her not to hesitate if she had a chance of future happiness – had underlined the words.

She whispered, 'I couldn't bear to lose you too.'

'You won't,' he promised. 'I was going to ask you to marry me, but I thought...'

'You thought it was too soon! Perhaps, when I tell you since Bertie returned from the sanatorium, after our year apart, we were never able to resume normal married life. I said it didn't matter, but, of course, it did. That's how it had to be, for half the years we were together.'

'It was the same for Joy and me, apart during the war, and then–'

'Shush. You remember you said it was important to let my emotions out?'

'Yes.'

'Well, doesn't that apply to both of us?'

'If you're sure–'

'I'm sure,' she said. 'Look, you go and collect a few things from upstairs. I'll be in my room when you return.'

She hung the yellow dress carefully in the closet, hunted in the top drawer of the chest, found what she was looking for: a silk night-dress she hadn't worn for years because it had been too tight. It was actually loose on her now.

Before she got into bed, smiling, she turned Mrs Norton's portrait to the wall.

Early next morning, she was the first to wake. She gently stroked Andrew's face, traced the outline of his lips. He shared her pillow, his arms still held her close. His eyelids flickered open.

'Hello,' he said drowsily.

'How do you feel this morning?'

'Wonderful. How about you?'

'I ought to feel sinful, but I don't! Andrew, does the age difference between us worry you?'

'Why should it? If I was seven years older than you, the question wouldn't arise.' His arms tightened around her waist. 'Let's spend the day in bed...'

'Now that *is* sinful,' she said, 'but – why not?'

NINETEEN

Cora didn't recognize the young man in uniform at first sight. He saw the uncertainty on her face when she opened the door to the flat.

'It's me, Cora – Tim, cap in hand! I should have rung first, sorry, but I came straight

265

here from the station. Aren't you going to invite me in?' He heaved up a bulging bag.

'Tim – of course! Yes, come in. The flat's in a bit of an upheaval, we do our main chores on a Saturday. This is Kim. Kim, meet Tim!'

'We were just about to stop for a cup of tea. Will you join us?' Kim asked.

She looked in the cupboard, located a tin of Spam, and set to, to make sandwiches.

Cora and Tim sat in the living-room, making awkward conversation.

'Your mother will be expecting you, won't she?'

'I didn't specify a time. As long as I'm there for supper,' he said.

'How long a leave have you got?'

'A fortnight, then back to barracks at Aldershot.'

'You *have* changed,' she observed.

'So have you. What happened to your hair?'

'I had it cut! Why, don't you approve?' she challenged, feeling put out.

'No,' he said candidly. 'I remembered your long locks. Not an Eton crop.'

'*Eton crop!* It is not! All my girlfriends like it.'

'Men,' he emphasized, 'like women to look feminine.'

'Now, now, you two, quarrelling already, have a bite to eat instead,' Kim said.

266

'I'm sorry.' Tim smiled disarmingly. 'I've been looking forward to seeing Cora again since we began corresponding: I've lost any social graces I had since joining the army, I'm afraid.'

After Tim had gone, Kim expressed her opinion. 'He's a nice young chap. He's keen to see you again. What are you going to do about it, Cora?'

'Well, I'm not thinking of leading him on. I do like him, despite the sparring. Maybe when he sees Dorothy again, he'll forget about me.'

'I know this is hurtful – d'you still believe Jimmy will come back into your life?'

'You know the answer. Probably not. But I *won't* give up hope.'

Kim was right, Tim was keen to see her again. On Monday evening he rang to say he was coming over, to take her to the cinema. 'Don't say you've got to wash your hair – even if you have, it can't take long to dry!' he said.

'Oh, all right then.' Aware of sounding ungracious, she added: 'Look forward to it!'

Cora hadn't sat in the back row of the pictures before. Other couples were already necking, as it was dubbed nowadays, although, as they brushed past the occupied seats, where none volunteered to stand up to let them pass easily to the other end of the row, she thought wryly: *necks* don't appear to have much to do with all that fervent activity! Maybe she should warn Tim that she wasn't about to follow suit?

Tim sensed her thoughts. He whispered in her ear: 'Sorry about all this – I was showing off, hoping to impress you by forking out for two one-and-nines!'

Cora giggled. 'I forgive you, so long as you come up with the chocs!'

'I remembered you couldn't resist liquorice allsorts; will they do?'

'*Would* you shut up,' came an irate voice from the row in front.

The quarter-pound box was empty after only ten minutes of the main film, *The Fallen Idol*. The performances of the leading actors, Ralph Richardson and the young Bobby Henrey were particularly poignant. Tim passed his clean handkerchief, which had been carefully folded in the top pocket of his best suit, to Cora. She even allowed him to squeeze her hand when, at the film's climax, they sat on the edge of their seats.

Tim had left his bicycle in the hallway of the flat – there was no need for him to rush for the last bus. Cora hesitated, then invited him in for a cup of cocoa.

Kim, they discovered, had already retired for the night. There was a note on the table: 'Hope you had a good time. Make Tim a piece of toast – he's got a way to pedal!'

'Tactful, your friend Kim,' Tim said. 'Well,

are you going to oblige?'

Kim had left bread ready sliced on a plate, and the butter dish.

'I'll make cocoa while you use the grill. Don't burn the toast!' Cora said firmly.

They discussed the film while Tim spread most of their precious butter ration on his toast, which he'd had to scrape on one side, despite Cora's warning.

'The cinema programme changes on Saturday – care to go again?' he asked.

'Sorry, I'm going home for the weekend. Dede will be back from California then, and Eliza has something important to tell us both, she says. Very mysterious!'

'Can't you guess?'

Cora shook her head. 'No! Something happened perhaps, while Dede was away.'

He was fastening his cycle clips. 'Better go.'

She opened the door, but before she could click on the landing light, Tim took her by surprise: he cupped her face firmly with his hands then gave her a long, lingering kiss, which quite took her breath away. When he released her, she was speechless for a moment, then she rallied, accusing him: 'You've done that before, I can tell!'

'I told you I'd grown up quickly in the army. *You* can't claim to be inexperienced either, can you?'

Cora giggled. 'Snap! But you needn't think I've–'

'Gone all the way? Nor have I. It doesn't mean I don't think about it, though,' he added audaciously.

She flicked the switch then, and pointed down the stairs. 'Goodnight, Tim.'

'You're not cross with me? You'll see me again?'

''Course I will. I'm glad we're mates again,' she said.

Cora arrived in London on the Friday evening. She was bursting to know what Eliza had to impart, but Eliza wasn't saying until Dede was home, except: 'I shall need your support, I reckon, Cora.'

Andrew joined them for supper, but afterwards he departed upstairs.

'Oh, I've good news for you,' Eliza said, as they settled down to catch up on other events. 'When I rang Ginny yesterday she said she'd heard again from Jimmy. Seems he's still in Liverpool. He looked up a cousin of ours, and was invited to stay.'

'Did – did he mention *me?*'

'He sent his love to all the family.'

'That's not the same thing.' Cora's lip trembled.

Eliza gave her a hug. 'I know how you feel. At least now that Ginny has an address for him you can write, can't you?'

'I might do better than that; I could turn up on his doorstep!'

'You sound fierce, so I reckon you mean it! Don't be too impulsive, dearie.'

'I'm old enough to make up my own mind,' Cora said firmly.

'Ouch! Yes, you are. But think first, then do, is my motto.' Eliza blushed as she realized she'd just rushed headlong into a relationship with Andrew.

Cora thought, there's something different about Eliza – she's well, *glowing*. Surely that must be connected to any announcement she makes tomorrow?

'There is something I want to show you, Cora – I need your advice.' Eliza took up the writing-box where she kept her household bills and correspondence. She opened a small drawer at the back and took out a folded paper. 'Read this, dearie.'

Cora perused her father's last letter in silence. When she eventually looked up she said simply: 'So, he did love us, didn't he?'

'Yes, he did. I haven't shown this to Dede yet...'

'You feel she's too young – she might wonder about the – person he mentions.'

'Don't you?'

'Yes. Someone he knew, before he came back to us?'

'He did tell me a little about her, when we married. I said it was in the past, there was nothing for me to forgive. It was a shock to realize he'd met her again and not said.'

'Have you ... written as he requested?' Cora asked gently.

'No, I'm afraid I haven't. I made a couple of attempts, but tore them up. Cora, will you write to this Lindy Wright for me? She must know of your existence. You'll know how to put it, I don't.'

Cora refolded the letter. 'I'll do it this evening.'

Thank you. I miss you, you know, but Dede's growing up fast.'

'What *would* we have done without you, Eliza?'

'I'd have had a dull life without you, and dear Bertie, I think. Cora, will you keep his letter for me in Aunt Poll's box? It would come down to you eventually, anyway. I've read it so often I know it word for word. Help yourself to notepaper et cetera.' Eliza had purchased a new, unlined pad from Bloom's for this purpose.

It took Cora quite a time to carefully phrase the letter to the Canadian nurse. She put Eliza's address at the top of the page.

Dear Mrs Wright,
I am writing to you, as my father, Albert (Bertie) Kelly, wished you to be advised in the event of his death. Sadly, he passed away in February of this year.
Yours sincerely,
Cora Kelly (daughter).

Eliza had already purchased a postal order to cover the cost of sending the letter by airmail; Cora then wrote a brief covering note to the almoner at the sanatorium.

She yawned. 'It's been a long day for me. Is it all right if I go to bed?'

'Yes, of course. Goodnight, then.' Eliza glanced at the clock.

'Shall I use the bathroom before you?'

'Yes, you do that.' Eliza paused. 'I'm just popping upstairs to ask Andrew something. I won't be long...'

'It's only nine o'clock. Your bedtime is up to you, Eliza!'

'If you don't mind, then?'

'Of course I don't mind. See you in the morning.'

Glimpsing the light from that room, Eliza tapped on Andrew's bedroom door. He drew her in. 'I thought I'd have an early night. I was already missing you.'

'I think Cora's guessed something's up.'

His arms went round her. 'Just as well you're going to confess all tomorrow, then.'

'Not *all*, Andrew. I don't want to shock her, confess we've been sleeping together all week. We must restrain ourselves until we get married.'

'We'd better make a date as soon as possible, then. How long can you stay now?'

'Long enough,' she whispered.

Dede was full of her holiday news. She'd so enjoyed helping to amuse the little boys. 'I've decided to become a children's nurse,' she announced.

'That's interesting,' Eliza observed, 'I thought you weren't keen on babies.'

'I wasn't. Mal says they're all smells and yells at times, but they're hard to resist when they give you a toothless smile. I agree with that.'

It was Sunday teatime. Cora had helped Eliza make a welcome-home spread. She'd have to leave for the station herself in an hour's time.

'Goody, chocolate cake!' Dede said.

'I'm afraid I licked the spoon – Eliza said I should save it for you,' Cora admitted.

'Leave the sandwiches for five minutes, Andrew's joining us.' Eliza poured tea with an unsteady hand, spilling some in the saucers.

She was glad when Andrew took his seat at the table. 'Eat up; then, when I say, can I have your attention?'

Dede looked at Cora. Cora winked at her. *Nothing to worry about*, was unsaid between them.

Ten minutes ticked by, then Eliza said: 'Right, are you listening?'

The girls both nodded.

It didn't come out exactly as Eliza intended. 'Andrew and I, well, with your approval, of course, think it would be a good thing if–'

'We've decided to get married, in other words,' Andrew said equably.

'Oh, is that all? Can I have another piece of cake?' Dede asked.

Then they all dissolved into relieved laughter.

'It's what Dad would have wanted,' Cora assured them, recalling what Bertie had said in his letter.

'Where will we live?' Dede wanted to know. 'I don't want to change school again.'

'We're not moving. When Andrew moves in with us, we'll let the other flat again.'

'Will you still work at Bloom's?'

Andrew answered for Eliza. 'Your mum enjoys it, so why not? I shall be changing my job though, if I get my degree I hope to move on, to a pharmacy in one of the London hospitals. It's what I was aiming for, before the war.'

'When will the wedding be?' Cora wondered.

'Soon. Just a quiet affair.'

'You said that last time!' Dede was tactless as always.

Eliza gave Andrew's hand a squeeze. Sooner the better, she thought, for they'd been rather reckless, and although she doubted it would happen just like that, after all this time, wouldn't it be wonderful, if she became pregnant in her fortieth year?

TWENTY

July, 1948

Eliza didn't have any difficulty deciding what to wear for her wedding. It would be the yellow dress, with a matching silk rose from Bloom's bridal display, pinned in her hair. The dress, which she hadn't worn since after the day she bought it, was now a little tight round the waist, she thought ruefully. She'd recovered her appetite; that was good, of course, but she decided she'd have to cut back on the cakes.

Cora teased Eliza's hair into a halo of ringlets. 'I'm thinking of growing mine again, then I could have a perm and curly hair too, it was always my ambition as a child!'

'You'd regret the perm, I think, but short hair is very suitable for the role you're going to play today, eh?'

'*Best man!* I'm honoured Andrew asked me. I ought to wear trousers, but I hope my new costume will do.'

'I like the kick-pleat at the back: you're

slim, so you can wear a hobble skirt.'

'I'm glad you're so happy again, Eliza, it means a lot to us.'

'I hope folk don't think I'm marrying on the rebound.'

'What did Dad say in his letter? *Don't hesitate!* I know I wouldn't if...'

'If Jimmy came back and wanted to be with you,' Eliza said softly.

'Don't make me cry today. My mascara will run.' Cora blinked away a stray tear.

'Mascara, what's that?' Eliza enquired, too innocently, then they both giggled.

'Like me to do your eyelashes?'

'No fear! Andrew can take me – unvarnished!'

'Oh Eliza,' Cora exclaimed, 'I do love you!'

Dede came bouncing into the room. 'I made the bridegroom a cup of tea as you said. Is the best man ready to accompany him? You'd better leave me in charge of Mum, Cora. I'll keep an eye out for the taxi.'

'You should go by taxi, too,' Eliza worried.

'Nonsense,' Cora said briskly. 'The walk will do us good. It's not that far, and a lovely day. See you at the town hall then, don't be late!'

When she'd departed Dede barred Eliza from looking out of the window. 'No looking at each other before the ceremony!'

'You and your superstitions,' Eliza said

fondly. 'You look so grown-up today, Dede.'
Cora had made her sister a swirling skirt in
a brilliant shade of blue, with a little 'mon-
key jacket' to match, with sparkling silver
buttons.

'I feel like a peacock! Still, it could be my
last chance to be a bridesmaid: Cora's
nineteen and the only boyfriend she has is
Tim, and you can't really count him.'

'You'd better not repeat that. He's coming
to the wedding, after all!' Eliza quickly suppressed a small sigh. She'd only one regret,
that again she was not to marry in church.
*Dear Lord, bless us anyway. Grant us a long
and happy life together.*

There were just the five of them at the
ceremony, but outside the town hall, when
they emerged, there was a small crowd of
well-wishers, including work colleagues of
Andrew's. Confetti was thrown, Eliza was
presented with a lucky silver cardboard
horseshoe, and cameras clicked busily.

'Shame Mrs Bloom couldn't be here, as
it's the Jewish Sabbath,' Eliza said.

The taxi drove them to a local restaurant
for the wedding breakfast.

This was the generous wedding gift of her
employers: the Blooms had insisted.

'Eat up,' Cora encouraged Dede. 'You'll
be on short commons back at my flat!'

They'd arranged the wedding to coincide
with the long summer holiday from school.

Dede was excited at the prospect of staying with Cora and Kim in Canterbury for a few days while Eliza and Andrew were on their honeymoon.

It was a proper lunch: asparagus soup and crusty rolls, followed by poached salmon and spinach, with peach sorbet for dessert.

'Real coffee,' Eliza sipped hers appreciatively. 'Cream, too!'

The wedding cake was a soft, iced sponge, like the one at her first marriage. Food rationing was still in place, after all. She wrapped the tiny decorative figures: the bride and groom, in her paper napkin. She recognized these napkins with a smile: more items from the bridal display at the shop, which she had arranged herself.

They travelled together to the main-line station but parted company there. The train to Canterbury arrived first, Tim carried the baggage aboard, while the girls hugged and kissed Eliza. It was an emotional few moments, during which Andrew stood back tactfully. Then Cora pumped his hand, and said: 'Didn't it all go splendidly?' Dede was less inhibited, offering her cheek for his kiss.

'We've time for a cup of tea,' Andrew observed, as they waved them off.

As they stirred the weak liquid in the thick white cups with the one spoon chained to the counter, they smiled rather sheepishly at each other. Eliza wondered if there was confetti in her hair, although the carnation in Andrew's buttonhole was a giveaway.

'Hereford,' she mused. 'Will we be in the country?'

'Mmm. More hilly there than in your beloved Norfolk! I hope you've packed some flat shoes for walking,' he said.

'Your aunt – she's the one who brought you up, when your parents were abroad?' Eliza realized she actually knew very little of his early life before he met and married Joy.

'Well, I was at boarding school in term-time, but I spent all my holidays with her.'

'I hope she'll approve of me...' Consider me good enough for him, she thought.

'Why on earth shouldn't she? She didn't marry herself, but she was more of a mother to me, still is, than her sister, my mother.'

'Your parents sound rather grand.' Andrew's father was an attaché in a foreign embassy.

'Do they? You had better luck with *your* family, I think. Aunt Carrie's looking forward to meeting you. She has a busy social life in the village, so don't worry, we'll have plenty of time to ourselves. We'll catch up on all we don't know about each other.'

They finished their tea. Time to wait on the platform, with his arm round her waist.

The first hint to Eliza of what to expect was when Aunt Carrie's chauffeur met them at the station in an ancient, but gleaming Daimler car. As their luggage was stowed in the boot Eliza and Andrew settled back on the sumptuous leather rear seat. She groped for his hand and he gripped hers reassuringly. 'The car comes out of the ark, darling. Aunt Carrie's as hard up as most are, postwar. She supplements money she inherited by selling garden produce in the farmers' market. Dommett, our driver doubles as gardener. He and his wife, the housekeeper and cook, live in the lodge on the estate.'

Estate! Eliza thought, in trepidation.

It was almost dusk when they turned into a long gravel drive and drew up outside Heartsease Hall. It wasn't as impressive as Eliza had imagined: a rather ugly red-brick Victorian edifice with a stout oak front door. As Dommett helped Eliza alight they were suddenly surrounded by four small barking dogs. Seeing the alarm on Eliza's face, Dommett said soothingly, 'The Dachshund gang, Mrs Livingstone. They don't bite.'

Mrs Livingstone: Eliza hadn't yet absorbed her new identity. It would be some time before she stopped thinking of herself as Eliza Kelly, or even Eliza Quinn.

The Dachshunds, whose silky coats brushed the ground and almost obscured their short legs, didn't actually bite, but they certainly nipped, targeting visiting ankles.

'Ouch!' Eliza exclaimed, unsure what to do.

'Dogs, desist!' a loud voice cried.

Eliza looked up as her attackers dispersed. A large woman, wearing a thick tartan skirt, despite the balmy evening, a tweed jacket and wellington boots, had come round the side of the house in pursuit of the dogs. She held out her hand in greeting.

'I'm so sorry. I'd just escorted them round the grounds, to make sure they didn't piddle indoors, which they tend to do when they get over-excited – typical females, you know. Come in, Eliza, do. Andrew, why didn't you carry your wife over the threshold? She'd have preserved her stockings then.'

'The door wasn't open,' Andrew reminded her mildly. 'As if you hadn't realized Eliza, this is my Aunt Carrie.'

'Excuse my attire, I'll effect a quick change, while Mrs Dommett takes you to your room to settle in and unpack. Dinner in thirty minutes.'

Eliza and Andrew, carrying their cases, followed the diminutive housekeeper up the winding stairs. 'Watch out for the holes in the carpet,' Andrew whispered.

The guest bedroom was at the end of a corridor, next to a cavernous bathroom.

'Plenty of hot water if you want a bath,' Mrs Dommett said. 'I'll leave you to it.'

'Not exactly the Dorchester,' Andrew observed ruefully. The large room was full of gloomy furniture, including a vast bed, but there were garden flowers in a jug on the dressing-table, and a note with the one scrawled word, WELCOME!

Eliza took up one of the towels piled on a chair, located her washbag. 'I won't take too long. Fancy, I've never had two baths in one day before!'

The taps on the bath were difficult to turn; she had to call Andrew to help. She stood there, with the towel draped round her, feeling shy and uncertain. What had she done, marrying someone she really didn't know at all?

'There.' He tested the water. 'More warm than hot, I think. Well, try it, anyway.'

Eliza let the towel drop, aware that he was waiting for her reaction. She stepped in the water, sinking down in its depths. 'Just right,' she said.

He hesitated by the door, then: 'It's been a long two months, Eliza, since we were able to express our feelings for each other. I was wondering, remembering that wonderful week, whether – there was anything you wanted to tell me?'

She lathered her arms with the soapy flannel. He's noticed my tummy isn't as flat as it was, she thought. She didn't look at him as she answered: 'No, Andrew. I'm not pregnant, if that's what you're worried about. Would you ... have minded if I was?'

'More important, would you, Eliza?' He

didn't wait for an answer. 'I've gained a ready-made family, which I really appreciate, but you've spent years, including hard times, bringing up your girls. I don't want to tie you down with babies all over again. You deserve a long honeymoon!'

She managed a smile. 'Let's make it last the rest of our lives then!'

Aunt Carrie was an entertaining companion at dinner. 'More of a high tea,' she said wryly, 'We eat simply these days. Freshwater fish: Dommett angled 'em out of the river. This is our own butter, made from goats' milk. Andrew, I won't be offended if you have your main meal out most days. Ross-on-Wye is a good place for restaurants.'

'Can we walk there?' Eliza ventured, wondering what to do with the bones from the fish – was it good manners to place them on the side of her plate?

'My dear, didn't I say? Dommett has oiled the squeaks, so to speak, out of the Morris Eight. There's a half-can of petrol in the boot: enough to get you to the nearest garage, anyway. You learned to drive in the army I presume, Andrew?'

'Yes.' He was struggling with fish bits, too, Eliza saw. 'Thanks, Aunt Carrie.'

'Now, Eliza tell me all about yourself!' It was a command not to be ignored.

Eliza had prepared herself for this and

decided what she should say. 'I brought up my friend's two little girls, after she died. Later, I married their father. He was drafted to a coalmine in Kent during the war, and we lived in a village there. We returned to London not long before Bertie died. He'd been in poor health for some time. Andrew became a good friend, as well as our tenant. He helped us through a difficult time.'

'It was to your mutual advantage, I presume, to marry sooner rather than later?'

Eliza digested this. 'I'm not sure what exactly you mean?'

'My dear, don't look so apprehensive! I understand you own your property. You had more to offer than my nephew. He doesn't rely on his parents in any way. However, he will inherit this pile, run-down as it is, from me. But I don't intend to up sticks until they carry me out of here, as it were.'

'Andrew certainly didn't marry me for my money, because I haven't any!'

'Aunt Carrie, may I have the final word on the subject?' Andrew asked.

'That's usually my prerogative!'

'I want you to understand that I married Eliza for love. I'm so fortunate to have been given a second chance of happiness.'

'So am I,' Eliza averred.

'Dessert,' announced Mrs Dommett. 'Last picking of the raspberries.'

Andrew leaned over Eliza's plate and

deftly removed a tiny white grub. She began to giggle, she couldn't help herself. Then they were all shaking with laughter and the tension evaporated.

'You'll do, Eliza,' Aunt Came observed, patting her hand. 'You'll do very well. Andrew's a very lucky fellow.'

They retired upstairs at ten.

'Your aunt's a demon with the cards,' Eliza said ruefully. 'Cora might have been a match for her, but not me.' She hung her clothes in the closet.

'Stop wasting time,' Andrew said. He was already in bed. 'I'm afraid it's the same lumpy mattress that I recall – there've been no new furnishings since I've known this place.'

She slipped into bed beside him, switched off the lamp. 'Andrew...'

'Mmm?' he murmured, drawing her to him.

'Thank you for saying you married me because you love me.'

'Well, it's true. How about you?'

'I love you, too,' she said simply. 'But it took me by surprise...'

'I've got a surprise lined up for you tomorrow.'

'Oh? And how about tonight?'

'It's our wedding night isn't it? What d'you expect?' he teased.

'You *know* the answer to that,' Eliza said

286

tenderly, as she nestled in his arms.

They were rather out of breath when they reached their goal the following morning: the beautiful Italianate church of St Catherine, high above the village of Hoarwithy in the valley below. The bell was already ringing for matins.

'Not much point in bringing the car,' Andrew said. 'Difficult to park up here.'

'Oh, Andrew, you must have known the only thing missing for me yesterday, was going to church. Thank you!'

'I'm not a regular churchgoer myself, but this is definitely the place for a spiritual uplift. It's only about eighty years old; there was a small chapel here originally, it was built by the vicar of Hentland – you'll find the interior *amazing*. Come on, we'd better follow the crowd inside!'

Their eyes were greeted by white marble columns, an altar and a pulpit inlaid with glorious colours; a golden dome with Christ depicted in mosaic. Pugin angels looked down from stained-glass windows.

They sat quietly at the rear of the church, drinking it all in. Andrew touched the worn golden wedding band on Eliza's finger: she had insisted that her mother's ring be used again. 'It's important to me, it's all I have of hers,' she'd said.

'Say a prayer for me, I'm not good at that

sort of thing,' he whispered.

Eliza looked up at the mosaic. Her lips moved silently. *Lord, bless our marriage. Please let us always be as happy as we are today.*

TWENTY-ONE

Kim inserted her key in the flat door. She turned, realizing that Cora was lingering still in the hall downstairs. 'What are you doing, Cora?' she called.

Cora bounded up the stairs, clutching her bag in one hand, and a long blue envelope in the other. 'Post! A letter which Eliza has readdressed to me. I think I can guess who it is from.'

'Stop guessing and open it, while I put the kettle on. Fancy one of Dede's buns?'

'Bit stale by now, I reckon, but I'm hungry. Oh...'

'What's up?' Kim enquired.

'It's a *long* letter.' Cora waved it at her. 'I didn't expect that.' She began to read.

Dear Cora Kelly,
I apologize for not replying sooner to your letter. It was a shock to hear of Bertie's death because when we said goodbye at the sanatorium he appeared to have made a

288

good recovery from his illness.

I am not sure how much you know about the link between your father and me. We met some time after he parted from his first wife, your mother. He was honest with me insofar as he told me that he would not divorce her to marry me. I was very much in love with him – we were together for five years, but I know that he saw your mother, and you, on occasion during that period. Eventually, we parted. This was a traumatic time, and I do not wish to say more about the subject in case Bertie never enlightened his family, in particular, your stepmother Eliza.

In the spring of 1936 I returned to Canada, not telling Bertie I was pregnant, it seemed best to make a complete break. He didn't need any more complications in his life. I was reunited with an old schoolfriend, who offered to marry me, and accept the baby. Your half-brother Louis Wright is now twelve years old. Unfortunately, my marriage did not last. Louis stayed with my parents, while I returned to my nursing career in Britain just before the outbreak of the war.

I would like to assure you, and your step-mother, that I never contacted Bertie, that our meeting again in Scotland surprised us both. He told me then how happy and settled he was with his family, and I could see that he had changed. How could I tell him about his son? I learned he had another daughter, exactly the same age as Louis!

You will no doubt read between the lines and suspect that I never stopped loving Bertie. Indeed, he was the love of my life. Before Louis is much older I want to tell him about his real father. May I also tell him that he has two sisters who would like to meet him one day? Yours sincerely,

Lindy Wright.

Kim's voice sounded far away. 'What's up, Cora? Not bad news, I hope.' Cora held out the letter. 'Here, read this. I don't keep secrets from you.'

Kim digested it in silence. Then she handed the letter back to Cora.

'What are you going to do? Show it to Eliza? You have to consider Dede, too.'

'I don't feel I can tell Eliza just yet, when she and Andrew are settling down to married life. I'm sure she didn't know anything about another child – how could she, when Dad wasn't aware of his existence himself?'

'This would have been more hurtful to your own mother I think,' Kim said.

'I won't rush into answering the letter,' Cora decided.

'Has it upset you?'

'In some ways. Oh, I believe Dad was faithful to Eliza, but he admitted to being unstable in his youth. He certainly let my mum down badly.'

290

'Another cup of tea?' Kim asked briskly. 'Then *I've* got some news for you.' When she'd replenished their cups, she added: 'I've had an unexpected proposal!'

'Kim! I presume you mean someone's asked you to marry him?'

'Don't sound so incredulous! Not some-one. Arthur Clarke from Personnel.'

'Mr Clarke? Oh, I know you mentioned you'd been invited out for a meal a few times when I was in London for the week-end. But he's...'

'Older than me, I know. Early forties, never been married, but has a lot to offer.'

'In what way?' Cora demanded. 'You've never been materially minded, Kim.'

'I'm not. We were working in the same section during the war – he was engaged to one of my friends. She was killed in a raid. He had an award for bravery. We met up again when I came here, but we've only become close recently. He's glad of the company, and so am I; after all, I'll be on my own again when you leave here.'

'Who said I'm leaving?'

'I don't think it will be too long before you receive a proposal yourself, my dear.'

'Surely you're not thinking that Tim...?'

'Well, he rushes round to see you directly he comes home on leave. Don't tell me you're not fond of him, eh?'

'We've been pals since we were ten years

291

old! What about Dorothy?'

'I think you were the only one who saw a romance between the two of them.'

'Kim, you know I'm in love with Jimmy...'

'Sometimes you have to settle for something less complicated. Friendship is a good start and can lead to love, if you work at it. That's what I hope, anyway.'

'You're going to accept Mr Clarke, I can tell!'

'Don't worry, we're taking things slowly. You and I will be flat-sharing a while yet.'

'I keep my friends for ever,' Cora asserted. 'Even though I don't see some of them very often – in fact, I haven't seen my oldest friend Naomi since 1940! *We* must never lose touch, Kim – promise?'

'I promise,' Kim said solemnly.

'When are you taking your holiday?' Tim asked. They were spending the day at Brighton. It was almost the end of the summer season and the last day excursion by train.

They were walking barefoot gingerly over the pebbles to paddle in the shallows.

'Middle of September,' Cora answered. There was a strong breeze: strands of her hair, longer now, blew across her face, obscuring her vision. She brushed it back with chilled fingers. 'I should have brought a warm jersey. Oo-er!' she exclaimed, as the water washed over her feet and then receded.

'Watch out!' Tim said sharply as the shale shifted and they found themselves sinking up to their calves in heavy, wet sand.

They scrambled out, retreated back up the beach to where they had left their towels and shoes. Tim looked ruefully at his soaked trousers. 'I should have rolled them up further! Did you get very wet, Cora?'

'Only the hem of my skirt,' she said, squeezing out the salt water.

'Here, put my jacket round your shoulders,' he offered. He looked up. 'It's starting to rain. We'd better make a run for one of the shelters along the front.'

Most of the visitors had already departed for their holiday lodgings; it was hardly the day for a picnic lunch. From their hard bench, under cover, they watched the pleasure boats returning to their moorings. A few hardy souls disembarked.

'I was hoping we'd have a boat trip this afternoon.' Cora sighed.

'It might clear up later on. Shall we have our sandwiches now?' Tim asked.

'Wait 'til we've warmed up a bit.' She shivered.

Tim slipped his arm casually round her back. 'That help?'

'Thanks. But don't get any ideas.'

'What – in this public place?'

'No public about that I can see.'

'In that case...' He deliberately pulled her to him. 'You taste all salty,' he murmured, before he kissed her.

After a few minutes she pummelled on his chest. 'That's enough, Tim.'

'You know it's never enough.' He released her reluctantly. 'You must realize how I feel about you, Cora. When I'm demobbed next year I hope to work in a garage as a motor mechanic.'

'Andrew would certainly recommend you. He said you did an excellent job on the 1938 Morris Eight his aunt gave him. He needs a car now he's employed at the hospital.'

'The army did me a favour, training me. Meanwhile, why can't we be engaged?'

'Tim, we're too young. Your mother wouldn't like it.'

'I won't live at home after I'm demobbed, you know. Dorothy says she won't either, after her three years at university. Mum spent all that time, bringing me up on her own, Jack, likewise with Dorothy. They deserve to sit back and enjoy their life together, now.'

'I agree with you there. I feel like that about Eliza and Andrew. Oh, they're still responsible for Dede, but they've got used to me being independent. Tim, things haven't changed for me, in one respect.'

'You're still hankering after that cousin of yours, I suppose.'

'Jimmy's not related to me at all, he's Eliza's nephew.'

'Well?'

'I *have* to find out whether he wants me in his life, or not.'

'And if he doesn't?'

'Oh, Tim, forgive me for hurting you, but ... he's the one for me, even if he doesn't acknowledge it.'

He sat silent for some time, deep in thought. Then he said abruptly, 'You should speak to him *soon*. I think the rain's set in. We'd best pack up and return home on an earlier train. I won't see you again Cora, until you let me know Jimmy's answer.'

Later, back at the flat, she confided in Kim.

'Have you decided where you're going for your holiday?' Kim asked.

'I have now. I'm off to Liverpool, to see Jimmy,' Cora said.

Having made her mind up, there was no deterring Cora. As she'd never been further than to Norfolk on her own, she went to London after work the following Friday evening to talk to Eliza and Andrew. It was after eleven before Dede could be persuaded off to bed.

'Have you got in touch with Jimmy yet?' Eliza asked. 'I hear Ginny sent you his address.'

Cora shook her head. 'I want to surprise him. If he knew I was coming, he might take off again.'

'Well, you must have somewhere to stay. Jimmy has a room at our cousin Brendan's. He has a houseful it seems. There's Maureen, Brendan's sister. I haven't seen her in years but we get a card from her at Christmas. I'll write and ask if she can put you up.'

'Would she tell her brother, d'you think?'

'I don't imagine she would, if I explained the reason, Cora.'

Andrew had been quiet while this exchange was going on. Now he said: 'I could drive you to Liverpool, Cora. Otherwise, Eliza will be worrying you'll get lost.'

'It's a big city,' Eliza said defensively. 'And it's nearly two hundred miles from London.'

'That's really kind of you, Andrew,' Cora said gratefully, 'but it's probably best if I travel by train. I know that petrol is still a problem and you need your car to get to work. But I hope you can think of someone to meet me at journey's end.'

Eliza sighed. 'I'd feel happier if you weren't travelling on your own, but I'll see what I can arrange.'

'I'll see you off this end,' Andrew offered.

After Andrew departed tactfully to bed, Eliza asked; 'Are you going to tell me now?'

'You read me like a book!' Cora opened her bag, took out Lindy's letter.

'I wondered when you were going to show it to me.' Eliza unfolded the paper. When she had finished reading, she refolded the letter. She looked at Cora. 'She seems like a nice woman. It can't have been easy, bringing up a child on her own.'

'*You* had two of us to care for,' Cora pointed out, 'before you married our Dad.'

'I was fortunate as well. I was resigned to being single all my life until Biddy bequeathed me the most precious thing she had, her children.'

'Would you have liked a baby of your own?' Cora wondered.

'I was pregnant once, but I miscarried. Bertie and I ... well, it didn't happen again.'

'It's not too late now, is it?'

Eliza wiped her eyes. 'No, but it's getting that way. Andrew is very different from your father. He wants me to have an easier life, to look after me.

'You must have a look at what he's done upstairs, with help from Dede. We're expecting the new tenants, a young couple with a new baby, next week. We got rid of most of that antiquated furniture and bought more modern furnishings. It all looks bright and cheerful now.'

'That's good. But you didn't say whether Andrew wants a family or not.'

'The honeymoon isn't over yet...'

'I won't probe any more. I can see how

happy you are, Eliza. Now, what do you think I should do about Mrs Wright's letter?'

'I hope you will agree to get in touch with her son later on. Shall I talk to Dede?'

'Would you? All I can think of at the moment is seeing Jimmy again!'

'Is everything sorted out?' Andrew asked when Eliza joined him in bed. His breath fanned her face. Eliza was distracted by his caressing hands on her bare skin. She'd given up the flannel pyjamas and so had he.

'I believe so,' she murmured.

'You've made me so happy Eliza. I feel positive again. The new job, all *this*...'

Just one thing missing, she thought. But it's not fair to mention that. This quiet, kind man has hidden depths: he is a wonderful lover.

TWENTY-TWO

Cora had been settled in her seat in the train for an hour or so, buoyed up by the anticipation and excitement of it all, when she experienced sudden doubts about the outcome of her journey to Liverpool.

'There's something else I ought to tell you,' Eliza had said the previous evening.

'You won't put me off now,' Cora asserted.

'When Maureen rang to confirm that she'd put you up and that Brendan will meet you at the station – he won't say anything to Jimmy – she told me that Jimmy seems settled in Liverpool. He's working as a shipping clerk in an office at the docks. She also mentioned he is close to Brendan's daughter, Mary. It was she who got him the job.'

'Well, they're cousins aren't they?'

'A couple of times removed. Cora, you must have wondered why Jimmy couldn't settle back at the farm...'

'It was because of what he went through as a prisoner of war, wasn't it?'

'Not only that. Ginny and I believe it was because he still had feelings for Helen.'

'He was getting over that! He and I ... well, if I'd been older, last time we met...'

'Don't get your hopes up too high, that's all,' counselled wise Eliza.

Now, Cora suddenly realized that the young mother with the baby in the opposite seat was trying to attract her attention.

'Sorry, I was miles away,' she apologized.

'I said, I need me bag down from the rack. I can't lift it, with the baby in me arms and I can't put her down. Could you...?'

'Of course.' Instantly, Cora was on her feet, reaching up for the bag. There were three men rustling their newspapers at the other end of the carriage, but they obviously didn't want to be involved. Cora wasn't surprised, for the baby had been sick.

'Thanks,' the wan-faced woman said in a cockney twang.

'Will it help if I unzip the bag for you?' Cora asked, hoping the infant's mother wouldn't ask her to hold it, not until it had been cleaned up, anyway.

'Thanks. There's a small towel with a damp flannel rolled inside, at the top.'

Cora spread the newspaper that Andrew had bought for her to read on the seat next to the baby. She quashed the thought that she'd intended to cut out the cartoon of Teddy Tail to send to Helen's little boys. 'Here, you can lay the baby on this, then wrap the soiled things in the paper.'

'Thanks,' the young mother repeated.

When the baby girl was clad in a clean dress and woolly jacket, Cora offered to take her, while her mother tidied up.

'The baby doesn't look ill,' she observed.

'Oh, she isn't; she often brings up some milk after her feed.'

The two smiled at each other. They were about the same age.

'I'm Nan, and this is Vicki. She's eight weeks old.'

'She's very bonny,' Cora said sincerely, adding, 'And I'm Cora. Are you going to Liverpool, too? It's a long journey with such a little one.'

Nan lowered her voice, glancing at the imperturbable men. 'Vicki's father left me before she was born. Not a word since. A friend tipped me off he'd moved back to Liverpool, where he came from. I borrowed the fare from me Gran. I know he won't want me, 'specially with the baby, but I have to try.'

Cora had already noted that her companion didn't wear a wedding ring. 'I understand,' she said softly, 'because I'm in a similar situation. I need to know whether someone wants me in his life or not.'

'At least your chap didn't leave you in the lurch, and expecting, like, eh?'

'No, it didn't go that far.'

'Then why bother? I'd have had too much pride if it wasn't for Vicki.'

Cora winced. Was she about to make a fool of herself? Maybe Nan was the lucky one, she thought, seeing the baby asleep in her mother's arms.

They were steaming into Crewe. The silent men jumped up, one spoke to the others at last. 'Well, we made good time, but I shall complain about the state of the carriage. Bloody nationalization! The railways aren't what they were before the war.'

The doors slammed shut and the journey resumed.

'Will you give Vicki her bottle for me?' Nan asked Cora. 'I need a fag to calm me down. Me last one, unless you..?' Her hands shook a little as she struck a match.

301

'I don't smoke,' Cora replied, hoping she didn't sound judgemental. She prayed the baby wouldn't be sick again, over what she fondly thought of as her Best Man costume. She'd so wanted Jimmy to see her looking her best.

Lime Street Station. There, waiting on the platform, was Brendan, in uniform. He was off duty but had kept it on, so she could recognize him.

He spotted Cora waving out of the window and hurried along towards her. As Cora was about to alight, Nan asked fearfully: 'What are the police doing here?'

'He's a relative of mine. Why, you're not in any trouble are you?'

Nan didn't answer that, she said instead: 'Can you carry Vicki through the barrier for me? Then I can find a taxi, leave my bags, and come back for her. I'll be as quick as I can.' She thrust the baby in Cora's arms and disappeared in the jostling crowd.

'What's this?' Brendan, a burly man in his early fifties, asked when Cora stood beside him, with the hiccuping baby.

'I'm not sure... I'm as surprised as you are!'

'I think you've been left holding the baby,' he said grimly. 'Come on!'

A scrap of paper drifted to the ground as Cora shifted the baby to a more comfort-

302

able position. Brendan stooped to retrieve it. They read the pencilled scrawl. PLEASE TAKE GOOD CARE OF VICKI.

'First stop police station. They'll likely say you'd best keep her over the weekend, or 'til we find her mother. Maureen's a part-time midwife, she's looked after young 'uns in an emergency for us before. She'll take it in her stride.'

'But Nan's got the baby's things – her bottle...' Cora realized.

Then they saw the shabby canvas bag lying on the platform, abandoned too.

It was getting on towards eight o'clock before they left the police station. There were statements to make; a doctor was summoned to ensure the baby was in good health. It was agreed that unofficially they would delay action a few hours because in cases such as these the mother very often had second thoughts.

The doctor said: 'The child has been well cared for. Her mother probably acted on impulse. She handed her baby to someone she felt she could trust. She'll be back.'

Meanwhile, Brendan telephoned Maureen to tell her of the unexpected events.

He reported: 'Jimmy's already there: Maureen invited him for supper. She's had to tell him what's what; I'm afraid your surprise is spoilt. Maureen says they'll eat now, if you don't mind. Which reminds me, I must ring Mary, or she'll be worrying.'

A police car took them to Maureen's – not a small terraced house by the docks as Cora had imagined, having seen an old photograph of Eliza's family home – but a semi-detached house on a post-war estate. Brendan pointed out his own house, just around the corner from his sister's.

'Families stick together if they can,' Brendan told Cora. 'Liverpool, like London, suffered a great deal in the bombing. But the city is recovering, and will no doubt be the better for it. They've already resumed building the cathedral. Can you believe it, work started on that in 1904, but it was held up by two world wars? Folk think that's a good sign.'

The door opened as the car drew up to the kerb. Maureen rushed to take the baby from Cora. Brendan unloaded the luggage, as Maureen cried: 'Here you are at last!'

Cora was tired, overwrought and hungry. She couldn't help herself: tears slipped down her cheeks as she saw how much Maureen resembled Eliza. She was older, of course, but still red-haired, plump and smiling. 'Come in, my dear!'

No sign of Jimmy. Cora thought woefully; he must have been fed up, gone home. The baby's wetted on my best skirt, I haven't combed my hair, put on lipstick, maybe it's just as well.

'I'll be off, after I've taken the cases in,' Brendan said. 'I'll ring if I have any news.'

Cora followed Maureen into the neat hall. 'I'll just settle the baby in the laundry basket, like all my waifs and strays, then I'll dish up your supper. Go in the parlour, Jimmy's waiting for you.'

'I can't see him looking like this,' Cora sniffled.

'Oh, well, the bathroom's top of the stairs, and your room next door to it. Come down when you're ready, eh?'

'Please tell Jimmy to go first. I must help you with the baby. I'll see him tomorrow, that's if he wants to see me...'

'I'm sure he does. Now, what experience have you with babies, Cora?'

'Not a lot,' Cora admitted. 'Just with my sister, and that was years ago.'

'Then you might as well leave little Vicki to me. Why not go to bed, you look worn out. I'll bring your supper up when the baby is settled.'

'Thank you, Maureen. Like Eliza, you know how to sort things out!'

She was reminded later of her first visit to California, when Eliza had brought her supper in on a tray. It wasn't bread, hot milk and honey this time, but tasty shepherd's pie, which was easier to manage with a spoon, sitting propped up in the big double bed. Maureen waited until she had eaten as much as she could manage, then handed her a mug of tea.

'See you in the morning dear! Don't hurry to get up. I'd best ring Eliza now and tell her all's as well as it can be, in the circumstance.'

Cora didn't expect to sleep soundly, but she did. The knocking on the front door in the early hours didn't rouse her. She wasn't aware that Nan had turned up weeping at the police station, that a kindly colleague of Brendan's had brought her to Maureen's to be reunited with her baby.

Maureen had made Nan egg on toast and told her: 'Eat up. Don't try to explain it all tonight. You can sleep in my bed, with the baby beside you. I'll go in with Cora.'

Cora opened her eyes in the morning to see Maureen, already washed and dressed, brushing her hair before the dressing-table mirror.

'Maureen, is the baby all right?' Cora asked.

Maureen turned, smiled. 'Oh, she's all right indeed. Her mum came back for her, as Brendan said she would. The police won't press charges. She's in my bed, they're both still asleep.'

'What will happen now?'

'She's welcome to stay for a while, 'til she gets herself sorted out. And you?'

'I'll see Jimmy today.' Cora said.

TWENTY-THREE

It was a new experience for Nan, sitting in the bath, with the baby on her lap, 'washing all me cares away,' as she said to Cora when she was invited in, after a polite knock on the door.

Cora gestured with the big towel. 'Maureen said to bring Vicki downstairs. She'll get her dressed and give her a bottle while you finish up here, Nan.'

Nan was obviously reluctant to leave the warm water, discreetly laced with Dettol, or to squeeze out the sponge, after she passed the baby to Cora. She swished her legs like a child and tilted her head back to rinse the soap from her hair.

Cora thought, she'll feel so much better for being clean all over. Maureen, she knew, had already consigned Nan's grubby clothes to the bubbling water in the kitchen copper. 'I don't usually tackle the washing on a Sunday, but needs must.'

There was a parcel of women's and children's clothing at the top of the linen cupboard. 'They might come in handy, not much in their bags,' said practical Maureen.

They ate their breakfast in the kitchen, sitting on wooden stools at a long table pushed against the wall. Maureen, flushed from her exertions, bustled around, wearing a wrap-around print apron over her Sunday clothes. She had fetched new-laid eggs from the coop in the small back garden where she kept a trio of bantams.

'Scrambled 'em,' she said cheerfully, 'as there wasn't enough for one each.'

Cora thought she not only has a look of both Eliza and Ginny, she has their generous spirit where youngsters are concerned. Brendan is kind, too. Nan is being lifted from her misery, her current hopelessness, like me, as a small girl in Californy.

Nan sat beside Cora, not saying much, but enjoying the good food. She'd clipped her damp, fine, mousey hair back from her face and she looked younger today in a simple cotton frock and pink cardigan. Yesterday Cora had guessed that they were around the same age; now she wondered if Nan was younger.

Maureen had been thinking the same, for she sat down at last, the other side of Nan and asked: 'Feel like explaining a few things, Nan? I could tell last night wasn't a good time to talk. How old are you, for instance?'

'Nearly seventeen,' Nan admitted.

'Your family throw you out did they, when they found out about the baby?'

'They wanted me to get Vicki adopted. I

308

was willing, until after she was born, then I knew I couldn't never part with her. I had a blazin' row with me dad. He said, find the bloke what got me into trouble – make him face up to his responsibilities. That's why I come to Liverpool.' Her face crumpled and she began to sob. 'I just thought – he ain't going to listen to me, if I've got Vicki in me arms. When I saw the policeman I panicked, and handed her to Cora. She'd been real kind to me, on the train.'

'Then?' Maureen prompted gently.

'I caught a tram, cos I couldn't afford a taxi like I pretended, then I walked a good way and got properly lost. I had to walk back the way I come, and a man told me where the lodging house was, down by the docks. I was ever so scared, being on me own. Round about midnight, I finally found him. He was drunk, he had a woman with him and he slammed his door in my face. I stumbled down lots of steps in the dark, 'cos he was staying at the top of the house, and the landlord come out of his flat. He told me to go to the church or the police station. The church was shut, I couldn't find a priest, so I did the other thing. They brought me here. That's it.'

Maureen put her arms round the girl and hugged her tight. 'They brought you to the right place, love. I'll help you get back on your feet. Stop crying, and stop worrying.'

Someone was rapping on the front door. Maureen smiled. 'That'll be your young man, Cora. A good sign, him coming early like this. Take him in the parlour and we'll stay out of your way in here. Good luck!'

Cora paused briefly by the mirror in the hall. Do I look all right? Will he be upset that I had my hair cut short? She was wearing maroon-coloured slacks, with a pink chenille T-shirt which clung to her curves and made her feel self-conscious. She ruffled her hair with her fingers.

She opened the door. He was standing on the step, smartly dressed in a white shirt, fawn trousers, a tie and checked sports jacket. Jimmy had cropped hair too, the unruly curls slicked back with hair oil. But his smile was the same, and he sounded like the old Jimmy when he said: 'Hey, aren't you going to ask me in?'

Cora nodded; he followed her into the parlour. Jimmy went straight to the window. 'Maureen hasn't pulled the curtains yet – not like her.' Sunlight streamed into the room, as he jerked the curtain cords.

He turned, still smiling. 'What took you so long, Cora? I thought you would have sought me out months ago!'

She was speechless, shaking her head now in disbelief. How could he say that?

The smile vanished. For a moment he appeared uncertain, then he crossed the room in a bound, wrapped his arms round her. She refused to respond to the embrace.

She said, in a fierce little voice: 'How can you joke about it? Don't you realize how worried I – we all were? You could have written to me, but you obviously didn't care.'

'I did care – I *do* Cora! Mum told me you had a boyfriend. I thought it could spoil things for you, if I got in touch and told you how I felt.'

'How do you feel?' she demanded. 'Why did you run away?'

He released her then. 'Let's sit down. I should have realized you'd be angry with me.' They sat at either end of the sofa. 'I couldn't fit in at home – I guess I always was the odd one out, but Mum made me feel special, and Mal – well, he tolerated me when I was a boy. Things became very tense between us when I returned after the war. I had experiences I couldn't talk about, and Mal couldn't forget what had happened between Helen and me before I went away – nor could she. When I met you again I thought I could start with a clean sheet, but then I realized it was unfair to expect you to take me on, with all my problems. Maybe I'll never get back to normal again, whatever normal is. The best solution was to leave California. I drifted for a bit, then I found the family here, and they were my salvation.'

'Mary? You ... fell in love with her?' Cora

had to know.

He looked at her in astonishment. 'Mary and her husband moved in with Brendan after his wife died. They've all been so good to me. Mary wangled me the job in her office. She's longing to meet you! I was told to bring you back for Sunday dinner.' He moved closer. 'You look like a boy with your hair like that,' he added softly.

'And you look like Denis Compton, the Brylcreem Boy,' she retorted with a grin.

'Do you forgive me?' he asked.

'Yes, except for the comment you just made.'

'The rest of you is all girl – bosom heaving with indignation–'

'Stop ogling my bosom and I'll prove to you that I forgive you.'

He threaded his fingers in her hair just as he had, she recalled, the day they were on the beach at California, drew her close and kissed her firmly on her parted lips. She responded eagerly, as she had never been able to do with Tim.

'You still love me, I can tell,' he told her exultantly.

'Of course I do!'

'What about the boyfriend?'

'He knows about you. He'll be hurt, and I'm sorry about that, but I'm not letting you get away from me again, Jimmy Brookes!'

'What happens next?' he asked.

'You'll have to marry me, you really will: certainly nothing further is going to happen here today! I can guess what you're thinking! What d'you say?'

'I've still got nothing much to offer you,' he admitted.

'Oh, I've got plenty to offer you! First, after I leave here at the end of the week I must see Eliza. I need her permission. She'll expect me to get married from home.'

'When is this wedding going to be?' He sounded bemused.

'How about next spring? I'll be twenty in May. I know it sounds a long way off, but we need to start saving up, don't we? You and I ought to go to Californy for Christmas, to make it all right with your family, because *they* must be with us on our special day. After we're married we'll find somewhere to live up here, and maybe I'll get a transfer to the Liverpool exchange! Any objections, Jimmy? If so, tell me now.'

'No objections, but I can tell who's going to wear the trousers,' he joked.

'Well, I'm wearing them today, but I promise to be in a frock on our wedding day!'

'Only one way I know to shut you up...' This was like the Jimmy of old. Much later, when they came up for air, decidedly dishevelled, he queried: 'Did I tell you I love you?'

'You didn't have to,' she gasped, 'It's

obvious, isn't it?'

'As your boss, Jimmy, I'm giving you the next three days off,' Mary declared, when she heard the news a second time, for Maureen had rung her while Cora and Jimmy were on the way over. 'You must show her Liverpool, warts and all; being in love, Cora will think it's a grand place, as we do. Welcome to the Quinn clan Cora, my dear.'

She thought, I'll really be one of this family, not a waif and stray like Nan, which I almost was, when Eliza took me on. What a warm-hearted lot they are. I'm so lucky.

Andrew was there with the car, to meet her off the train. 'Eliza was worried you'd change your mind, and stay in Liverpool,' he told her, with a wry grin.

'No, I may have rushed into an engagement,' she flashed the inexpensive ring on her finger, 'but we have to consider others as well as ourselves. Eliza taught me that.'

'Congratulations. You're quite a girl, you know, Cora!'

'So Jimmy keeps telling me,' she said demurely. 'You'll give me away at my wedding, won't you, Andrew?'

'I'd be honoured to. Dede, naturally, is already planning her bridesmaid's outfit!'

'And darling Eliza – is she pleased for us?'

'I can confirm that she is. We hope you'll

be as happy as we are, Cora.'

They were turning into their road now. Cora had something to say before they went indoors. 'Andrew, d'you know what would make your marriage perfect for Eliza?'

'I'm not sure what you mean, I thought it was, just about.' He sounded hurt.

'Eliza would dearly love a baby – your baby! She won't say, because she's not sure you feel the same way. There, I shouldn't have interfered, but I have. Sorry.'

The car had stopped. The front door opened and Eliza and Dede came rushing down the path to greet Cora.

Andrew said quickly and quietly: 'Don't be sorry, you've given me something to think about. Well, out you get – let the hugging and questioning begin!'

Tomorrow, Cora thought ruefully, I'll be back in Canterbury, and have to recount every last detail – almost! of my week in Liverpool to Kim!

'Another wedding,' Eliza said dreamily when she and Andrew eventually got to bed, after all the talking. 'In our local church too, that's fitting, for she'll feel near to her parents there. I'm so happy for Cora. I hope Jimmy will live up to the promises he made. But I wish she wasn't going to live so far away. She can't come back and forth as easily or cheaply as she does from Kent. I'll miss

Cora. We've been through so much together.'

He said softly: 'How about a second family? I've come around to that idea.'

'Oh, Andrew, you don't know how much that means to me!'

'I do now.'

'That's good, because, well, I didn't know how to tell you, but you remember our wedding night at Aunt Carrie's?'

'How could I forget it ... lumpy bed and all, eh? Well?'

'It must have been then! Two months ago, I had a shock when I realized I might be pregnant, because we'd been careful, but obviously not careful enough!'

He held her close. 'That's a relief! I thought we'd be in for an anxious time, trying for a baby, and it might not happen. Now we needn't worry, darling.'

'It might not be as easy as it would be if I was younger,' she reminded him.

'What's the point of working in a hospital if I can't get the best advice for my wife?'

'The only drawback I can think of is that as mother of the bride, I'll be the one who needs a large bunch of flowers, if the baby doesn't arrive before the wedding!'

'You're not going to tell the girls yet?'

'Not until I've had it confirmed. So long as you're glad about it.'

'I am,' he said. He caressed the almost imperceptible swelling of her body. 'It's a big responsibility, a baby. I'll try to be a good father, I promise.'

'You'll be the best,' she told him, with confidence.

Cora and Dede were still whispering happily in their room.

'Did Jimmy ask: "will you do me the honour of marrying me?"' Dede wanted to know.

'Actually,' Cora giggled at the thought, 'I told him we were getting married! He didn't stand a chance, poor chap. You know what I'm like when I get overexcited.'

'What about poor old Tim?'

'I'll write to him very soon. I must tell him before I ask Dorothy to be a bridesmaid.'

'You'll ask him to the wedding, won't you, though?'

'I will, but he might decide not to come. I shall understand if he declines.'

'Oh, in all the excitement I clean forgot to tell you – I had a letter from Canada! From Louis, the boy Mum told me is my half-brother. He said he'd like to be my pen-pal, as we're both twelve. Mum said you know about him, too: you'd written to his mother. It'll be like you writing to Naomi, won't it?'

'I'd love to see Naomi again. We were younger than you are when we last met.'

'Ask her to your wedding too, then!'

317

'D'you know, I might. We really must stop talking and try to go to sleep, Dede.'

'I know, but I'm so excited – just think, I could be an aunty in a year or two!'

Cora thought, we might both have a little sister or brother before that happens. She said firmly, 'You'll have a long wait, I believe. Turn over, and close your eyes!'

TWENTY-FOUR

In the middle of November, two months after her visit to Liverpool, Cora had the first inkling that something was wrong. She hadn't heard from Jimmy at all this month, when up until now he had answered all her letters. Oh, he hadn't got carried away and written reams as she had, and he'd hardly referred to the wedding plans; he was obviously content to leave all that to her, but he signed off, 'with my love, Jimmy.'

Kim observed her friend's daily disappointment when no letter arrived postmarked Liverpool. Cora was definitely not her usual cheerful self. She waited until Friday evening to broach the subject. Cora was toying with her supper.

'What's up?' Kim asked.

Cora pushed her plate away. 'I keep thinking, maybe I rushed Jimmy into agreeing to a wedding, and all the rest of it. Looking back, it was too easy.'

'Forgive me for saying this, but do you think he's having second thoughts?'

'I ... I don't know.'

'Is that why you haven't started sewing your wedding dress yet?'

'It seemed I might be tempting fate,' Cora admitted miserably.

'Look, my dear, you could be upsetting yourself over nothing at all.'

'But you don't believe that, do you?'

Kim leaned across the table and covered Cora's clenched hands with her own. 'Ring him up, ask him. You have to know.'

'Right, I will! After the post comes tomorrow...' She managed a smile. 'What's your news? Have *you* set a date yet?'

Kim hesitated a moment. 'I wasn't going to say anything just yet, but, well, I imagine you've realized that I'll have to resign my post when I marry Arthur. It's against the rules for husbands and wives to work together.'

'I suppose I did know, but as it seemed unlikely ever to apply to me, I dismissed it,' Cora exclaimed. 'Tell me the rest!'

'We've decided to spend Christmas together in Arthur's house – to see how we get on under the same roof! If that goes well, we thought we'd get married in the New Year. There! I've said it. I'm afraid it will mean you'll have to find new digs, as I know you can't afford to stay here on your own. However, I thought, it won't be for too long, before Cora gets married herself and departs for Liverpool. Also, I was aware you hoped to be in Norfolk for Christmas.'

'Look, I still could be! Or I'll go home to my family and cry on their broad shoulders,' Cora said with a show of bravado. 'Though it's all baby talk there just now.'

'You're glad for Eliza and Andrew, aren't you?'

'Of course I am. It will be an important bond between the two of them, because Dede and I are not actually related to Eliza, as you know. It's rather different for Dede, because she never knew our real mother. Do you and Arthur hope for a family, Kim?'

'We haven't discussed it. That side of things... I'm not sure it will happen,' Kim mused. 'Anyway, Arthur is buying me a portable typewriter. I said: if I'm to be a lady of leisure I'm not very good at flower arranging. I'll write my wartime memoirs, instead!'

There was a letter from Jimmy on Saturday. Kim left Cora to open it in private.

Dear Cora,
There is no easy way for me to say this.
It would not be right for me to marry you. My inner demons are still with me. I can't expect you to give up your youth and aspir-

ations in life, it would all end in despair and disappointment.

For a short time I believed it would work, that we could be happy. I know you had our future mapped out, but it is better to end it now than later.

I will write to my mother, and I am sorry you will have the task of letting all the others know.

Dear Cora, forgive me, if you can. I do care for you, I always will, but you deserve a better man than me.

I may move on, I don't know. I hoped to stay in Liverpool, but probably I should go.

Love from Jimmy.

(You don't need to answer this letter.)

Almost blinded by tears, Cora reached down Aunt Poll's box from the shelf in her bedroom. She opened it, adjusted the contents to bury the letter where she couldn't see it, with all her hopes for the future. On an impulse, she tugged off her ring and added that. Something rolled into her lap. She was sitting on the side of her bed, and she wiped her eyes on the sheet. It was the marble which Tim had given her as a keepsake. She clutched it tightly in her hand.

Some time later, when Kim was aware that the awful sobbing had ceased, she came into the room, carrying two cups of steaming tea.

Cora sat up, dry-eyed now.

'You don't have to say anything,' Kim assured her. 'Would you like me to stay?'

Cora nodded. Kim put the cups on the bedside table, sat down beside her.

The minutes ticked by, then Cora said: 'It's over, Kim. He says he loves me, but he can't marry me. It was all too good to be true, wasn't it? Now I have to tell the family there won't be a wedding – not ever.'

'Better to end it now,' Kim said gently, 'Than after the event. Why don't you go home today – you should be with your family at a time like this.'

Cora was suddenly galvanized into action. 'Yes, you're right. I can make the next train if I hurry. I'll just drink my tea – thank you for that. Will you ring Eliza and say I'm on my way?'

'Of course I will. And I'll call a taxi, first, shall I?'

'Please. Don't worry, Kim. I'll be all right.'

They were there to meet her off the train; Eliza, Andrew and Dede. Had Kim said anything about the reason for the unexpected visit, Cora wondered?

Dede sat in the front seat of the car, while Eliza and Cora were in the back.

'What's up?' Eliza whispered to her.

'Kim didn't tell you?'

'No, but I just knew something was wrong...'

'I heard from Jimmy: the wedding's off,' Cora said flatly.

'Oh, my dear – don't say any more now.'

They were soon home. Cora went straight to the bedroom she shared with Dede. Eliza gave a warning glance at Dede not to follow. She said briskly to Andrew: 'Fish and chips for lunch, I reckon. Will you and Dede fetch it?' It would give her and Cora a chance to chat, she thought.

When the front door closed Eliza hurried to do just that.

'You look well Eliza.' Cora looked quite composed, if pale and puffy-eyed.

'I am. But I've had to take to wearing smocks, as you can see. Mrs Bloom makes me sit on a stool behind the counter, and clucks round me like a mother hen. Dede is attempting to knit a baby's vest, more grey than white, but it'll be fine after a wash. Now, you obviously aren't feeling too good. Like to tell me about it?'

'Jimmy has jilted me. He's called the wedding off. There's nothing I or anyone else can say, to make him change his mind. I feel... I've made a fool of myself, Eliza.'

Eliza stroked Cora's fringe out of her eyes. 'Your hair's growing. You mustn't blame yourself. Jimmy's not been, well, right, since he came back from the prison camp. How could he be – incarcerated for almost five years? He's realized, rather late, that it

323

wouldn't be fair to marry you. I'm ashamed to admit, Cora, for a moment I wondered if you were about to confide that you were pregnant too and that Jimmy wasn't going to stand by you.'

Cora flinched. 'We didn't go that far. I wish we had. I would have had something to remember – a night or two of love! Does that shock you, Eliza?'

'No, it doesn't. Do you want to say more about it?'

'I'd rather pretend this is a normal week-end home. Try to put it to the back of my mind. I'll get in touch with the others concerned next week. If Dede asks, though, I'll tell her.'

'You'll be with us for Christmas after all?' Eliza asked.

'At the moment, I think I'll likely decide to stay in Canterbury.'

'Oh. At least you'll have Kim with you, I won't worry that you're on your own.'

Cora thought; I can't tell her Kim will be away. I can't spoil Christmas here for them. She put her hand in her pocket, gripped the marble. It helps to hold that tight to prevent me crying.

Christmas Eve, and Kim was ready packed to go, waiting for Arthur to collect her after a full day's work. He lived in the house where he had been born, which he had inherited from his parents, in the countryside outside Canterbury.

'Are you sure you'll be all right on your own?' she asked Cora anxiously.

'Quite sure. I appreciate the paper chains, and the food you insisted on getting in for me to cook. I'll have the wireless for company.'

'And downstair's cat. Don't forget to feed him over the next two days.'

'I won't. Isn't that Arthur's car outside?'

'Yes. I'll ring you Christmas morning, I promise!'

'Not too early,' Cora called after her, 'I plan to have a long lie-in.' She said to herself, I might even spend most of Christmas in bed. At least I'll be warm there.

When Kim had gone Cora stuffed the chicken, garlanded it with sausages and streaky bacon, put it in the oven. Kim wouldn't have approved, she knew, but she intended to have a lazy Christmas day, in or out of bed. Eliza had sent a small homemade plum-pudding and half a dozen mince pies. These would just need reheating tomorrow morning. She peeled a couple of potatoes and a few sprouts, to cook them too.

Kim had filled the fruit bowl, and a dish with Kentish cobnuts. She had even filled a pillowcase with Cora's Christmas presents. 'I'll leave the cards for you,' she said. The one card Cora hoped for hadn't come, of course. There was no word from Jimmy. But thcy hadn't forgotten her in Liverpool. She had made an impression on them during her brief stay apparently, she thought ruefully. Maureen had written in her card: *Thinking of you,* and signed it with much love from herself, Nan and Vicki, who were still with her. Brendan's greeting was from himself, Mary and her husband Gerry.

It was past eleven when she finished in the kitchen. She gave a sigh of satisfaction. Keeping busy had damped down any errant thoughts. Now for a bath. She hoped that the water was hot enough. She shampooed her hair, as Nan had that day, in the same water. She'd warmed the towel and her pyjamas on the clothes horse by the gas fire.

The urgent knocking on the front door startled her. Who on earth could it be, at this late hour? Almost Christmas Day, she thought, glancing at the clock. She wound a smaller towel turbanwise round her damp hair, turned on the landing light, and went cautiously downstairs. 'Who is it?' she called out.

'Tim. I got a lift back from camp. Sorry it's so late. Can I come in? It's cold out here.' She heard the stamping of boots on the step.

'What on earth...' she exclaimed, but she slid back the chain and opened the door. 'You're lucky I wasn't already in bed,' she reproved him.

Tim was in uniform, with a kitbag slung over his shoulder. He said simply: 'I had to come. It's not right for you to be on your own. Dorothy wrote to me and said what had happened. She was worried when you told her Kim wouldn't be here. I hope you'll let me stay tonight, but I'll have to go home some time tomorrow, I promised Mum I would.' He sniffed the air. 'Something smells good!'

'Are you hungry?' she asked, hanging his greatcoat on a hook. 'Shall we have a taste of Christmas dinner tonight?'

'I wouldn't say no,' he admitted.

'Hot chicken sandwich then. You can carve it. Got your bayonet?'

'Glad to see you're still joking,' he said.

'Got to, even though my heart is breaking, eh?'

'You didn't write and tell me things had changed,' he said, as he sliced the meat.

'Well, they had, and they hadn't...'

'You mean, I still haven't a chance?'

'I didn't say that. I ... I'm glad you're still my friend, Tim. I'm glad you're here.'

'That's enough for now.' He took a large bite of his sandwich. 'Can I stay?'

'You can sleep in Kim's bed. I'm sure she wouldn't mind. Anyway, I'm not going to ring and ask her at this time of night, am I?'

She took the turban off her hair, shook her head. 'Do you mind if I brush it to dry it by the fire?'

'Hang on, and I'll do it for you, if you like,' he offered. 'I'm glad you've grown it.'

'About two inches since last I saw you!' she said. He stood behind her and gently teased out the tangles.

Her eyes were closing and she was drifting off to sleep when he ceased brushing. 'There, that's done. You ought to get to bed, we'll talk in the morning.'

'You can tuck me up, but that's all,' she murmured.

'Come on then,' he said, keeping his arm round her until she slipped under the covers. He tucked the covers round her firmly, switched off the light. 'See you in the morning. Happy Christmas!' He leaned over the bed to give her a quick kiss, no more.

'Happy Christmas,' she answered. Maybe it would be, after all, she thought. His kiss had been warm, comforting, but not demanding. She needed that right now.

EPILOGUE

May 1950

'What a day!' Cora cried happily, as her new husband piled their luggage on the rack above their heads. 'Can we pull the blind down on the window for privacy?'

'You've been watching too many Hollywood films,' he said. 'British Railways would not approve. Especially in broad daylight.' He glanced down at his trouser turn-ups. 'They won't appreciate all this confetti either, I think. Stop shaking your hat like that. It's all over the floor. We could get fined for leaving litter.'

'Don't you like my hat? Or my silver grosgrain costume?' The jacket was nipped in at the waist, the skirt was slim and calf-length: you couldn't stride out in it, Cora thought.

'You look very smart, but I preferred your orange-blossom headdress, and that beautiful floaty white wedding dress. You fulfilled all my dreams in that...'

'You only get married once. Oh, well I suppose that's not always so, but when I said "I do" I meant it!'

'So did I. I can't believe that only a year

and a half ago we weren't even together.'

'Yes we were! In my flat for Christmas. Remember?'

'In separate beds. Remember? I'm not sure my mother believed that story.'

She had the grace to blush. 'I'd had a lucky escape, only I didn't realize it. I was heartbroken, you know I was. If I had married Jimmy I'd have been following in my mum's footsteps when she married my dad. Jimmy was aware of that, he couldn't bring himself to marry me, then let me down. He'll always have a special place in my heart, you must know that.'

'Yes, I do know,' Tim said. 'It was all we hoped for, the wedding, wasn't it? And everyone enjoyed the reception, I think. The church hall was a good place to hold it. Friends and family were generous with their contributions to the feast.' He patted his stomach.

'Mmm. All my favourite people! Didn't Dorothy look smashing?'

'My best man certainly thought so. Mind you, he's only a humble mechanic like me and Dorothy's set to become a famous scientist. Shame your friend Naomi couldn't make it. I was hoping to meet her at long last.'

'She's taking her finals this year. Isn't Eliza's baby the sweetest thing? She's so much like her mother, red curls and all. Did I tell you they called her after that special church they visited on their honeymoon – Catherine?'

'You did. Several times. Is that a hint? Our church being All Saints...'

'You still can't resist teasing me, Tim Titchley, can you?'

He grinned. 'That's because I've had plenty of practice in that over the years.'

'I know they've only just met, and I'm so glad he and his mother could come to our wedding, but our young half-brother Louis soon learned how to rattle Dede, eh? I'm glad Lindy and Eliza got on so well, it could have been awkward them having Dad in common. I heard Eliza inviting them to lunch tomorrow.'

'Dede's going to be a stunner when she grows up,' he said.

'Like me? Go on, you'd better agree!'

'I do. Let me prove it...'

They didn't realize that the train was pulling into a station, and that folk were hurrying past their carriage window with broad smiles on their faces. They didn't need to read the label crafty Dede had tied to the door handle, JUST MARRIED.

'I can hardly wait until tonight,' he whispered.

'We'll be on our way to Californy then,' she whispered back.

'I'll put Catherine to bed,' Dede offered,

when they were back home after a very full day. After most of the guests had departed there had been plenty of washing-up to tackle.

'Would you? I'd be really grateful.' Eliza sighed. 'I just want to put my feet up.'

Andrew eased her shoes off, and she twitched her toes thankfully.

'It all went off very well,' he observed. 'As the bride's mother you had nearly as many compliments as the bride. That shade of green is just your colour.'

'Oi, what about me,' Dede put in.

'You looked wonderful, too,' Andrew said gallantly.

'In spite of Catherine wiping her fingers down my dress?'

'I thought that was made from water-marked silk,' he returned, straight-faced.

'D'you think anyone noticed?' Eliza asked Andrew, when Dede had departed with the baby, carrying her on her hip. She was an experienced older sister now.

'Noticed what?'

'That I'm expecting again. And getting on for forty-two!'

'You look younger every day, honestly. We agreed to have a second baby as soon as we could, then call it a day, didn't we? But you should take it easier this time.'

'I'm not the only one! Fancy Helen having four on the trot like that. I was sorry they couldn't come.'

'She's a sensible girl. Mal hasn't got time to stray.'

'He's very different from his brother. Poor Jimmy – he reminds me so much of Bertie. He still isn't settled. Last time Ginny heard from him he was back in Liverpool. I'm so thankful Cora and Tim found each other again.'

'She won't forget Jimmy, I think,' Andrew said. 'I'm sure it's the same for you, with Bertie, Eliza, as for me. I'll always cherish the memory of dear Joy.'

'You're right, of course: you usually are. But Tim's like you, the Rock of Gibraltar.'

'Thanks very much,' he said, before kissing her. 'I gather that's a compliment?'

'The very best,' she assured him.

'Bottom bunk or top?' Cora enquired.

'Either, as long as you share it with me!'

'Bottom, then.' She giggled. 'Mind you, I've eaten so much at dinner I've probably expanded several inches.' She slid over to the far side of the bunk. 'I might burst out of my nightdress. I hope not, because it cost me a week's wages.'

'I shan't worry if you do.' He looked at her appreciatively. 'There's not much of it, for your money! D'you expect me to shave again?' Tim yawned.

'You'll do as you are,' she said. 'What can

you see out of the window?'

'Porthole,' he corrected her. 'Water, that's all. No fish.' He turned her to face him. 'You smell delicious... You *are* delicious...' He jumped into bed. 'Ow, what's that?'

'Your marble,' she giggled. 'I don't have a pocket, so it rolled out from under the pillow when you leapt in.'

Somewhere music was playing. 'Put another nickel in,' Cora murmured, 'in the nickelodeon – all I want is music, music, music...'

'All I want is *you*,' Tim said.

As Cora twined her arms round his neck, she sang a snatch of an older song. 'Californy here we come!'

'Who'd have thought we'd be going on our honeymoon to another California, in America?' she asked. 'Thanks to my mother's sister, my long-lost aunt!'

'You certainly started something, writing to her about our wedding,' Tim said fondly. 'But that's quite enough singing for tonight, don't you think?'

The publishers hope that this book has given you enjoyable reading. Large Print Books are especially designed to be as easy to see and hold as possible. If you wish a complete list of our books please ask at your local library or write directly to:

Magna Large Print Books
Magna House, Long Preston,
Skipton, North Yorkshire.
BD23 4ND

This Large Print Book, for people
who cannot read normal print,
is published under the auspices of

THE ULVERSCROFT FOUNDATION